EVIL AT HEART

Also by Chelsea Cain

The Gretchen Lowell series

Heartsick

Sweetheart

Also

Confessions of a Teen Sleuth: A Parody

The Hippie Handbook:
How to Tie-Dye a T-Shirt, Flash a Peace Sign, and
Other Essential Skills for the Carefree Life

Dharma Girl: A Road Trip
Across the American Generations

Edited by Chelsea Cain

Wild Child:
Girlhoods in the Counterculture

CHELSEA CAIN

EVIL AT HEART

MACMILLAN

First published 2009 by Macmillan
an imprint of Pan Macmillan Ltd
Pan Macmillan, 20 New Wharf Road, London N1 9RR
Basingstoke and Oxford
Associated companies throughout the world
www.panmacmillan.com

ISBN 978-0-230-01591-3 HB
ISBN 978-0-230-71086-3 TPB

1 3 5 7 9 8 6 4 2

A CIP catalogue record for this book is available from
the British Library.

Typeset by SetSystems Ltd, Saffron Walden, Essex
Printed in the UK by CPI Mackays, Chatham ME5 8TD

Visit www.panmacmillan.com to read more about all our books
and to buy them. You will also find features, author interviews and
news of any author events, and you can sign up for e-newsletters
so that you're always first to hear about our new releases.

For Eliza Fantastic Mohan,

who continues to live up to her name

Acknowledgements

Special thanks to Karissa Cain, for her invaluable assistance and for putting up with me. My editor Kelley Ragland is the super smartest. I am so lucky to be with St Martin's, and everyone there deserves fancy presents and excellent wine, especially Andrew Martin, George Witte, Sally Richardson, Matthew Shear, Hector DeJean, Tara Cibelli, Nancy Trypuc, Matthew Baldacci and Matt Martz.

Several friends have wasted time reading this book-in-progress. They include Lidia Yuknavitch, Andy Mingo, Chuck Palahniuk, Monica Drake, Mary Wysong, Diana Jordan, Erin Leonard, Jim Frost, Suzy Vitello, Cheryl Strayed, and my husband, Marc Mohan. They have each made this book better.

I would not be anywhere without Joy Harris and Adam Reed at The Joy Harris Literary Agency. I also want to thank the Men and Women of the Multnomah Corrections Department because I told them I would and because those people don't get thanked enough. Thanks to my book group – or rather Tracey Massey's book group – for letting me come only when my own books are on the docket. Caroline Schiller and Claus-Martin Carlsberg, you two still have the very best story. I used many fun death facts that I found in *Final Exits: The Illustrated Encyclopedia of How We Die* by Michael Largo, and recommend it highly for the paranoid or merely curious.

And lastly, I want to thank Nancy Eris Hebert, a reader and flight attendant who made sure my name reached the sky, and who died before I could thank her.

1

The rest stop off I-84 on the Oregon side of the Columbia River was vile, even by rest-stop standards. Graffiti covered the white subway-tile walls; the paper-towel and toilet-paper dispensers had been emptied, their contents now strewn on the concrete floor. Two of the metal stall doors were pulled off their top hinges and hung at odd angles. It smelled like a parking-garage stairwell, that peculiar marriage of urine and cement.

Eighteen miles from the nearest bathroom, and they end up at a rest stop trashed by hooligans. There was no alternative. Amy put her hands on her hips and stared at her eleven-year-old daughter.

'Come on, Dakota,' she said.

Dakota's blue eyes widened. 'I'm not going in there,' she said.

This is what the whole road trip had been like. They had been making the annual drive up from Bakersfield to see Erik's family in Hood River every summer since Dakota had been a toddler. She had always loved it. This year she had spent the whole trip texting friends and listening to her iPod. Maybe if Dakota hadn't been such a little jackass for the last two days, Amy would have been more sympathetic.

'Just squat over the bowl,' Amy said.

Dakota bit her lip, leaving a glob of pink lip gloss on her front tooth. 'It's gross,' she said.

'Want me to see if the men's room is any better?' Amy asked.

Dakota's cheeks flushed. 'No way,' she said.

'You said you had to go,' Amy said. In fact, after not going in the restaurant they had stopped at for dinner, Dakota had quickly begun insisting that her bladder was going to burst and that if it did she was going to use it to seek emancipated minor status under California law. Amy didn't even know what the fuck that was, but it seemed serious. So here they were, at a rest stop in the middle of nowhere.

There was a banging at the door. 'What are you guys doing in there?' Erik called. They were twenty minutes from his sister's house. If they didn't get there soon, Amy knew that Erik was going to lose it. He had already been white-knuckling the wheel for the past ten miles. Who was she kidding? She was the one who was going to lose it.

'She doesn't want to use any of the toilets,' Amy called to her husband.

'Then come outside and go behind a tree,' Erik called back.

'Dad!' Dakota said.

Amy pushed open the door to the last stall. It was cleaner

than the rest, or at least less filthy. Toilet paper in the dispenser. No visible human waste. That was a start. 'What about this one?' Amy asked her daughter.

Dakota took a few tentative steps up behind her and peered into the toilet bowl. 'There's something in there,' she said, pointing limply to the pale pink water in the bowl.

Amy didn't have time to explain to her daughter the effect of beets on pee. 'Just flush it,' Amy said. She turned and walked over to the row of white sinks and waited. She heard the toilet flush and felt a little bit of the tension bleed from her shoulders. They would be on the road soon. Erik's sister would have wine waiting. Erik's sister always had wine waiting.

'Mom?' Amy heard her daughter ask.

What now?

Amy turned and saw her daughter standing in the stall, the metal door swung open. Dakota's face was white, blank, her hands balled into fists. The toilet was overflowing, water spilling over the lid onto the floor, forming a puddle that seemed to almost have a tide. Only there was something in the water. It swirled with veins of red. It looked almost menstrual. And for a second Amy thought, *Did Dakota get her period?*

The bloody water streaked down along the outside of the white toilet bowl, onto the floor, under Dakota's sneakers, and towards where Amy stood frozen. There was something in the toilet, something that had bobbed to the surface and now sat at rim level. A piece of something raw. Flesh. Like some maniac had skinned and drowned a rat. It sat on the edge of the bowl for a moment and then slopped onto the floor and slid forward, skimming Dakota's sneaker and disappearing under the next stall.

Dakota shrieked and scrambled forward out of the stall into Amy's arms, not even looking back when her iPod slipped from her hands and landed at the base of the toilet with a deadening splash.

Amy forced herself to swallow the warm saliva that rose in her throat, marshalling her will not to gag. It wasn't a rat. It was definitely not a rat.

'Mom?' Dakota said.

'Yes?' Amy whispered. The iPod was still playing. Amy could hear some tinny pop song coming out of the half-submerged white earbuds. Then, just like that, it stopped.

'I don't have to go to the bathroom any more,' Dakota said.

2

Detective Henry Sobol lifted the evidence bag out of the rest-stop bathroom sink. The contents, four fistfuls of severed flesh, three of which had been plunged from the toilet, glistened under the clear plastic. It was heavier than it looked – dark, almost purple – and the large medallions of flesh were frayed, like they had been cut with a serrated blade. Blood and toilet water formed a triangle of pink juice at the corner of the bag. It didn't have the sanitized look of the clean, plump, pink meat under cling film at the supermarket; something had been killed for this. Or someone had tried to make a kebab out of roadkill.

'Tell me again where you found this?' Henry said.

The state cop who'd called him stood next to Henry with his 'Smokey Bear' hat in his hands. The bathroom's fluorescent lights gave his skin a pale green sheen. 'The john,' the state trooper said, tilting his head towards an open stall. 'Got a nine-one-one call. Family reported some blood in the bathroom. I responded.' He shrugged. 'Plunged it. That came up.' Maybe it wasn't the lighting, Henry thought.

5

Maybe the trooper was green because he was sick to his stomach. The trooper swallowed hard. 'Medical examiner thinks it's a spleen.'

The Hood River County medical examiner stared at Henry, nodding slightly. He was wearing a DaKine T-shirt and cargo shorts, and had the weathered skin that everyone in Hood River seemed to have, thick from snowboarding and windsurfing and whatever the hell else they did out here.

Henry scratched the top of his shaved head with his free hand. 'It doesn't look like a spleen to me,' he said.

Claire Masland appeared next to him, her gold badge on a lanyard around her neck. Two hours ago they had been at his apartment. She'd had fewer clothes on then.

The ME lifted his hands to his hips. 'I'm sorry,' he said. 'Let me clarify.' He made a chopping motion with one hand. 'It's a spleen that's been cut up. And jammed in a toilet.'

Henry laid the gory package back into the sink.

This is what it had been like over the past two months, since the Beauty Killer, Gretchen Lowell, had escaped. The Beauty Killer Task Force worked around the clock, tracking down tips. It had taken them ten years to catch her the first time. This time they knew what she looked like. The task force had doubled. And still Henry wasn't sure they'd ever catch her. They wasted too much time following false leads. A suicide in the river. A drive-by in North Portland. It didn't matter what it was, people thought that Gretchen Lowell was behind it.

Henry knew it was hysteria. Gretchen didn't have a victim profile. She'd claimed to have killed two hundred people.

They'd convicted her of killing twenty-six, adding another twenty to the list once she was in jail. Men, women, black, white, it didn't matter. Gretchen was an equal-opportunity serial killer. But she was also a megalomaniac, and she always left a signature.

Claire wandered away. Henry was already thinking about getting home. *Co-ed Confidential* was on Cinemax at eleven and Claire had said she'd watch it with him. He cleared his throat. 'Some kids probably bought an organ at a butcher shop,' he said. 'Thought they'd scare the crap out of someone.'

'Maybe,' the ME said. 'Can't tell until I get it back to the lab. But the size looks right to be human.'

The state cop gripped his hat a little tighter. 'We figured we should call you guys,' he said.

Gretchen had removed some of her victims' spleens. Both pre- and post-mortem. But she left bodies in her wake, not organs. 'It's not Gretchen Lowell,' Henry said. It wasn't right. No body. No signature. 'It's not her style.'

'Henry,' Claire said. 'Look at this.'

Henry turned towards Claire. She was facing the opposite wall, past the stalls. There was seepage where the toilet had flooded onto the concrete floor and Henry had to navigate around it, his attention shifting between his new black cowboy boots and the reflection of his large frame in the puddle. When he got to Claire, he looked up.

The graffiti was recent. Other pencilled and scratched musings had been marked over by the thick, neat red lines. The same shape, rendered over and over again. The hairs on the back of Henry's neck stood up, his shoulders tightened. 'Fuck,' he said.

'We need to tell Archie,' Claire said softly.

'Archie Sheridan?' the state cop asked. He stepped forward, his black boots slapping through the puddle.

Archie had run the task force that had hunted Gretchen. It had made him the most famous cop in the state. For better or worse.

'I heard he was getting inpatient treatment,' the ME said from the sink.

Inpatient treatment, Henry thought. That was a nice euphemism for it. 'Officially he's a citizen until he gets his psych clearance,' Henry said.

'You have to call him,' Claire said again.

Henry looked back up at the wall. Hundreds of tiny hearts, executed perfectly with what looked to be a red permanent marker. They covered everything, obliterated everything. The heart was Gretchen's signature. She carved it on all of her victims. She'd carved it on Archie.

And now she was back.

3

It was long past visiting hours at the Providence Medical Centre psych ward. Henry rode the back elevator up to a small waiting room with a locked door, a telephone, two chairs, and a table with a sign-in sheet and a stack of Al-Anon brochures. He didn't sign the sign-in sheet. No one ever did.

He picked up the phone. It automatically connected to the nurse's station inside and in a moment a female voice picked up.

'Can I help you?' the voice said. She didn't sound like she meant it.

'I need to see Archie Sheridan,' Henry said. He didn't recognize her voice. He didn't know the night-shift nurses. 'My name's Henry Sobol. It's police business.'

There was an extended pause. 'Hold on,' the voice said.

After a few minutes the door buzzed and then popped open, revealing a tired-looking woman in scrubs and a Peruvian cardigan. 'I'm only letting you in because he said he'd see you,' she said with a tight-lipped smile.

'I know the way,' Henry said. 'I'm here three times a week.'

'I'll walk you anyway,' the nurse said.

There were no TVs in the rooms, but Henry could hear the Animal Planet channel blasting from the break room. Animal Planet was always on in the break room. Henry didn't know why.

The place had been shocking at first. Fluorescent lights, tile linoleum floors, patients in green scrubs. Everywhere you looked were reminders of suicide – the patients wore socks so they couldn't hang themselves with their shoelaces, the garbage bags were paper so patients couldn't pull the plastic ones over their heads, the utensils were plastic so patients couldn't stab themselves in their jugulars, the mirrors in the rooms were metal sheets so patients couldn't use the shards to fillet their wrists; there were no outlets in the rooms that could be used for electrocution, no electrical cords that could be used for nooses.

Archie had now had two run-ins with Gretchen Lowell, each of which had left him near death. He was addicted to painkillers. She'd done a number on his psyche. Henry, more than anyone, knew he needed rehab, knew he needed a mountain of analysis. But what he hadn't expected was that once Archie got in, he wouldn't want to get out.

The night nurse followed Henry into Archie's room.

Archie's room-mate was asleep, snoring loudly, that particular kind of wet, choking apnea that was a product of being overweight and heavily sedated. It was the kind of thing that would drive you crazy, if you weren't already crazy to begin with.

The caged sconce over Archie's bed was on and he was sitting up, on top of the white sheets, the wafer-thin pillow folded behind his curly brown hair, a thick biography open on his lap. He had graduated from scrubs the month before, and now got to wear his own clothes, a sweatshirt and corduroys, slippers instead of socks. He'd lost weight and from a distance he looked like the man Henry had met fifteen years before, good-looking, healthy. Whole.

Up close, the furrows on Archie's forehead and worry lines around his eyes told a different story.

Archie's dark eyes fixed on Henry, and Henry felt a strange unease. Archie's affect had changed. Henry didn't know if it was the meds they had him on, or the fact that he'd been high on painkillers for two years and now he wasn't. It was like he had grown older, stiller. Sometimes Henry couldn't believe he was only forty.

'What's happened?' Archie asked.

Henry shot a look up at the camera mounted in the top corner of the room. It still made him feel strange, being monitored like a prisoner. He pulled up the guest chair on Archie's side of the room – light plastic, so you couldn't hurt someone if you threw it – and sat.

'Can I have a minute?' Henry asked the nurse.

'Don't wake Frank,' she said, and stepped out of the room. Henry looked at Frank. A sheen of saliva collected at the corner of Frank's mouth.

Henry swung his head back to Archie.

'There's a crime scene,' Henry said. He reached into the front pocket of his black jeans and pulled out a pack of gum. 'They found a spleen at a rest stop east on eighty-four. There are hearts drawn on the wall. I need you to come take a look.'

Archie didn't react at all; he just sat looking at Henry, not moving, not blinking, not saying anything. Frank made a gurgling sound like a dying chicken. A tiny light blinked red on the surveillance camera. Henry slid a piece of gum from the pack and unwrapped it and put it in his mouth. It was liquorice-flavoured, warm and soft from being in his pocket. He held out the pack to Archie.

Archie said, 'It's not her.'

Henry folded the gum back in his hand and repocketed it. He would never understand Gretchen's pull on Archie. He knew about Stockholm syndrome. He'd read half a dozen books on it since Archie's captivity. He understood his friend's obsession. They'd hunted her for a decade, living and breathing her, working her crime scenes. Only to discover that she was right under their noses posing as a psychiatrist consulting on the case. It had been hard on all of them— hardest on Archie. 'What if it is?' Henry said.

'She said she would stop killing,' Archie said. The corner of his mouth twisted. 'She promised me.'

'Maybe she had her fingers crossed,' Henry said.

Archie's eyes fell back to his book, and then he slowly closed it and set it on the table next to his bed. He lifted his chin. 'You still there?' he said in a loud voice.

There was a split-second pause and then the night nurse appeared in the doorway.

'They never go far,' Archie told Henry with a faint smile. His eyes flicked to the nurse. 'I'll need to get a day pass,' he said. And then, almost as an afterthought, 'And shoes.'

'He's needed at a crime scene,' Henry said.

'You don't have to convince her,' Archie said. 'I've been here two months. They want me out of here. Thing is, they can't make me leave the ward until I tell them I won't kill myself. And I've got excellent health insurance.'

'A pass shouldn't be a problem, Mr Sheridan,' the night nurse said.

'*Detective* Sheridan,' Henry said. The night nurse looked at him, an eyebrow raised. 'It's "Detective",' Henry said. 'Not "Mister".'

4

Archie had been to that rest stop before. He remembered the brown picnic tables out front, where he and Debbie had sat, slowly getting soaked in the drizzle, while the kids ran in circles on the grass. They had been on their way up to Timberline Lodge, to take the kids up to see snow. Eighty-four was not the fastest route, but it was the most scenic. They had made it as far as Hood River when Archie got a call about another victim. A sixty-two-year-old black man had been found in a Target parking lot, filleted from sternum to pelvis, his small intestine stuffed in his open mouth. It was like Gretchen had known that Archie was going out of town and wanted to teach him a lesson.

'Well,' Debbie had said as they pulled around to head home. 'It was a pretty drive.'

There were nice rest stops along the Gorge, projects built under Roosevelt's Works Progress Administration that looked like stone cottages plucked from an enchanted forest. This wasn't one of them. This rest stop was a breeze-block rectangle, painted Forest Service brown, an entrance for men on one side, women on the other. No free coffee here. There were two patrol cars out front, but they didn't have their lights on. They had closed the women's entrance off to the public, but the men's room was still open. Archie counted four more cars in the parking lot. A man in a baseball cap headed into the men's room. A woman threw a ball for her dog. A second woman, a blonde, got into a dark Ford Explorer. Archie felt his body stiffen. He was careful not to look back, not to let Henry notice him react.

Sometimes a blonde was just a blonde.

Beyond the boundaries of the blurry yellow light thrown by the rest stop's floodlights was vast darkness: no cloud cover, no light from the city. The Gorge sky was filled with stars. An unyielding dry breeze moved through the trees, and the brown grass crunched under Archie's feet. You never had to mow your lawn in August in Portland, unless you watered it. Two months ago, the grass had still been green.

'Everything's dead,' Archie said to Henry. Henry was wearing black jeans, a black T-shirt, cowboy boots, and a black leather jacket. But he was a step ahead and didn't hear him. Archie ducked under the tape and followed Henry into the rest-stop bathroom.

A flash went off. Archie blinked, momentarily blinded. As his eyes refocused he saw a state trooper with a big digital camera. The trooper was in his late twenties, Archie guessed, his dark hair receding prematurely above each temple, his face a little doughy. But he had even features and straight teeth and the build of an ex-jock, and the silver, five-point badge pinned to his chest was polished to a high sheen.

The state-trooper uniform was ridiculous – the big hat, the epaulettes, the blue pants with light blue stripes down the sides; they looked like park rangers who'd lost a fight with a blueberry. But this guy wore it well. He almost looked like a real cop. The trooper looked up and lifted his thick eyebrows at Archie. 'Hey,' the trooper said. 'Hey, it's you.'

Archie tried to force his mouth into a friendly smile. It had been like that since Gretchen had taken him captive, this sort of morbid celebrity. There had been a paperback best-seller, *The Last Victim*, about his kidnapping, and a TV movie. Gretchen's escape from prison and their subsequent second run-in had only made it worse.

'Let him look around,' Henry told the trooper.

A leathery-skinned man dressed for a day hike stood by the sink.

'Can I go now?' he asked Henry.

'A few more minutes,' Henry said.

Archie reached into his pocket looking for the brass pillbox of Vicodin he usually had. It was reflex. He knew it wasn't there. They had taken it at the hospital, along with his cell phone and the belt Debbie had given him on their last Christmas together. He hadn't known what to do with his hands since. He settled on putting both of them in his pants pockets and focused on taking in the scene. The bathroom was familiar. The scratched sheet-metal mirror. The too-bright white walls. The fluorescent lights. It was not unlike his room at the psych ward. With at least one noticeable difference. The bathroom had been trashed. 'Malicious mischief', they called it, a term that Archie had always liked. Of the six stalls, five had been deliberately clogged with toilet paper and faeces, a stew of brown sludge and disintegrating paper. The metal stall doors hung off their hinges. Someone had urinated on the floor. The porous concrete had absorbed most of it, but there were still a few standing puddles, reflecting the jumpy white fluorescents above. Pipe noise echoed in the room, water rushing, foot-steps, everything louder, distorted. Archie leaned across the overflow to peer into the last stall, the one where they'd found the body parts. It was the cleanest of the stalls, the toilet seat still attached, the hinges intact. They had wanted someone to use that stall, to flush, to find the bloody surprise. They had wanted the drama.

An iPod in a yellow jelly case lay facedown on the floor at Archie's feet.

Another flash went off. Archie turned to see the state trooper lower his camera. 'Sorry,' the trooper said.

Claire Masland walked in. He hadn't seen her in two months, but she didn't let on. She smiled briskly, ran a hand through her short dark hair, and said, 'Hi, Archie.'

She was wearing jeans and a T-shirt with a picture of a bear on it and black motorcycle boots. Archie took a step toward her and picked a cat hair off her shirt. Henry had cats. 'Hi, Claire,' Archie said.

Claire broke the seal on a water bottle she had in her hand and took a slug. 'You seen the wall?' she asked.

'Show me,' Archie said.

It looked like the hearts had all been drawn by the same person. The same shape, two plump humps, a sharp point.

The marker line thickness was consistent. It must have taken whoever did it a while, because there were a couple of hundred hearts. Careful, methodical. Not the same person who'd torn apart the bathroom. Someone else.

Another flash.

If Gretchen had done this, there would be more. This was a woman who'd pulled a victim's small intestine out with a crochet hook. Her aim was not to disturb. Her aim was to terrorize. A spleen in a trashed public toilet was gross. But it was not up to Gretchen's pay grade. 'Anyone check the back of the toilet?' Archie asked.

The others looked at each other. The state trooper shrugged.

Archie went back to the stall, stepped over the iPod, and walked through the overflow to the toilet. Most public restrooms these days had tanks built into the wall, steel bowls, and lasers that could tell when you'd got off the pot so the automatic flusher could kick in.

The great toilet-upgrade revolution had not yet reached this particular Gorge highway rest stop. This toilet had a tank on the back. Archie picked up the heavy porcelain lid and slid it over, resting it perpendicularly on the back of the tank.

What he saw in the water made his stomach turn.

Henry, Claire, the ME, and the state trooper all crowded in as close as they could get without getting their feet wet.

'Well?' Claire asked.

'Hand me a container,' Archie said. His voice was calm. He was glad he could still do that. He could see something horrible and not let it show. He'd learned a long time ago that the more dangerous the situation, the more crucial it was to remain in control.

The ME disappeared for a moment and returned with a six-inch clear plastic tub, the sort of thing a deli might pack potato salad in. Archie stretched an arm back for the tub, and then lowered the tub into the back of the tank and scooped up a healthy amount of the contents.

He held it up for the others to see.

The state trooper lifted his hands to his face, scrambled to the next-door stall, and vomited.

'Jesus,' Claire said.

It looked like eyeball soup. Archie had managed to scoop up four eyeballs, and he could see at least two more still in the tank. They had been cleanly removed from their sockets – whole, plump, iridescent white orbs, mottled with red tissue, each iris a pupilless pale blue. Some floated. Some just sort of hung in the water, like pearl onions in a jar.

The plastic tub had a recycling symbol on it. Archie wondered if the ME would rinse it out and reuse it when they were done.

He handed the tub to the ME. 'Why don't you keep an eye on this,' Archie said.

The trooper came back around, wiping his chin with a paper towel he must have picked up off the floor.

Archie walked back over to the wall of hearts. No rapid pulse, his breathing normal. It must have been the anti-anxiety meds. Gretchen was out there. She was killing again. And he wasn't afraid.

Archie laughed.

Two months earlier, in a hospital bed, his throat cut, nearly dead, he and Gretchen had made a deal. He'd tried to sacrifice himself to catch her. But once again, she'd managed to pull him back from the brink of pastoral darkness. She wanted him alive. So he agreed not to blow his brains out, and she agreed not to murder anyone.

Now the deal was off.

Archie felt Henry's hand on his shoulder.

No one moved. The only sound was the steady hum of one of the toilets running.

'I shouldn't have brought you here,' Henry said.

The ME held the plastic tub of eyes up to the flickering light. The eyeballs bobbed and spun.

'So what do we do now?' the trooper asked finally.

'Seal the scene,' Archie said. 'Call in the task force.' Archie looked around the bathroom. 'See if you can turn up any more parts.'

The trooper's face glowed. 'It's her,' he said. 'Gretchen-fucking-Lowell.' He slowly shook his head and tried to hide his lopsided grin.

Archie had seen it before. The naked exhilaration young cops brought to the Beauty Killer crime scenes. Like they were in on something special. Like they might be the ones to catch her.

'I didn't mean—' the trooper hesitated, his cheeks colouring, '—I thought it was exciting.' He glanced down at his boots, then back up at Archie. 'Did she do that to your neck?'

'Yeah,' Archie said, not moving. 'She did that to my neck.'

The trooper's eyes darted away again, somewhere over Archie's shoulder. 'Sorry,' he said.

'Don't be,' Archie said. 'I was unconscious.'

The trooper's hand went up past the knot of his blue tie, to the collar of his dress shirt, and Archie noticed a high-school ring. 'You're lucky,' the trooper said. And then, after a brief pause, the trooper clarified, 'To be alive.'

Lucky. The trooper didn't want to catch Gretchen. He just wanted to meet her. 'You can ask me if you want,' Archie said.

'Archie, come on,' said Henry.

'No,' Archie said. He beckoned with his hand. 'Go ahead. Ask me.'

Someone flushed a toilet in the men's room on the other side of the wall and the tinny sound of rushing water filled the room. Archie could see Claire in the periphery of his vision give Henry a look. Henry didn't move.

The trooper's cheeks were scarlet now. He looked down again, then up. His eyes shone. A high-school football player, Archie decided. A quarterback. You didn't have to have a college degree to join the state cops.

'What's she like?' the trooper asked.

Archie stepped forward and took the trooper's free hand in his and lifted it to his own neck. 'Feel that,' Archie said gently, guiding the trooper's fingertips over the thick scar on his neck. The trooper didn't pull away, didn't cringe, instead he leaned forward, his eyes following the line of Archie's scar, still raw and fibrous, still sensitive to the touch. Archie could see the pulse in the trooper's neck quicken. Archie moved the trooper's hand over an inch. 'The jugular is here,' he said, pressing the trooper's fingers into his neck so he could feel the arterial cord pulsing beneath the flesh. 'Gretchen knows where to cut,' Archie said. 'I didn't get lucky. If she'd wanted me dead, I'd be dead.' Archie let go of the trooper's hand and the trooper slowly withdrew it. 'What's she like?' Archie repeated softly. He put his hand on the trooper's shoulder and leaned forward, so his face was inches from his. Gretchen was a beautiful, sensual, charismatic, manipulative bitch, the object of Archie's sexual obsession, his torturer, and the person who knew him best in the world. 'She's a serial killer,' Archie said. He smiled and gave the trooper's shoulder an avuncular pat. 'If you ever lay eyes on her, shoot her.'

Archie turned to Henry. 'I'm ready to go back to the loony bin,' he said.

5

Susan Ward made her way quickly down the hospital corridor. It was 9 a.m. and she was already in a bad mood. There
was something going on out in the Gorge and Ian had sent
Derek Rogers to cover it instead of her. She'd already
called Derek eleven times. This was number twelve.

'What do they mean "body parts"?' she asked him. She was
having trouble holding her phone to her ear, keeping her paper
cup of coffee from spilling, and digging through her purse for
an Altoid to mask the taste of the cigarette she'd smoked in
the hospital parking garage.

'They're not saying,' Derek said. He had been out there
most of the night and it sounded like the novelty was wearing
off. 'But they've got half the Beauty Killer Task Force out
here and FBI and volunteers searching the woods.'

It would be big news if there hadn't already been so much
Gretchen Lowell pandemonium. The *Herald* had run a
front-page story about her every day since she'd escaped.
She'd been spotted in Italy, Florida, Thailand, and Churchill,
Manitoba. All the freaks who'd ever claimed to have been

abducted by aliens were now claiming that they'd seen the Beauty Killer. Crimes all over the world were being attributed to her. If you believed the twenty-four-hour news channels, she'd murdered a family in Thailand and then made it to England to kill a fishmonger by sundown.

'Keep me posted,' Susan said. 'I'm at the hospital.'

'When are you going to give up?' Derek said.

Susan wedged the phone between her ear and her shoulder and managed to locate the Altoids tin in a purse full of balled receipts, pens, gum wrappers, and used tissue. 'Maybe this week he'll see me,' she said.

'If Ian finds out you're working on a book, he'll pop his ponytail,' Derek said.

Susan pressed the button for the elevator up to the psych ward. Ian had given Derek the crime beat after Susan's mentor, Quentin Parker, had been killed. Susan told herself she didn't care. She had some projects up her sleeve that might get her out of the newspaper business once and for all. The sooner the better, the way things were going. She just needed to get Archie to talk to her.

'Hello?' Derek said.

'Did you know,' Susan said, 'that since 1958 over four hundred people have died of an allergic reaction to sperm?'

There was a pause. 'Uh, no,' Derek said.

The elevator dinged and the silver doors slid open. 'I've got to go,' Susan said. She popped an Altoid in her mouth and dropped the tin back in her purse. 'I'm here.'

6

They wouldn't let Susan in. They never did. Her name wasn't on Archie's list of approved visitors. But Susan buzzed and sent the nurse back to ask if Archie would see her, and when the nurse came back, like always, and said no, not today, but he says hi, Susan took a chair in the psych-ward waiting room. If she came often enough, and sat long enough, eventually, she hoped, Archie would relent.

And if he didn't, well, it was a nice quiet place to get some work done.

There were two chairs, both pee-coloured moulded plastic, and Susan always sat in the left one. 'Waiting room' was generous. It was more like a waiting closet. No windows. Just five feet square, filled by two chairs and a card table stacked with mental-health brochures. Susan was halfway through her coffee and had taken a break from her laptop to read a leaflet about adult hyperactive attention deficit disorder when the elevator doors opened and out stepped Henry Sobol.

He lifted his eyebrows when he saw her. 'Purple, huh?' he said.

'It's called "Plum Passion",' Susan said, touching her violet hair. It had been turquoise. Before that, pink. Susan threw a glance at the psych-ward door. If Henry was here to talk to Archie, maybe the thing at the Gorge did have something to do with Gretchen. 'Are you here because of the rest stop?' she asked.

'Just visiting a friend,' Henry said.

Henry didn't visit in the mornings. At least he'd never come while she was there.

'You can trust me,' Susan said. She knew that Henry didn't believe her. And maybe it wasn't even true. But Susan wanted it to be.

Henry started to reach for the call button, but then hesitated and turned back to her. 'You know what a journalist is?' he asked.

'What?' Susan asked.

Henry's expression didn't flicker. 'A dead reporter.'

'Ouch,' Susan said.

'I stole it,' Henry said.

Susan leaned forward. 'You hear the one about the woman who got pulled over for speeding?' she asked. Susan never remembered jokes. But she'd heard her mother tell this one so many times it had stuck.

'Don't tell it if it's not dirty,' Henry said.

Susan brushed a lock of purple hair out of her eyes. 'The cop asks why she is in such a hurry,' she said, 'and the woman explains that she is late for work. "I suppose you're a doctor," the cop says, "and someone's life hangs in the

balance." "No," the woman says, "I'm an asshole stretcher."'
Susan giggled. Henry's face clouded. It occurred to Susan at
this moment that maybe Henry wouldn't like this joke, but
there was no turning back, so she went on. '"An asshole
stretcher," the cop says, "what's that?" "It's where you start
with one finger," the woman says.' Susan lifted one of her
fingers and wiggled it for effect. '"And then work in a second
until you've got your whole hand in there."' Susan demon-
strated, like she was stuffing a turkey. '"And then the other
hand and you keep stretching until it's about six feet."' She
pantomimed it. '"What do you do with a six-foot asshole?"
the cop asks.'

'Let me guess,' Henry said. 'Give him a badge.'

Susan dropped her hands back in her lap. 'You've heard
it,' she said.

Henry pressed the buzzer. 'Mine was better,' he said.

'I can write a good book about this case,' Susan said.
'Something important even, maybe.' They both knew what
that meant. Not like *The Last Victim*. 'Gretchen is a celebrity
to some people. I want to explore that. I want to understand
the cultural fascination with violence.'

'Come on, Susan,' Henry said, lifting his hand to the back
of his neck. 'Let him move on.'

'You know what I'm working on now?' Susan said. 'It's a
bathroom book. A thousand weird ways people die. Like how
many people a year are killed by falling coconuts.'

'How many?' Henry asked.

'About a hundred and fifty,' Susan said. 'They're really

dangerous.' She raised her finger again. 'The point is I can't do this Gretchen book without him.' She gave Henry a pleading look.

A female voice cracked over the intercom. 'Can I help you?' the voice said.

'Finally,' Henry muttered. 'It's Henry Sobol to see Archie Sheridan,' he said.

'I'll be right there,' the voice said brightly.

Susan wasn't ready to give up. 'I watched her cut his throat,' she said. She and Henry had both been there. Susan had held a dish towel on Archie's neck, felt his warm blood soak the cloth. She blamed herself for Gretchen's escape. She wondered if Henry blamed her, too. Susan had, after all, in a blaze of panic, provided Gretchen with access to a gun.

Henry looked her up and down and then frowned. Susan thought he was going to say something snarky about her hair. But instead he squinted at her and said, 'You take care of yourself, right?'

'I take vitamins.' Susan said.

Henry sighed. 'I'm talking about varying your route to work,' he said. 'Locking your door at night. That sort of thing.'

The hair on Susan's arms stood up. Henry would only ask her that if he thought there was a chance she might be in danger. 'Oh, God,' she said. 'You think it might actually be her.'

'Just take precautions,' Henry said. 'Can you do that?'

A knot of anxiety tightened around Susan's throat. Take precautions? She'd moved back in with her mother. They hadn't locked the front door of their house for as long as Susan could remember, until two months ago. Since then, Susan's mother, Bliss, had lost eight keys. 'What happened out there?' Susan asked. 'Is there something you guys aren't releasing?'

The door opened and a nurse appeared.

'I shouldn't have said anything,' Henry said to Susan.

'You think I don't think about her all the time?' Susan said. 'I see her face everywhere I go. It's on every channel. I saw a kid downtown yesterday selling RUN, GRETCHEN T-shirts. They sell these heart-shaped digital key chains that count the days since she's escaped. In LA, you can get a Gretchen Lowell manicure. French pink with blood-red tips.'

The nurse stared at Susan. Susan didn't care.

'If she's back in the area,' Susan said, 'the people have a right to know. You have to go public.'

Henry walked through the door.

'I'll wait here,' Susan said. The door closed. Susan sank back in her chair. If Gretchen was back, she'd pick them all off one by one, just for fun.

She called Derek again.

He didn't pick up.

Susan dug into her purse, pulled out her car keys, and checked the digital readout on the key chain. Gretchen had been at large for seventy-six days and counting.

If she made it a hundred, a bar downtown had promised to serve free Bloody Marys to the first one hundred blondes who walked through the door.

If you were going to be murdered, you might as well be drunk.

7

The clay was the last thing on Archie's mind, but he rolled it under his hand anyway, until it was a smooth ball. They were ten minutes into morning craft period. Archie was sitting across the table from his room-mate, Frank. Craft period. Gretchen was out there somewhere killing again, but safe inside the funny farm, he was playing with clay.

Archie didn't mind the craft projects. He didn't mind Frank's snoring, or the group therapy sessions, or the slippers. He had come to like being told when to eat and when to sleep. The fewer responsibilities he had, the less chance there was he'd fuck them up.

He was locked up. And he was free. His team, the task force he'd led for the better part of his career, was out there looking for Gretchen Lowell without him. And for the first time in forever he didn't care. If Gretchen wanted him dead, she'd kill him. It didn't matter where he was. They wouldn't catch her. Not unless she wanted to be caught.

Then Henry walked in. And Archie felt, despite himself, a stirring of his old obsession.

Henry dragged a seat over from another table and sat down with Archie and Frank.

'Goat spleen,' Henry said. 'Human eyes.'

Most of the other patients were outside on the caged balcony smoking, and, except for the TV blasting Animal Planet, the common room was quiet. Archie looked across the table at Frank. He was concentrating on his clay and didn't look up.

Henry leaned forward and tilted his head towards Frank. 'Can I talk in front of him?' he asked.

'Frank and I don't have secrets,' Archie said. 'Do we, Frank?'

'Clay feels like babies,' Frank said.

Henry cleared his throat. 'Okay, then,' he said. He scratched his ear and looked at Archie. 'The ME says we've got three pairs of eyes.'

'Pairs,' Archie said. 'That's good.' He smiled at Henry. 'Otherwise we'd be looking for pirates.'

Henry continued. 'All three appear to be a few years old. The ME thinks they were preserved in formaldehyde before they were dumped in the tank.'

Archie continued to rotate his palm over the orb of clay on the table. 'Match anything?' he asked. He kept his face neutral and his eyes on his hand, trying to focus on the clay.

'Nothing in the regional database. We're looking wider. You thinking we'll turn up some corpses to match?'

'Gretchen never took out anyone's eyes.'

'Gretchen never did anything,' Henry said, 'until she did.'

Archie rubbed his eyes with his hand. They'd given him

a sedative when he'd got back the night before, and he still felt groggy from it. 'Beef up Debbie's protection detail,' he said with a sigh. He didn't think Gretchen would go after Debbie and the kids again. She had already terrorized him once with that trick, and she didn't like to repeat herself. But the protection might buy his family some peace of mind.

'Already done,' Henry said. 'Vancouver PD's got a car outside her house. The kids get escorts to school. Everything we talked about.' Henry spread his moustache with a thumb and forefinger. 'I want you to consider leaving town.'

'Boca Raton's nice,' Frank said.

'Gretchen will find me anywhere I go,' Archie said. There was no emotion to it. It was merely a fact.

Henry folded his big arms on the table and leaned forward. 'But the press might not,' he said. 'You don't know what it's like out there. The city council is considering a curfew. There's a company that gives goddamn Gretchen Lowell tours.' His neck reddened as he talked. 'They've got these buses with her face painted on the side. Why do you think Debbie moved to Vancouver? Property taxes?'

On Animal Planet, a vet was trying to save a cat who'd been hit by a car. Archie had seen the episode eight times before. The cat ended up dying.

The killing wasn't going to stop until Gretchen wanted it to.

'I want to help,' Archie said. 'I'll consult from here.'

Frank hunched over the table across from Archie, working his clay into a two-foot-long roll the width of a thumb.

'Leave town. I'll find another bughouse for you, if you want. In New Hampshire. Somewhere far away.'

The truth was, New Hampshire sounded nice. Far away sounded nice. But no one knew the Beauty Killer case files like Archie did. Henry needed Archie. And Archie knew it. 'Call me if anything develops,' Archie said. 'I'm around.'

'The last time I called,' Henry said, 'some woman told me she was going to get you and then wandered away and never came back.'

There was only one phone patients were allowed to use. Incoming calls only. When it rang, everybody lunged for it.

'They shouldn't let crazy people answer the phone,' Henry said.

Frank looked up from his clay roll and smiled.

'Crazy people are the only people here,' said Archie.

Henry leaned back in his chair, crossed his arms, and rested his chin on his chest. 'So are you just going to hide out here the rest of your life?' he asked.

Archie didn't have an answer.

Henry watched him, jaw working, the muscle popping under the skin. Archie could almost see him trying out different arguments. 'No one knows,' Henry said finally. 'You clear a psych exam you can come back to work. You're still a fucking hero out there. Fucking Philip Marlowe.'

Frank's eyes shot up, alarmed, from behind his glasses. 'No bad language here.'

'Sorry, Frank,' Henry said. He leaned forward and worked his jaw some more before continuing. 'Don't leave the ward,' Henry said to Archie. 'I need to know that you're safe.'

Archie had hospital privileges. He could roam anywhere he wanted, as long as he was back for evening meds. They called it Level Four. Archie had been a Level One when he'd checked himself in. He'd clawed his way up from high-risk to mildly disturbed.

'Never,' Archie said. 'Who'd hang out with Frank?'

Frank had started folding the clay snake he'd made back on itself, back and forth, again and again.

Henry raised an eyebrow and looked over at Frank. 'What are you working on there, buddy?' Henry asked him.

Frank's eyes flicked up to the TV, and then he smiled down at his clay. 'Cat intestines,' he said.

Henry threw a glance at Archie. 'Nice,' he said.

The door to the balcony opened and people started coming back in, their blank stares momentarily enlivened by nicotine. There was a group therapy session starting in a few minutes. 'You need to go,' Archie said to Henry.

Henry stood up. He hesitated. 'Susan Ward's out there,' he said.

'I know,' Archie said. 'She likes to steal the Wi-Fi.'

'You don't want to see her?' Henry said.

The truth was that Archie had come close to letting her in a few times. But he'd always caught himself. Entangling Susan in his life was the last thing she needed. 'I want to finish my craft project,' Archie said.

Henry planted his hands in his pockets and turned to leave. 'Think about what I said,' he said to Archie, starting for the door. 'I hear fall's nice in New England.'

'Henry,' Archie said, stopping him. His voice was steel,

the clay strangled in his hand. 'You need to issue a shoot-to-kill order. We can't let her get away again.'

'That's the sanest thing you've said in months, my friend,' Henry said.

Frank chuckled. It was the first time Archie had ever heard him laugh. It was an unsettling sound, like a child crying.

8

The Beauty Killer Body Tour stopped four times a day at Pittock Mansion. Randy pulled the bus over, and all the tourists would file out with the guide, pay their admission to the mansion, and then be led through the house to the spot on the grounds where Gretchen Lowell had dumped the body of a disembowelled oral surgeon named Matthew Fowler. The guide would point to the spot in the grass where they'd found him, and the fuckers would take pictures of it.

Randy waited in the bus.

Portlanders had been getting their wedding pictures taken at the 1914 stone palace since one of the Pittock grandsons had sold the house to the city in the sixties.

He wondered how many wedding photos now had assholes in RUN, GRETCHEN T-shirts wandering around in the background.

It was ten o'clock. The next stop was a motel in North Portland where Gretchen had jammed some poor schmuck's dismembered penis in an ice machine. Randy liked that one. He liked to see the faces on the tourists when the guide flipped open the lid on the ice machine and they saw the rubber dildo the motel owner kept in there for laughs.

Laughs.

He needed another job.

He pulled off his BEAUTY KILLER BODY TOURS T-shirt, turned it inside out, put it back on, and got out of the bus for a cigarette. He wasn't supposed to leave the bus unattended, but fuck it. What were they going to do? Dismember his penis?

The tourists were inside, no doubt admiring the curved marble staircase at seven bucks a pop, so Randy lit up and walked around to the front of the house. They didn't charge admission into the yard. The Beauty Killer Tour could have taken tourists right to the spot where Fowler had died, but instead they made the tourists pay to go inside the mansion first. It kept the Pittock people happy, and everyone got a little bit richer thanks to Portland's favourite serial killer.

The mansion was a thousand feet above Portland, and on a clear day the view was something spectacular. Today you couldn't see shit. Not Mount Hood. Not Mount Saint Helens. Definitely not Mount Adams. Just grey clouds that looked to be about a mile thick. It was for the best. They needed the rain. The whole city had shrivelled up over the last few months.

Randy walked to the edge, overlooking the foliage-thick cliffside that led down to the city, and tossed his cigarette over the black chain-link fence.

He immediately realized what he'd done. The brush on the hillside was like kindling. An arson rap was the last thing he needed. He stood at the fence and scanned the hillside to make sure the cherry tip had extinguished – and that's when he saw it. At first he thought it was an old, deflated basketball. It was nestled in the brush, like someone had tossed it from exactly where Randy was standing. But as he leaned over to get a better look, he realized, with unusually sudden clarity, that it was a head.

He lost his footing, and had to scramble, flapping his arms, to keep from falling. When he was upright, he started running, as fast as he could, for the mansion.

He was only vaguely aware of the smoke snaking up the hillside behind him.

9

Susan glanced down at the array of self-defence sprays laid out on the passenger seat of her car. Pepper spray. Mace. Some toxic herbal spray her mom had made her out of nutmeg. She swept them into her open purse, started the car, and headed out of the hospital parking garage.

Body parts.

She looked up at the sky. It hadn't rained since early July, but today there was no blue sky in sight. The Gorge rest stop was forty-five minutes away. She could make it in thirty – unless it started raining.

She fed a Jimi Hendrix CD into her car stereo, and was turning out of the medical campus, when her phone vibrated in her lap and nearly caused her to steer into a Ford Explorer. Susan slammed on her brakes, causing her purse to spew most of its contents on the floor. The woman behind the wheel of the Explorer had blonde hair. Her head was turned, and Susan couldn't see her face. But there was something about the hair.

Susan's body went cold.

Gretchen.

Susan couldn't move for a moment. Her car stalled, and she snapped to and laid on her horn, hoping to get the woman to look up, but the woman kept going.

Susan glanced across the street where a billboard with Gretchen's face on it advertised a special edition of *America's Sexiest Serial Killers*. Another blonde drove by.

Susan shook her head, restarted the Saab's engine, and pulled onto Glisan Street.

This was ridiculous.

Gretchen was long gone. And if she wasn't – well, Gretchen Lowell wouldn't be caught dead in a Ford Explorer.

The phone in her lap vibrated again and Susan flinched.

She closed her eyes. This couldn't continue. At this rate she'd be dead of a coronary before she turned thirty.

The phone. She picked it up off her lap and answered it. She could barely make out the voice on the other end over the wail of electric guitar coming through her dash speakers. 'What?' she said.

The voice got louder. 'Hello?' It was a man's voice. She didn't recognize it. He sounded confused. 'Hello?' he said again.

Susan turned down her car stereo. 'Sorry,' she said. *'Are You Experienced.'*

'Am I what?' he asked.

'Not you,' Susan said. 'The album. Hendrix. *Are You Experienced.'* It must have been lunch break at the hospital because traffic was crawling. 'Can I help you?' Susan asked.

'Susan Ward?' the man said.

Her full name. Susan's fingers tightened around her sheepskin steering-wheel cover. She knew where this was going. 'I sent in that student loan payment yesterday,' she said. She was lying. 'Swear.'

There was a pause. 'What?' the man asked.

This part of Glisan was all flower shops and bars. 'Is this about my student loan?' Susan asked.

'No,' the man said.

Susan mentally inventoried the bills stacked next to the *Vogue* on her coffee table. 'Visa?' Susan guessed.

'I'm not a bill collector,' the man said.

'Oh, good,' Susan said. The light at the upcoming inter-section was red and Susan came to a stop behind a long line of cars. It started to rain and she turned on the windshield wipers, which needed replacing and only made visibility worse.

'I want to talk to you about a story,' the man said.

Susan's fingers tightened again. Another pissed-off reader. Excellent. Why did people feel the need to let her know every time they found her irritating? 'If you have a problem with something I've written, the best thing to do is write a letter to the editor,' she said.

'You wrote to me on my website,' he said. 'You said you were interested in writing about our group.'

Susan had written to hundreds of Gretchen Lowell fan sites over the last few weeks asking for interviews and information. 'Who are you?' she asked. 'What site?'

'There's a body at three-nine-seven North Fargo,' the man said.

Not funny. 'Who is this?' Susan asked.

'Someone who appreciates beauty,' he said.

There was something deadly serious in the man's voice that gave her a sudden chill.

'Is this for real?' Susan asked.

Someone behind her honked and she looked up to see that the light had changed.

She turned around to see a man in a black SUV giving her the finger. She hit the gas. 'Hello?' she said into the phone. She looked at the phone LCD screen. Disconnected.

Susan's heart was racing now. She pulled over to the kerb, letting the guy in the SUV whip around her without even giving him a dirty look. 'What the fuck?' Susan said quietly. She highlighted the incoming number and called it back.

No one answered. No voice mail. It was a local area code. But she didn't recognize the number.

If there was a body, why tell *her*? Why not call the police? Should she call the police? That would be silly. Bothering them based on some weird phone call. Henry would think it was another joke.

But if it *was* real, and that guy *was* from one of those Beauty Killer fan clubs, then she'd really have a book. She'd have her pick of agents. Archie might even agree to be interviewed. And she'd have a great opening chapter . . .

What was the address? Fuck. Three something? Three-nine-seven? Susan looked around for a pen, and found several on the floor of the passenger seat. She grabbed a candy wrapper out of where she'd stuffed it in a cubbyhole in the car door and turned it inside out. *Fargo.* She wrote that down on the white inside of the wrapper. It was *North Fargo.* Three-nine-seven *North Fargo.* She was almost positive.

The Gorge would have to wait.

10

There were eight therapy sessions a day at the Providence psych ward. Archie went to four. Two mental-health groups. Two substance-abuse groups. Archie wasn't sure why they bothered breaking them up. It was all the same people. Most of them went to every session. It was something to do in between episodes of *Emergency Vets*.

'Do you want to stay?' Sarah Rosenberg asked him.

'No,' Archie said. He'd helped push the tables to the side, and then to arrange the chairs in a circle at the centre of the room. 'This is the schizophrenics and bipolars session. The depressives aren't meeting until two.'

'Your sense of humour is returning,' she said.

'Is that a good sign?' Archie asked.

He followed her across the hall to one of the individual counselling rooms. He met with Rosenberg every day for twenty-five minutes. Why twenty-five and not an even thirty, he didn't know. But he guessed it had something to do with insurance.

'How's Debbie?' she asked.

Archie sat down in one of the two brown Naugahyde chairs that faced each other in the room. A light rain slapped against the window. 'Probably a little tense,' he said.

Rosenberg sat in the opposite chair and set her coffee cup on the armrest. 'What's happened?'

Archie didn't know how much Henry had made public. 'I just think it must be exhausting. Living out there, knowing that Gretchen could show up at any time.'

'Does she like Vancouver?' Rosenberg asked.

'Being in a different state makes her feel safer,' Archie said. The truth was they didn't talk much. She brought the kids by once a week to visit him, but she didn't stay. She'd started seeing an alternative-energy entrepreneur, whatever the hell that was. They'd drop the kids off and go get a bite to eat downtown. 'I try not to make it complicated for her.'

Rosenberg tilted her head and looked hard at Archie. 'It's important to you that she feel safe,' she said.

Archie leaned his head on the back of his chair and looked up at the ceiling. There was a sprinkler overhead. Just in case he burst into flame. 'Yes.'

They were quiet for a moment.

Archie could hear someone shouting in the next room.

'Do *you* feel safe?' Rosenberg asked.

Archie lifted his head back up and wagged his finger at her. 'I think I know where you're going with this,' he said.

Rosenberg sat forward, resting her elbows on her thighs. 'You're off the painkillers. Your health has stabilized. You need to check yourself out of here. They have an excellent outpatient programme. You'll get a lot of support.'

Archie shook his head. Even if he wanted out, he had nowhere to go. 'My liver enzymes are still high,' he said.

'Frankly, with the amount of Vicodin you took I'm amazed you're not on the transplant list,' Rosenberg said. 'If you want me to let you stay, you need to make an effort. You need to practise functioning outside this hospital. You're Level Four. Go for a walk.'

The rain was picking up. Archie looked out the window. The ground was too dry. It would flood. 'She's out there,' he said. He could feel her. It was a stupid thing to think. People couldn't feel each other's presence. He wasn't psychic. He didn't believe in auras, or souls, or cosmic connections. But still he knew – as much as he knew anything – that Gretchen was never very far from him.

Rosenberg put her hand on his and looked him in the eye. 'There will always be serial killers,' she said. 'There will always be bears in the woods.' She gave his hand a squeeze. 'Bad things happen. People die.'

Archie couldn't concentrate. The shouting from across the hall was getting louder. A woman's voice, but Archie couldn't make out whose.

He wondered what was on Animal Planet right now.

Rosenberg sat staring at him. Waiting. That's what being on the psych ward was like, everyone watching you all the time waiting for you to twitch or scream or say you were better, thanks for everything.

Archie had been good at waiting. It was a useful skill when you were interviewing witnesses. Gentle silence. Almost everyone felt the need to fill it, and that's when the details surfaced. People would tell you anything, just to avoid sitting quietly.

But Archie still wasn't used to being the one expected to do the talking. He pulled his hand out from under hers. 'Just ask the questions,' he said. The questions, and he could go. The sessions with Rosenberg always ended with the same three questions. Anything changed since yesterday? Rate your mood. Any immediate concerns?

'If you get out of here,' Rosenberg said, 'you can still have a life.'

What life? He'd driven his family away. His job was tenuous. He had nowhere to live. The only thing he had was Gretchen.

He'd have to leave, of course. He knew that. But not yet.

He was not ready to leave yet.

He had one card and he decided to play it. He looked her in the eye. 'I'm still a danger to myself,' he said. He knew that as long as he said it, they couldn't force him out. But for the first time in two months, it was a lie. He didn't want to die. The deal with Gretchen was off. She'd threatened to kill again if he killed himself, and now she'd started to kill again anyway. He was free to do it, with only his own blood on his hands.

And he didn't want to die.

He wanted to kill her. He wanted to kill Gretchen. That's why he had to stay inside. Because if he let himself back into the world, he would hunt her down and he would hurt her.

Rosenberg frowned and her eyebrows knitted. 'At some point you're going to have to forgive yourself.'

Forgive himself. Right. Archie rubbed the back of his neck with one hand and allowed himself a wry chuckle. 'Sarah,' he said. 'I had sex with a serial killer.'

Rosenberg didn't miss a beat. 'Which part do you hate yourself for more?' she asked.

She waited.

But the silent treatment didn't work.

There was too much shouting from across the hall.

Archie looked up toward the door.

'They can handle it,' Rosenberg said.

A crashing sound echoed through the walls. They both knew what it was. A plastic chair hitting shatterproof glass.

Archie stood.

More shouting.

'Call security,' someone yelled.

Archie went through the door and into the hall. Rosenberg was behind him, two nurses were coming around the corner. Autopilot kicked in. Through the door. Three people scrambled out past him as he entered. There were five people left in the room. The counsellor, crouched, bleeding, behind an overturned desk. Two women standing frozen by the wall. Frank, still sitting in a plastic chair, knees apart, a dazed grin on his face. And the woman standing in the centre of the room, hunched, crying, gripping a shard of something hard and bloody.

'Oh, for fuck's sake,' said Archie.

The woman's name was Courtenay Taggart. She'd been transferred up from the ER with bandaged wrists, and had then managed to peel up a piece of Formica off the built-in bedside table in her room and had tried to finish the job. She'd been on suicide watch ever since. They'd taken everything out of her room except a mattress. Her door was never closed. A staff member sat in a chair outside her door 24–7. Archie had seen her a few times through the doorway as he passed by in the hall, lying on her bed like a child.

She spun toward him now, and lifted the shard to the soft flesh of her neck. Apparently she'd found another source of Formica.

'What are you doing, Courtenay?' Archie asked.

He guessed she was about twenty. She might have looked younger if she'd been wearing civilian clothes and not green hospital pyjamas. Her dyed-blonde hair was pulled back. Her face was flushed sunburn-pink. She had a nice face, round cheeks, and the kind of skin that had never seen a blemish.

She opened her mouth to say something and then Archie saw her eyes dart behind him. He turned his head and saw one of the ward orderlies moving cautiously in from the door. He was a young guy, all ninety-degree angles, strong and stocky, with hair buzzed short and a square face. Archie had seen him in the halls, pushing a mop or wheeling a meal cart.

'Put it down,' the orderly said.

Courtenay looked right at the orderly and pushed the piece of Formica into her neck.

One of the women huddled near the wall gasped.

'Get out,' Courtenay screamed at the orderly, her pretty face twisting, sending forth a spray of saliva and snot.

'It's okay,' the orderly said. 'My name's George. What's yours?'

Archie cringed. *Don't admit you don't know her name.* The orderly's expression was earnest, palms held out and up, posture neutral. He had probably taken a seminar on hostage situations. Introduce yourself. Establish a rapport. Stall.

'Courtenay,' Archie said, trying to distract her from the orderly. 'What can I do for you?'

She nodded toward the orderly. 'I don't want him here,' she said. A bead of blood ran down her neck.

'Go,' Archie told the orderly, mustering all his authority. Archie looked around the room. 'Everyone go,' he said. The woman who'd gasped started crying, and hugged the woman with her. The counsellor crouched frozen on the floor. Frank sat in his chair, smiling.

Archie needed to clear the room. There were too many people. He needed Courtenay calm. Angry, excited people made bad decisions. There were already too many unpredictable elements. Hostages were bad enough to manage. Mentally unstable hostages made things very dangerous.

Archie turned to the orderly. 'Trust me,' he said, lowering his voice. 'I know how to do this. Get out.' The orderly glanced over at Courtenay. Then he turned back to Archie, nodded, and backed away. As he did, it was like a seal had been broken. The counsellor ran for the door, gripping his bleeding arm, and the two women went out behind him. Frank didn't move.

The telephone started to ring.

'Security will be here in a few minutes,' a nurse called to Archie from the door.

It was the three of them then: Archie, Courtenay, and Frank.

Courtenay's nostrils flared with each breath and her knuckles were white around the shard of Formica.

'Everything's going to be fine,' Archie said softly. He slowly extended his hand. 'Please give that to me.'

Courtenay looked him in the eye and pushed the Formica deeper into her neck, and blood trickled down her chest.

'You don't have to do that,' Archie said.

She let up on the Formica, the colour returning to her hand. Tears streamed down her cheeks. 'I'm fat,' she said.

She wasn't fat. She wasn't even generously proportioned. Her pyjamas hung a size too big over her body. This was what had driven her to attack a counsellor and jam a countertop into her neck?

'It's the lithium,' said Frank from his chair.

'You're not fat,' Archie said. 'So if that's why you're cutting yourself with a countertop, it's massively moronic.'

The phone was still ringing.

Behind him, Archie could hear chaos in the hall. People shouting. Someone crying. Psych wards were like pre-schools – tantrums were contagious.

Courtenay cocked her head at Archie. 'How did you do it?' she asked.

Archie wondered if she could somehow see it on him, like he could see her bandages. 'Pills,' he said.

'Do you have kids?' she asked.

'Two,' Archie said. 'Six and eight.'

The phone continued, insistent. It was all Archie could do not to rip it out of the wall.

Frank started to stand up and move for it.

'Frank, sit down,' Archie said.

Frank looked up, startled by Archie's tone, and then lifted a finger at the phone. 'It's for me,' he said. 'It's my sister.'

'It's not important,' Archie said through clenched teeth.

Courtenay wiped some snot off her lip with her forearm. 'I cut my wrists,' she said. 'But I did it wrong. I went horizontally. You're supposed to go vertically. Did you know that?'

'Yeah,' Archie said.

Frank grinned. 'Remember, kids,' he said in a sing-song voice, 'it's up the road, not across the street.'

'Frank,' Archie warned.

Courtenay shook her head sadly. 'I didn't know.'

Her knuckles whitened again and her elbow lifted, and Archie knew he only had a second to stop her from hurting herself again.

'You can't get to the carotid artery with that,' he said quickly. 'It's not sharp enough.'

He stepped forward and pulled back his collar, exposing the scar on his neck. 'Look,' he told her, and he lifted his chin and took another step to her, so she could see the ugly rope of scar tissue that Gretchen had left on him. Courtenay wanted to be beautiful.

'You'll just end up mutilating yourself,' Archie said.

Courtenay's mouth opened as her eyes dropped to his neck. She blinked rapidly, then let the Formica fall to the floor and dabbed at her self-inflicted wound with her fingers. 'Am I going to have a scar?' she asked, forehead creasing with dismay.

Archie moved to her and took her tenderly by the shoulders. It was both a gesture of comfort and to ensure that she wouldn't dive for the Formica. 'I don't think you'll even need stitches,' he said.

Three uniformed hospital security guards hurried into the room, with the orderly tagging behind them. The guards took Courtenay by each arm and led her mutely away, and then the room exploded in noise and motion.

Archie walked over to where the phone sat, still ringing, on an end table by the couch, and picked it up.

'Hello?' he said.

But on the other end there was only silence.

Archie hung up.

'I'm going to my room,' Archie told Rosenberg. 'I need a sweater.' It was true. He was suddenly very cold. It was probably the adrenalin drop. Hospitals were kept ten degrees colder than what anyone would find comfortable. Archie didn't know why. Maybe it was to keep patients like him from overstaying their welcome.

He had a green cardigan and a blue crew neck. They were in the bottom drawer of his dresser against the wall facing the foot of his bed. He was opening the drawer when he felt the vibration. He thought it was the medication at first. They were adjusting his Prozac dosage and he felt that sort of thing sometimes, electrical sensations that travelled down his arms, or lit up his brain at night. Brain zaps, the nurses called them, as if they were a perfectly normal side effect, like bloating.

But the vibration wasn't the medication.

It was a phone.

Archie froze. It had been two months since he had heard a vibrating cell phone, that odd low-frequency buzz, both a sound and a feeling. Fifteen years he'd carried a phone in his pocket. And in two months, he'd already forgotten it.

It was in his dresser.

He traced his fingers up along the dresser drawers, feeling for the telltale vibration. The buzzing stopped.

He opened the second drawer down.

The phone was half covered by a pair of pants, but it was there, clear as day. Archie glanced up at the camera mounted in the corner of the room. The camera didn't have the right angle to see it.

He reached into the drawer and pretended to be fascinated by an imaginary stain on a pair of corduroys while he fumbled with the phone with his other hand. He didn't take it out of the drawer. Five hundred and thirty-eight missed calls. One text message. Archie clicked on it.

'Darling,' it read. 'Feel better?'

Archie's body stiffened. Gretchen.

She'd got someone to put it there, some hospital employee who probably thought the phone was for Archie to keep in touch with a loved one.

It was the second phone she'd found a way to get to him. He'd discovered the first one the second week he'd been there. It was taped under the sink in the bathroom. He'd thrown it away in the bathroom trash, jamming it under half a roll of toilet paper so the custodial staff wouldn't see it.

This time Archie slipped the phone out of the drawer, and put it in his pocket.

He was Level Four. Rosenberg had said he should go for a walk.

11

Three-nine-seven North Fargo was the scariest house in sight. The old bungalow sat abandoned on an empty block that had long ago turned to urban meadow. Its asbestos siding was painted a shade of brown that even in its prime must have embarrassed the neighbours, and its asphalt roof was more moss than shingles. Sheets of plywood covered the windows. The words KEEP OUT were spray-painted across the plywood that covered the front door. If Susan had been scouting locations for a horror movie, she would not have had to look further.

It had to be a prank. It was too perfect.

Susan sat in her car at the kerb and craned her head around to look up and down the street. It was late morning, and no one was around. There were no other houses on that block, and the church parking lot across the street was empty. She considered the possibilities. What if there *was* a body in there? It was feasible. Some beer-fuelled college kids had sneaked inside to party or to read Longfellow or something, and found some dead junkie or homeless person and then didn't want to report it because they didn't want to get hassled for trespassing.

Sure. That made perfect sense.

Or maybe it was a trap. A *Herald* headline flashed in Susan's mind: **Intrepid Reporter Murdered After Walking into Beauty Killer Ambush.** *Journalist*, Susan corrected herself, remembering Henry's joke.

Susan pulled out a cigarette, lit it, and stared some more at the house.

This was ridiculous. She was being dramatic. Get it over with, Nancy Drew.

She tossed her cigarette out into the rain, grabbed her purse full of mace, and got out of the car.

Look like you're supposed to be there. Quentin Parker had taught her that. Look like you're supposed to be there and no one will ask you what the hell you're doing. He had always kept a clipboard in his car. No one questions a man with a clipboard, he'd said.

Susan went around to her trunk, where she kept her emergency reporter kit, and got out a flashlight and notebook, which she put in her purse, and an old clipboard. If someone in the church across the street was watching, she would look like she was trying to Rock the Vote, or maybe conducting a survey. *And how many corpses do you have inside, sir?*

She was wearing black jeans, black lace-up boots, and a black vest. Add the purple hair and red lipstick and she looked more like she should be working at the MAC cosmetics counter than conducting door-to-door surveys.

Did people even use clipboards any more?

Stride confidently. That's the other thing Parker had taught her. Susan tried to stride confidently, but it was a challenge since it was raining pretty hard and she had to tramp through a lot of dead weeds to get up the overgrown front walk.

The house, up close, was even worse off than it looked from the street. The porch, along with the stairs up to it, leaned slightly to the right, while the house itself seemed to lean slightly to the left. Susan walked around the side through knee-high grass. She put the clipboard under her arm. It was pointless. No one could see her anyway. Behind the back of the house she saw what she was looking for – a piece of plywood lay on the ground in front of a basement window that had been broken. You couldn't keep people out of abandoned houses. Not in this neighbourhood.

Susan got her flashlight out of her purse, flipped it on, and squatted near the window. The broken glass had been knocked out clean, so the window frame was free of shards. The natural light coming through the window illuminated a diffuse rectangle of concrete and broken glass below. Susan poked her head in, bracing herself on the window jamb with one hand, and reached the flashlight in as far as she could. It didn't reveal much. Pipes. Ducts. Concrete. It looked . . . basementy.

'Hello?' she said into the darkness. 'Did someone here order a pizza?'

The only sound she heard was a bus going by at the next intersection.

Was it breaking and entering if the window was already

broken? Or was it just entering? If she went in and didn't find anything, she'd go straight to the paper and never tell anyone. Susan couldn't believe she was actually considering this. And at the same time, she felt a shiver of delight. Six months ago, she was writing human-interest stories about zoo animals. This was a lot more exciting.

'I'm coming in,' she said. She stowed the flashlight back in her purse, dangled her legs through the window, and dropped down to the floor below. Broken glass crunched under her boots.

The house was quiet. Weirdly quiet. No central air, no water heater, no humming fridge, none of that ambient house sound.

She got the flashlight out again and turned it on. It illuminated so much dust in the air that the beam looked almost solid. A corner of the basement floor was flooded with brackish groundwater that had seeped in through the foundation. Beer cans, cigarette butts, and broken liquor bottles littered the floor. There was a vague smell of urine.

Susan shuddered. Suddenly covering an elephant's birthday party didn't seem so bad. She looked longingly up at the window she'd just come through. The sill was chin-high. She was skinny, but not strong. There was no way she'd be able to lift herself up to climb out. She was committed.

She took a few tentative steps and aimed the flashlight up the stairs. There were lots of things that could kill you in a house: radon, asbestos, toxic mould, formaldehyde, carbon monoxide, lead, polyurethane foam, fibreglass insulation. This house wasn't any more dangerous than any other.

'Anyone home?' she called. 'I'm gathering signatures,' she said. Her voice sounded hollow and nervous. 'To legalize pot?'

Nothing.

She saw something move. Just a flash. She jerked the flashlight beam to the left just in time to see the back end of a rat skitter past a beer can.

She made it halfway up the stairs in two steps. Not that she was scared of rats, she told herself – she was just suddenly in a very big hurry. The stairs led up to the kitchen. With all the windows covered, the first floor was even darker than the basement. She knew it was the kitchen only because of the cracked speckled linoleum on the floor. There were footprints in the dust on the floor, seemingly dozens, in random patterns, like there'd been a scuffle there, or a square dance.

There were no appliances in the kitchen any more, just empty wooden cupboards and fittings for gas pipes sticking out of the wall where an oven used to be. The sink was filled with more beer cans. There were no dead bodies.

Susan squeezed the flashlight in her armpit, and got her notebook and pen out of her purse. She had to hold the flashlight under her chin to see what she was writing, but she managed to take a few notes. *Footprints. Miller High Life cans. Really fucking spooky. Also, rat.*

She put the notebook and pen away, took the flashlight back in her hand, and followed the beam out of the kitchen into a dark hallway and towards the front of the house until she came to a bedsheet that blocked the entrance to the next room. The sheet had been nailed to the ceiling and hung to the floor like a makeshift door. Classy.

Rat-borne illnesses killed almost thirteen thousand people a year.

Susan heard another bus rumble by.

She felt strangely calm now. Like she was watching herself in a movie. Like she was one of those girls who go into the spooky house alone while the audience hides their faces and screams at her not to do it. The house was empty. She had done it. She'd crawled through a fucking basement window. She'd battled a rat. It was practically heroic. She was going to dine out on this story for months.

She just had to find her way out.

Her flashlight beam threw a yellow circle on the sheet. 'Hello?' she said. She listened, not expecting to hear anything, and then, slowly, pulled the sheet curtain to the side and walked into the room.

The first thing she noticed was that it was clean. Not regular clean. Weird clean. Crazy clean. Her flashlight beam reflected off the scrubbed hardwood floors. The walls and ceiling were a freshly painted white. It smelled different. Like disinfectant. Like a hospital.

Susan's stomach somersaulted as she panned her flashlight around. No furniture. No dust. No cobwebs. Whoever had been squatting there had been a real OCD case. Her flashlight swung past the open sliding door to another room, and stopped. Someone had hung clear plastic sheeting between the two rooms. Visqueen. Her mother kept a sheet of it over the compost pile.

She forgot what she was doing. She forgot that she was looking for a way out. She moved towards the plastic, flashlight in hand, but it was so thick that the beam of light couldn't penetrate it enough to see the other side. She tried to pull it aside but it was nailed up more securely than the sheet in the hall, and she had to duck down and squeeze through below where it was fastened.

She turned, straightened up, and lifted her flashlight to look around.

Something was in there.

The knot in Susan's stomach tightened. 'Hello?' she said.

It was under a sheet. Maybe a piece of furniture. People threw white sheets over furniture to protect it if they were going away for a while. Rich people, with second houses, in the twenties. It wasn't furniture. Old clothes? Something a squatter left, hoping to come back for later?

It wasn't old clothes.

Who was the guy who'd phoned her? And why?

Call the cops, her little voice said.

But instead she felt in her purse for the notebook and pen.

She traced the form on the floor with her flashlight. Surrounding it, like some sort of offering, were eight or ten big red plastic flashlights, none of them on.

Maybe it was some sort of renovation project.

It wasn't a renovation project.

'Okay,' Susan said. She moved tentatively forward, notebook and pen clutched in one hand, flashlight in the other. 'I'm going to look.' When she got to the form she knelt down, and the knees of her jeans pressed into something wet. She sat back on her heels and shone her flashlight on her legs. Blood.

She jumped to her feet. Blood was everywhere. The form was soaked in it. It pooled on the floor, a viscous jam, shiny in the flashlight beam. She opened her purse, snapped up her spray can of herbal mace, and held it out, index finger on the nozzle.

'Are you okay?' she asked in a tiny voice.

It sounded stupid even as she said it. There was no way someone could bleed that much and still be alive. *Don't look under the sheet.* She couldn't help it. She had to know. She held the flashlight overhead, an ad hoc bludgeoning instrument, and, grimacing, used the spray can of mace to ease the sheet back.

She took his face in all at once – a flash of eyebrows and acne scars, a slender nose, round face, and soft chin, all the details ordering in her brain to form a face, a young man, a guy her age. For a split second, she thought he was okay, that he'd start laughing, that it was all some stupid joke. He was wearing one of those silly hospital scrub caps, for Christ's sake, a purple one with cartoon elephants on it, like he was in some sort of costume. And his eyes were open. She let the breath she'd been holding escape in a gasp. Then her brain caught up with her.

The eyes weren't right. The lids were pulled back too far, his fixed stare barely visible under a cataract-like white glaze.

She jerked back, and her flashlight beam momentarily angled up, cutting a path to the opposite wall. For a second

Susan thought she was seeing things. She angled the flashlight up again, the beam trembling with her hand. The yellow ball of light slid across the wall, and Susan wanted to turn it off, wanted it to be dark, because even scary pitch-black would be better than this.

The wall had been painted white. But it had been decorated. Someone had covered the surface, almost every inch of it, with hundreds and hundreds of hand-drawn red hearts.

Get out of the house, her little voice screamed. But Susan didn't move. There was no fucking way she was going back into that basement.

She reached into her purse and felt around for her phone.

She called the paper first, and 911 second.

12

Henry stood in the rain on the hillside with Detective Martin Ngyun, staring down at the leathery head in the mud. The ferns and brush around the head were charred and the entire area was dusted with foam from a fire extinguisher. Henry could see a soot-blackened cigarette that had been stamped deeply into the dirt.

Henry peered up the hillside. The whole task force had responded. A busload of Beauty Killer tourists were standing at the top of the hill behind the crime-scene tape taking pictures. No keeping this one under wraps. They were probably tweeting as he stood there. 'Who put out the fire?' Henry asked Ngyun.

Ngyun had been on the task force for seven years. The only time off he'd ever taken was when the Blazers had made the finals. That hadn't turned out well at all.

'Some docent from the house,' Ngyun said, adjusting the bill of his Blazers cap against the rain. 'Seventy-two years old. Jumped the fence and climbed down the hillside with a fire extinguisher.'

Henry extended a hand, palm up. 'It's raining,' he said.

'Hadn't started yet,' Ngyun said.

The head had been severed from its body close to the jawbone. The rain was melting the fire-extinguisher foam and Henry could see that the skull showed through in places, and the hair had thinned and was matted with dirt. It was face-down, resting against the root of a weed. Henry looked up the hillside again. 'My guess is someone tossed it over the fence,' he said, his eyes following the angle of the slope. 'And it rolled down here.'

'Lucky it didn't roll any further,' Ngyun said. 'Never would have found it.' He frowned at the tangle of blackberries below. 'Probably dozens of heads down there.'

'I'll talk to the mayor about curfew,' Henry said. This was the new mayor. He'd taken the job two months ago, after the old mayor had blown his brains out in front of Archie.

'Yeah,' Ngyun said. 'Because no one gets murdered during the daytime.'

'It will appease the citizenry,' Henry said. He squatted, trying to get a better look at the head's features, but the angle of the face in the mud made it hard. 'Where's the ME?'

'On his way,' Ngyun said. He glanced at his watch. 'It's eleven. They said eleven-fifteen.'

Henry hesitated. He knew he'd catch hell from Robbins for moving the remains. But fuck it. He pushed the thing with the toe of his shoe, until it rolled face-up.

The holes where its nose, eyes, and mouth used to be were crawling with wiggling yellow maggots. No telling if the thing had its eyes gouged out, or just lost them to worms.

Claire called his name, and Henry looked up to see her standing with her hands on her hips looking down at them. Next to her, in a white Tyvek suit, was Lorenzo Robbins, of the medical examiners' department.

'Did you just kick my head?' Robbins said in disbelief.

Henry's phone rang. He'd never been so happy to get a phone call in his life. He smiled up at Robbins, held a finger out in a 'just a minute' gesture, and picked it up.

It was a sergeant from the North Portland precinct. 'We have something your task force might be interested in,' the sergeant said. 'A *Herald* reporter found a body that looks like it might be Beauty Killer-related.'

A *Herald* reporter. Take precautions, he'd told her. Be safe. Don't do anything stupid. 'Let me guess,' Henry said. 'Susan Ward.'

13

Archie sat on the floor, leaning up against the mauve wall in a bathroom on the first floor of the hospital.

He held the phone in his lap, rereading the text. '*Darling, feel better?*'

Archie put his head in his hands. Two years had passed and his ribs still ached from where she'd broken them. They probably always would. He moved his hands to his neck, and felt the length of the scar there, his freshest scar, two months old and still tender to the touch. Then he reached under the waist of his shirt and moved one of his hands over his older scars: the one that ran up his midsection, the smaller scars on his flank, and finally the heart-shaped reminder on his chest.

His mind turned to the butchery at the rest stop.

She would not stop killing.

Archie picked the phone up and pressed the top of it against his forehead, digging into the skin until his skull felt like it might split, and his head cleared. Fuck it.

He sat up and punched in a text. 'Where are you?'

He hit send and waited.

The toilet was beige with a mismatched white seat. There was a handicap grab bar next to it, and a hook to hang a purse on, and a feminine-hygiene-product waste receptacle. Archie looked up at the ceiling. White corkboard panels. A smoke detector. A sprinkler valve. Two white air vents were layered with years' worth of dust and grime. No one ever bothered to clean up there.

He glanced back at the phone. Nothing.

The rose-tile floor gleamed, even though the grout was brown. There was a round silver drain in the middle of the floor.

Someone rattled the handle of the bathroom door.

Archie looked up, startled. 'Occupied,' he called.

The phone vibrated. He looked at the screen. 'Do you miss me?'

Archie stared at the phone, calculating how to respond. A thousand options flew through his mind. He needed her to show herself. He needed her to think he was still in her thrall.

There was a knock on the door. 'Just a second,' Archie said.

A small brown house spider crawled out of the drain on the floor and scurried over the tiles towards the sink.

Archie typed, 'I want to see you,' and hit send.

An hourglass rotated on the phone screen. Then popped out of view. Message sent.

He looked up at the door, stood, flushed the toilet, and then held his hands under the sensor to turn on the water. The countertop was speckled peach and black Formica, the same colour and pattern that Courtenay had dug into her neck. It had probably come off the same roll.

Archie checked the phone. The only thing on the screen was the time: 11.23, 11.24, 11.25. He dried his hands with a paper towel and threw it in the grey rectangular trash can. A caricature of a lady skunk stared down at Archie from the Aire-Master air freshener.

Someone tried the door again. 'Just a second,' Archie called again, this time more loudly.

The door handle jiggled uselessly against the lock.

Archie ignored it this time. It was a hospital. There were dozens of public restrooms.

He set the phone on the speckled Formica and fixed his eyes on the screen, willing Gretchen to respond. 'Come on,' he said softly, gripping the edge of the counter. 'Come to me.'

The phone buzzed in his hand and a new text popped up. '*Knock knock.*'

Archie studied the words on the phone, and then, slowly, gazed up at the door. She was in the hospital. She was watching him right now. He put the phone back in his pocket and turned and took a step towards the door.

'Gretchen?' he said.

There was no response. Archie extended his arm, reached his hand out and carefully turned the lock. Then he folded his hand around the handle, took a deep breath, and pushed the door open.

There was no one on the other side. He turned his head. The hallway was empty. He reached up and touched his forehead. He was sweating. He looked at the phone and then shoved it in his pocket. He was letting her get to him again. It was a guess. She'd guessed that he'd call her from a locked room. It hadn't been her at the door. The person who'd been waiting had become impatient and left.

He had enough problems without adding paranoia to the list.

Archie could see a gift store at the far end of the corridor. He squinted at it, and recognized the book displayed in the window – *The Last Victim*. It had been two months since Archie had read a paper. If he was going to have a chance at finding her, he needed to catch up on the news. He started walking. Halfway down the corridor, he stopped and did a three-sixty. There was no one of interest around, but he could not escape the disquieting feeling that he was being watched.

14

Gretchen's photograph graced the front page of every newspaper the hospital gift store sold.

Archie picked up a copy of the *Herald*. **Day Number Seventy-six**, screamed the headline below her front-page photo. Archie leafed through it. No story about the rest stop. That would be in tomorrow's edition. There were four stories about Gretchen. But nothing new. Just the same rehashed details, the same quotes.

Archie closed the paper and looked at her picture on the front page again. It was her mugshot from two years ago. She was wearing the same clothes she'd had on in his final memories of being tortured. When she'd held him, and stroked his head, when he thought he was finally dying, and was so grateful to her for letting him.

Her blonde hair was brushed into a smooth ponytail, not a hair out of place.

Gretchen took a beautiful mugshot.

Something caught Archie's eye inside the gift store. Her image again, multiplied. He put the paper down and stepped inside, and then made his way past the gleaming foil balloons, the stuffed animals, the candy and sentimental cards, past the white-haired woman sitting behind a knick-knack-jammed counter, watching TV, and stopped in front of the magazine rack.

Twenty different magazines were displayed in plastic pockets on the wall. Almost every issue featured Gretchen as its cover girl.

The press had always loved Gretchen. She'd made headlines around the world. But he had never seen anything like this.

News magazines promised stories of her crimes and updates on the manhunt. Fashion magazines promised to help women make their hair look like hers. Cultural magazines questioned her influence. Entertainment magazines mused about potential casting for an upcoming feature about her.

The cover of *Portland Monthly* had an image of a tour bus plastered with Gretchen's face on it. **Gretchen Lowell,** the headline read. **Portland's Next Big Tourist Attraction?**

But the magazine that caught his eye was the current issue of *Newsweek*. It wasn't her airbrushed headshot on the cover that made his gut twist. It was the huge bold-letter headline – a single word:

INNOCENT?

15

The fingerprint tech rolled Susan's right index finger, left to right, over the sponge of dark purple ink. He'd done her thumb first, and was working his way to her pinkie. Elimination prints, they called them. Next time she broke into a house she was definitely wearing gloves.

'This better come off,' Susan said.

She was perched on the back of a police van, the cab's double doors open on either side of her, blocking the view of the gawkers who already lined the police tape that had just gone up a half-hour ago. The rain had stopped, but not before Susan's hair had gone frizzy. Police radios cracked, emergency lights flashed. Everyone walked with purpose. The blood on Susan's jeans had started to dry, stiffening the denim against her knees. She was trying to ignore it.

The fingerprint tech was sitting next to her, a police fingerprint card on the bed of the van between them. His hooded eyes didn't waver from his work, his balding head bowed over her hand beside her. 'Hold still,' he told Susan.

Henry cleared his throat and tapped his notebook with

his pen. He'd come out of the house ten minutes before, mouth set, eyes masked behind sunglasses, and had been grilling her ever since.

'How did this guy get your cell-phone number?' Henry asked.

'Everyone has it,' Susan said. 'It's on my e-mail signature. I'm a reporter. I need to be reachable.' She craned forward, trying to catch a glimpse of his notes. She should be the one asking him questions. For a reporter, she spent an awful lot of time being interviewed. 'So, I hear you found a head,' she said.

Henry angled his notebook towards his chest. 'I should arrest you for trespassing,' he said. 'What the fuck were you thinking?'

'I played the odds,' Susan said. She looked at her boots. They were caked with mud. She had probably tracked it all through the house. 'Who's the dead guy?' she asked.

Henry rubbed the back of his neck like it hurt.

Susan could hear more sirens in the distance. The fingerprint tech moved on to the next finger. She glanced, dismayed, at her purple fingertip. 'Seriously,' she said, 'that ink washes off, right?'

'The victim doesn't have ID,' Henry said, and Susan looked back up. 'The ME says male in his early twenties. Only been dead two to six hours.' Henry leaned toward her. It was a tiny motion, a shift in his stance of an inch, imperceptible to anyone watching, but Henry was a mountain, and it was all Susan could do not to cower. 'Tell me about the caller,' Henry said.

'Tell me about the head,' she said.

'We found a head,' Henry said. 'Pittock Mansion. We had to close off part of the backyard, but you can still take a tour of the house.' He scratched one eyebrow. 'I think they're charging extra.'

Susan pulled at her damp tank top. 'He didn't sound young,' she said of the caller. 'He didn't sound old. He said he was part of a Gretchen Lowell fan group.' She caught herself. 'I mean, not specifically. He said I'd written to him on his website, wanting to write about his group.' Henry held his pen to his notebook, apparently still waiting for her to say something worth writing down. She wound a piece of purple hair around a finger and tried to remember any other group she might have contacted – she used the Internet endlessly – but came up only with the Gretchen story. 'I've been contacting Beauty Killer fan sites.' She left out the part about him not recognizing Jimi Hendrix. She didn't think Henry would be interested.

Henry wrote something down. Susan lifted her chin to read it. 'SW PC.' He circled it. 'What the hell does that mean?' she asked.

'I'm going to need your hard drive,' he said.

He had to be kidding. 'No,' Susan said. And she felt the need to add, 'And I have a Mac, not a PC.'

Henry adjusted his sunglasses, pressing them more firmly into place. It wasn't sunny. But Susan wasn't sure this was the time to point that out. 'We need to trace your Internet history,' he said.

Susan shook her head. 'And have you find out how much time I spend Googling myself?' she said. 'No way.'

Henry lowered his head and looked up at her from under the aviators, and she knew then why he wore them. 'This is a murder investigation,' he said. 'You're obstructing justice.' He gritted his teeth. 'And pissing me off.'

'I'm a *journalist*,' she said, straightening up. 'I'm not turning my computer over to the police.' She'd told the cops when they first got there that she wasn't showing them her incoming call log. She was protecting a source. It was the code. Once you gave up a source, you could forget about anyone ever telling you anything again. Parker taught her that. He'd gone to jail to protect a source. 'Good luck getting a warrant,' she added. The fingerprint tech rolled her ring finger across the ink pad. There was dirt under the nail. 'Can you tell an ape fingerprint from a human one?' she asked him.

The tech didn't look up. He lifted her finger off the ink and pressed it in the centre of a square on the fingerprint card. Susan admired his focus. 'Yes,' he said.

Henry wrote something down. 'Do you think you'd recognize the caller's voice?' he asked.

Susan tried to replay the caller's voice in her head, but it eluded her. 'Maybe,' she said. She gazed down at her blood-stained jeans. Thank God for black denim. It could hide anything.

'The guy I found,' she said – she could still see his face, those egg-white eyes – 'how'd he die?'

'I think we can rule out natural causes,' Henry said.

Susan had knelt two feet away from the body, and got blood on her pants. The sheet was soaked with it. The guy had bled a lot. Like he'd been cut up. No, she thought, *operated* on. The hearts on the wall, Gretchen's signature, the fan site. Suddenly she knew. 'His spleen's gone, isn't it?' Susan asked. Henry's reaction was almost undetectable. But he flinched.

Someone had ripped out his spleen. Just like Gretchen had done to her victims, like she'd done to Archie. She had sliced Archie open without anaesthesia and cut it out of him. Then sent it to Henry in the mail. Susan's throat tightened and she had to swallow a few times before she could speak. 'Should I be in protection?' she asked.

Henry took off the sunglasses and looked at her. His shaved head was still shiny with rain. 'Leave town,' he said.

It was a good idea. Go to Mexico for a few months. Get some writing done. Maybe she could have done it, a few months ago, before she'd met Archie. 'I can't,' she said. 'I'm a journalist. I can't.'

Susan's pulse was racing. The fingerprint tech must have felt it because he looked up at her for the first time since he'd arrived. 'Koalas,' he said. 'You fingerprint a koala, it's almost impossible to tell the print from a human one.'

'Seriously?' Susan said.

He pressed her pinkie onto the cardstock. 'Fools us every time,' he said.

'Did you know,' Susan said, 'that in the past twenty years, nine children have been crushed to death by school cafeteria tables?'

The fingerprint tech glanced up worriedly. 'No,' he said.

Susan relaxed a little, and as she did her brain started to circle the details. Who had called her? 'Do you think she has a new accomplice?' Susan asked Henry. He didn't answer. Then something occurred to her. 'Accomplices?' she asked, stressing the plural. The crime scene flashed in her mind. 'There were ten flashlights.'

'One person could have set up all the flashlights,' Henry said, putting the sunglasses back on. 'We want to keep the flashlight thing out of the media, okay?'

'Maybe she had nine accomplices,' Susan said. 'Like a serial-killer baseball team. Or maybe she's trying people out. You know, she cuts one of them from the team after every kill. The last guy alive gets to be her murder buddy.'

Henry was not amused. 'Tell me about these fan sites,' he said.

'People paint pictures of her and post them,' Susan said. 'They write her poetry. Fan fiction. I did a story about it a few weekends ago.' No reaction. Susan exhaled, exasperated. 'You don't even read the *Herald*, do you?'

'I get all my news from the *Daily Auto Trader*,' Henry said.

The fingerprint tech handed Susan a moist towelette. She scrubbed her fingers with it and the ink wiped right off. Whatever was in that towelette had to be toxic. 'I have to work,' Susan said, standing up. The fingerprint tech held out a plastic bag and she dropped the inky towelette in it.

Henry crossed his arms. 'I can't convince you to keep

some of what you saw to yourself?' he said. 'So as to, you know, avoid pande-fucking-monium?'

'No chance,' Susan said. 'Besides, you found a head. You don't think the citizens are going to freak out as it is?'

Henry grunted. 'You're getting to be a better reporter,' he said.

'Journalist,' she corrected him. She waved a hand at him and took a few steps away from the van.

'Wait,' Henry called, and she turned around. He stared at her, working his jaw, one hand behind his neck. Then his hand dropped, and he stepped towards her. 'I'm only telling you this because it's going to come out,' he said. 'And it might as well be you.' He sighed. 'There are some things about the rest stop we haven't made public.'

16

Archie sat on the gift-store floor, surrounded by magazines, the *Newsweek* open on his lap. Pictures of Gretchen smiled up from all around him on the carpet. He'd found twenty-seven stories about her in all. He'd read the *Newsweek* first. It was full of excuses. She wasn't to blame. It was society. We were all responsible.

Archie didn't remember society pressing a scalpel into his chest.

There were photographs of him, too. Standing at a crime scene. Leaving the hospital. The man she'd tried to kill twice. They portrayed him as some sort of hero. It made better copy, Archie guessed, than the truth. The details about their latest run-in were sketchy. Henry had managed to keep under wraps the specifics of how Archie had again found himself at Gretchen's mercy. He was recuperating from his injuries. She was at large.

Reality was murkier.

Archie touched the photograph of her in *Newsweek*. It had been taken outside the courthouse. She'd been turning away, her wrists in manacles, dressed in prison blue, hair loose, profile perfect, like an image off a coin. He lifted his hand, leaving a fingerprint on the page.

He turned over his hands and looked at his palms. He was sweating again.

God, he wanted a Vicodin.

He wiped his hands on the front of his pants, feeling the phone inside his pocket. He pulled it out. No new messages.

'If you're interested in her, we've got the book,' the old woman behind the counter said. Archie looked up. She'd unpacked several angels from the box and had lined them up in front of her on the counter, and now peered over them.

Archie saw himself then, sitting there, surrounded by magazines open to articles about the Beauty Killer, what he must look like. He put the phone back in his pocket.

The old woman tilted her head towards the window display where a stack of copies of *The Last Victim* were stacked next to a dozen copies of *The Five People You Meet in Heaven*.

Archie closed the *Newsweek*, got to his feet, and slid it back on its shelf behind him. 'I already own a copy,' he said.

He bent down to gather the magazines on the floor so he could reshelve them, and as he did he glanced up at the old woman. The small television still played behind her, and for a second, Archie thought he saw Gretchen's face on the screen. He stood there, frozen, in a sort of half squat, convinced he was seeing things, still riveted by the TV, as graphics spun onto the screen to form the words *Beauty Killer at Large: Day 76.*

The graphics burst into flame

Archie straightened. 'Turn it up,' he said.

The old woman looked at him sceptically. Then she slowly turned to glance at the TV screen, then back at him, and down to the magazines at his feet.

'Turn it up,' Archie said again. He moved forward, towards the counter and the TV.

She raised an eyebrow, paused, lifted another angel out of the box and set it on the counter, and then pulled a remote from the pocket of her polyester waistcoat and hit a button.

A newscaster appeared in an electric-blue KGW news channel raincoat holding a mic, with Pittock Mansion in the background. A human head had been found on the grounds. The image cut to another newscaster in another blue KGW raincoat standing in front of a boarded-up house. A body had been found in the house. Police weren't releasing any details.

In a wide shot, Archie caught a glimpse of Henry walking into the house.

Archie reached for the cell phone that was usually clipped to his belt, his fingers on the corduroy of his pants, finding nothing. His cell phone was locked away back at the ward.

But he had another one.

He slid his hand in his pocket and found the cell phone again. But he didn't pull it out.

The old woman was watching the TV now, eyebrows knitted, one hand still wrapped around the feet of the statue of an angel, knelt in prayer, a wire halo stuck into the top of its head.

'Can I use your phone?' Archie asked.

She had no reason to say yes, but she reached over and lifted the receiver off a beige desktop telephone and set it in Archie's hand. 'Dial nine,' she said.

Archie dialled nine, and then Henry's cell phone number. Henry picked up on the third ring.

'What's going on?' Archie asked him.

'Where are you calling from?' Henry asked.

'The hospital gift store,' Archie said. 'I needed a balloon.'

He could sense Henry hedge. Archie was on leave. He had no right to know anything about a police investigation. 'Susan Ward got a tip and found a body in an abandoned house on North Fargo,' Henry said. 'And someone dumped a head in the yard up at Pittock Mansion.'

They'd found one of Gretchen's victims on the grounds at Pittock Mansion just months before she was caught. She'd never repeated herself before. But it couldn't be a coincidence. 'Eyes?' Archie asked.

'The head's too decomposed to tell,' Henry said. 'Robbins is looking at it now. Body in the house has eyes. He's fresh. Killed sometime overnight.'

Archie glanced back at the TV screen where KGW news anchor Charlene Wood now stood at the scene interviewing a bystander. 'Is it Gretchen?' Archie said.

Henry exhaled. 'There are hearts drawn on the wall next to the body,' he said. 'Like at the rest stop. Susan called the paper. It went out on the wire. There are reporters everywhere.'

Archie felt his chest tighten again. 'Is Susan okay?' he asked.

'She's a pain in the ass,' Henry said. 'Won't give up the source who tipped her.'

Archie couldn't help but smile. 'Parker would be proud.'

'Yeah, well, it's fucking dandy that her journalistic testicles have dropped, but that doesn't help me much with the crime fighting,' Henry said. 'It looks like the victim's missing his spleen. That's not public yet,' he added. 'But it will be.'

The old woman unpacked another angel.

'I can send a car for you,' Henry said.

Archie turned and glanced behind him, back into the hall. He thought about telling Henry, but he couldn't without giving up the phone. What was he supposed to say? 'I think she's got someone inside the hospital who's spying on me'? 'I just have a feeling'?

He'd sound like a lunatic.

'I'm just not up for it,' Archie said. He didn't need to find her. She would find him. He was sure of it.

'Your family still coming tonight?' Henry asked.

Debbie brought the kids by every Wednesday. It was something Archie usually looked forward to, but with all the drama, he'd lost track of what day it was. 'They're still coming,' Archie said, rubbing his eyes.

'Say hi,' said Henry. He hesitated, and then, in a tone that made Archie wonder if Henry sensed something was wrong, he added: 'I'll check in later.'

'Okay,' Archie said. He dropped the receiver back into its cradle and glanced up at the TV. It had already gone back to *Perry Mason*.

'You're him, aren't you?' The old woman tilted her head again in the direction of the front window display.

'No,' Archie said.

She nodded. 'You're that detective.'

She picked up one of the angels and held it out to him. There was a brass plaque at the angel's feet with a pretty script. Three words.

Watch over me

She set it in his hand.

17

A **sign posted** in the elevator up to the psych ward read:

SHOULD THE ELEVATOR DOORS FAIL TO OPEN
DO NOT BECOME ALARMED, THERE IS LITTLE DANGER
OF RUNNING OUT OF AIR OR OF THIS ELEVATOR
DROPPING UNCONTROLLABLY.

'That's reassuring,' Archie said to the candy striper riding in the elevator next to him.

Her eyes widened.

'It's for the crazy people,' Archie explained. 'We panic easily.'

He wasn't making her more comfortable. He decided to stop talking. Then he noticed that she was holding an envelope in her hand with his name on it. The envelope was big and square and pink and hard to miss. The candy striper was fanning her face with it. Hospital volunteers weren't called candy stripers any more. Archie didn't know what they were called.

'That's for me,' Archie said.

She wasn't a teenager. College, maybe. She shot Archie a reflexive smile. 'I have to deliver it to the ward,' she said. 'Before I can go to lunch.'

The elevator doors opened and they both stepped out into the psych ward's minuscule lobby. The girl was hesitant.

'You've never been up here before,' Archie said.

'Are there psychos?' she whispered.

'Tons,' Archie said. He pressed the call buzzer. 'It's Archie Sheridan,' he said.

'Just a minute, Mr Sheridan,' a nurse's voice responded.

The girl looked down at the name on the card. 'I guess you are you,' she said.

'I'm pretty sure I still am,' Archie said. He noticed her nails then. French pink with blood-red tips. Women liked it when you complimented them. Archie didn't know much about women, but he knew that. 'I like your nails,' he said.

Her cheeks dimpled and she inspected a fluttering hand. 'It's called a "Beauty Killer",' she said. 'My manicurist says all the celebrities are doing it.'

Archie nearly choked. A Beauty Killer manicure? Everyone had lost their minds.

'Are you okay?' the girl asked.

Muffled hollering echoed from behind the door. Archie recognized the bellicose ranting of his room-mate, Frank.

The girl drew a sharp breath.

'He's harmless,' Archie assured her.

The girl tapped a foot and bit her bottom lip. 'What's taking them so long?'

'They're distracted,' Archie said. It took a few minutes and several staff members to subdue one of Frank's tantrums. He gave the girl what he hoped was a sane smile. From inside the ward, Frank howled something about devils. The girl stiffened. 'Why don't you just give me the card?' Archie suggested.

She considered it for a split second, then pushed the card into Archie's hand.

'Okay,' she said, hitting the elevator button. The doors opened immediately and she leaped inside. 'Nice angel,' she said as the doors slid closed.

Archie set the angel down on the table of Al-Anon brochures and examined the envelope.

There was no postmark, which meant that it hadn't come through the mail – someone had dropped it off at the hospital. The return address was 397 North Fargo. No name. The body had been found on Fargo. The address wasn't in Gretchen's handwriting, but it would not have been hard for her to find someone else to write it. Archie worked his finger under the flap and along the glue line, and pulled out the card.

The card was old-fashioned, the paper softened with age. Two red hearts were connected by a gold chain. Below the hearts was a white ribbon emblazoned with the words A VALENTINE MESSAGE. Archie opened the card. Printed inside, in pretty cursive, was a poem: 'May this chain / Be the one sweet tether / That binds your heart / And mine together.'

She could get to him anywhere. It was just a matter of time.

Frank's screaming quieted, and a nurse came and opened the door. Archie walked inside.

He left the angel on the table.

18

Susan sat glued to her computer at the *Herald*. She had copy due at two. And it was already quarter of.

Eyeballs in a toilet tank. Susan wondered if Gretchen had gouged them out while the people were still alive, or waited until after she'd murdered them. Either way, it made Susan's eyes ache just thinking about it.

The Pittock Mansion Head, as everyone was already calling it, had made national news. CNN quoted a source at the ME's office saying that the head's eyes were missing. They were running an online poll where you could guess what colour they were going to turn out to be. Brown was winning two to one.

The *Herald* was abuzz. The TVs bolted to the ceiling were all tuned to live reports from the house on Fargo and from the Gorge and from Pittock. There was talk already of doing another special issue. Susan was working on a first-person account of finding the body; Derek was working the news angle and Ian had sent two other reporters up to the mansion. Thanks to Henry, Susan had broken the additional details about the rest-stop story on the *Herald* web-site. The eyeballs. The hearts on the wall. The spleen. They'd go big on it the next day – front page, above the fold. Henry had promised a sketch of the dead guy in the house by deadline, so they could run it and see if anyone recognized him.

The cops had their Beauty Killer Task Force; the *Herald* had its own version – Susan and Derek, plus two other reporters, two editors, two photographers, a copy editor, and an intern. They'd profiled the families of victims. They'd tracked down people who claimed to have seen Gretchen Lowell since her escape. They'd interviewed anyone and everyone who'd ever had contact with her and lived. The only thing they hadn't done was a background on her. No one knew where Gretchen Lowell came from. There was a record of her being picked up for writing a bad cheque in Salt Lake City when she was nineteen. That was it. No school records. No birth certificate.

Just a lot of bodies and the few biographical details Gretchen had doled out in prison, most of which were probably lies. The lack of information had left the reporters covering the manhunt with little choice but to recycle the same interviews, the same experts, over and over again.

The thrill of the hunt had turned tedious and a gallows humour had taken root. A photograph of Gretchen Lowell peppered with darts hung on the wall. Ian had given everyone in the group mugs with Gretchen Lowell's face on them and the words *I'd kill for some coffee*.

'What did Gretchen Lowell give Archie Sheridan for

Valentine's Day?' the intern asked. She never remembered his name. She just thought of him as 'the intern'.

'Not in the mood,' Susan said, eyes on her monitor.

'His heart,' the intern said. 'Ha!' He was wearing a RUN, GRETCHEN T-shirt and Kissinger glasses that were either incredibly hip or deeply uncool – Susan hadn't figured out which. She glared at him, and he turned back to his computer.

'I'm forwarding it,' he said.

'You do that,' Susan said.

She went back to cramming her near-death experience into thirty inches. Advertising was tight, and it took more than a dead body and a serial killer to justify space for a story someone couldn't read, in one sitting, on a toilet.

She scrolled through her call log again and found the number of the man who'd phoned her with the address.

Parker had told her that back in the golden age of newspaper reporting, reporters had had to use reverse phone books to look up addresses from phone numbers. These were massive bound books provided by the phone company and kept under lock and key in a conference room cabinet. You had to get an editor to unlock the cabinet for you and then you had to look up what you wanted right then because you couldn't take the books back to your desk. The phone company sent new directories every year, so there was no guarantee the information was even up to date. But it was still a cool trick. Something to show people on the tour. Tell me your phone number and I'll tell you your address. Before Google, it was like magic.

Now anyone with a phone number could plug the digits into a free Internet search engine and have the corresponding address online in an instant. Plug the address into Google Earth and you could see a 360-degree street view of the house.

It sort of took the fun out of it.

Susan's search of the number from her phone log had not turned up a house. It had turned up a pay phone in North Portland.

There had been 2.1 million pay phones in the US in 1998. Now there were less than 840,000. (Probably even fewer, as it had been a few months since Susan had done her big pay-phone feature.) Cell phones hadn't been real good for Superman that way. But Oregon had thought ahead, and when pay phones started going the way of Big Mouth Billy Bass and laser discs, Oregon had passed legislation to preserve 'public interest pay phones' in areas where not everyone had the latest BlackBerry. Places like North Portland.

Susan plugged a nearby address into Google Earth and fooled around until she found an image with the pay phone in the background. No booth – just one of those half-shells with a big black phone-book binder dangling from a silver cord.

Then, on a lark, she plugged in the address of the house: 397 North Fargo. She was surprised by what came up.

Nothing.

No such address.

'Where's my copy?' Ian said.

Two o'clock.

Susan looked up to see her editor, Ian Harper, leaning a skinny hip on the edge of her desk. He pulled at his ponytail, a habit Susan had once found endearing and now just annoyed her. There were editors who didn't bother you until deadline, and editors who hovered. Ian was a helicopter.

She pried off her boots and pulled her legs up into a cross-legged position on her chair. 'How's the wife?' she asked.

Ian's mouth tensed. He looked around. No one had looked up. No one cared. The intern was busy tweeting his latest Gretchen Lowell joke. Most of the *Herald* staff listened to iPods while they worked. The vast and carpeted fifth floor was a cube farm of people sitting in silence, staring at glowing monitors.

'I want my thirty inches in a half hour,' he said. He reached up and slid a stray piece of brown hair back into his ponytail.

'I'm working on it,' Susan said.

He started reading over her shoulder. Susan positioned herself between him and the monitor.

'Don't bury the lead,' Ian said, tapping in the air towards the screen. 'That's your hook. Make the most of those two inches.'

Susan smiled sweetly. 'You would know,' she said.

The intern laughed.

Ian pushed off her desk and started back to his office. 'I want to see typing,' he said, not looking back.

Susan swivelled back to her monitor, wondering how

she'd ever slept with him. 'It's called "keyboarding" now,' she said.

A newspaper column inch was about thirty-five words. Thirty inches was 1,050 words. Susan always had to do the maths. She kept a solar calculator on her desk for just that purpose. Five hundred words in, five hundred fifty to go.

A stack of envelopes hit her desk. Derek. He grinned at her. He had a cleft in his chin. An actual cleft. Like Kirk Douglas. Susan had never met anyone with an actual cleft before Derek.

She caught him one morning in her bathroom cleaning out his cleft with a cotton bud.

'You got mail,' he said.

She glanced down at the pile of envelopes – some obviously press releases, some coaster-sized white envelopes with little-old-lady handwriting, and one bright pink envelope that looked to be some sort of card. 'You checked my box?'

'I was checking my box,' he said with a shrug. 'Our boxes are right next to each other.' He paused and gazed at her meaningfully, like their box proximity might be some sort of cosmic sign.

Susan threw a look at her overflowing in tray. 'Just put it in the pile,' she said.

Derek frowned. 'You need to reply to readers,' he said. 'It's part of marketing.'

'I would,' Susan said, 'but I'm out of Garfield stationery.'

Derek smoothed out a wrinkle in his khakis. 'You hate Garfield,' he said.

Susan splayed her hands. 'But I love lasagne,' she said. 'Ironic.' She pushed away from her desk and leaned back in her chair. 'I need to work, Derek. I'm on deadline.'

His eyes fell to her jeans. 'You've got blood on your pants,' he said.

She looked down at her shins. The blood had hardened into a smooth rust-coloured stain. Susan uncrossed her legs and lowered her socked feet to the floor. 'Thanks,' she said.

'I've got some OxiClean in my desk,' Derek said.

'That's good on stains,' the intern said.

Susan turned to the intern. 'Aren't you supposed to be writing a sidebar on spleens?' she said.

'Sorry,' the intern said.

'You get anything out of the PIO?' Susan asked Derek. One of the great things about covering real news was getting to use nifty acronyms for things like 'police information officer'.

'Nothing you didn't get from Sobol. They haven't identified the body yet. I did a little digging and found out that the house is owned by an old lady. She's been in a home for over fifteen years. Place has been vacant since she left. There's an oil tank on the property and radon in the basement. She couldn't sell it.' He scratched the cleft in his chin. 'I might go interview her. Human-interest angle. Funny thing is, she said that she'd already gotten two offers for the house since the news broke. I guess people want their very own Beauty Killer crime scene.'

'Sure,' Susan said. 'Open up a little B and B.'

Derek shrugged. 'What are you going to do,' he said. He turned and walked away, and sat back down at the desk he'd inherited from Parker a few months ago.

He never looked comfortable in it. It was too big for him.

19

They had cleaned up the blood spattered on the floor in the break room. Archie could still smell the bleach. Word on the ward was the counsellor had needed stitches; Courtenay hadn't. She was back in her room, in lockdown. She'd been singing the same song all afternoon. 'High Hopes'. You could hear it all the way down the hall. *He's got high hopes ... high apple pie, in the sky hopes.*

Archie hoped it was intended to be funny.

'My sister's coming to visit,' Frank said from the couch.

'Yeah, Frank,' Archie said.

Archie had showered and put on clean clothes and brushed his teeth after dinner. They ate at five o'clock, like old people. Now he was drinking coffee out of a mug that had a cartoon of letters spelling MONDAY laid out on a psychiatrist's couch. In a voice balloon, Monday is saying, 'Everybody hates me.'

Archie took a sip out of the mug and glanced up at the clock. Six-thirty. Debbie was always on time. He watched the hands meet at the bottom of the clock, then looked over at the door to the break room. Debbie stood there, leaning against the door jamb, smiling at him. Her summer tan, acquired from gardening, had faded. No garden at her secure Vancouver apartment. Still, she was more beautiful than ever. Short dark hair, a black sundress, bare arms crossed, silver bracelets on her wrists. She looked younger, almost happy.

Ben and Sara burst in on either side of her and ran to Archie. As time passed, they looked more and more like her. Her freckles. Her fine, straight hair. Her long limbs. It made Archie glad to see so little of himself in them, as if they might be spared some essential suffering. He hugged them both, inhaling the sweet smell of shampoo in their dark hair, holding them each a second longer than they wanted.

They were changing schools in the fall. But even if Debbie hadn't moved, she'd never have allowed them to go back to their old elementary school. Not after what had happened there. It was the first place Gretchen had gone after her escape.

'Give your dad and me a minute,' Debbie said. The kids looked back at her, and Archie nodded and kissed them both again on the top of their heads and watched as they went and sat on the couch in front of the television.

Sara pried her sneakers off and pulled her legs up under her on the couch as she sat down next to Frank. It was after dinner and everyone except Frank and Archie was outside smoking. Free period.

Emergency Vets was still on. It must have been an all-day showing.

'Is this the one where the cat dies?' Sara asked Frank.

'Ferret episode,' Frank said.

'Good,' Sara said.

Debbie waited a moment, until the kids were absorbed in the show, and then walked over to where Archie was sitting. 'What's going on?' she asked him. Her arms were still crossed. He could smell her. The same shampoo as the kids, but other scents mixed in – a musky lotion, and a perfume he didn't recognize.

They'd fallen in love in college, nearly twenty years ago. He still had a hard time imagining his life without her. But he was careful that she didn't see it. He didn't want to make things harder than they already were.

'What?' he said, thinking of the phone in his pocket.

'She's back,' Debbie said.

'She's a serial killer,' Archie said. 'It was just a matter of time before it started again.'

'I thought she'd run,' Debbie said. 'That she was far away.' She made a helpless gesture with her hands. 'On an ice raft somewhere.'

'I guess she got bored killing Inuit,' Archie said.

The door to the balcony opened and two women came in and sat down at a table near the TV. One of the women had been in the hallway during Courtenay's breakdown.

'When will this end?' Debbie said, closing her eyes.

'When she's dead,' Archie said simply.

Debbie opened her eyes and looked at him. Then she turned and looked at the kids. The vets on TV were operating on a ferret who'd swallowed a Matchbox police car. Ben and Sara and Frank were sitting side by side, riveted.

'I'll fix this,' Archie said quietly. 'No matter what it takes.'

Debbie slowly turned back to Archie. 'How will you fix it?' she said. 'You're in a mental hospital.'

'I like to think of it more as a "booby hatch",' Archie said.

'I've got media camped outside my house,' Debbie said. She sat down, across from him at the table, where Henry had been earlier that morning. 'That Charlene Wood person from Channel Eight showed up and started broadcasting live from in front of our building,' she said. She glanced back over at the kids and lowered her voice. 'Like a pre-game show. Like Gretchen's going to show up there at the top of the hour.'

'She won't bother you this time,' Archie said.

Debbie flinched and then she set her jaw and her eyes narrowed. 'I forgot how well you know her,' she said. *Know her.* The words sat, ugly, between them. He deserved it. He deserved any vitriol she wished to dish out. His betrayal of their vows had been epic.

Debbie shook her head. 'I'm sorry,' she said.

'I'm the adulterer,' Archie said. He was lucky, he knew, that she let him see the children at all. 'What I meant to say,' he said, 'is that I know how she thinks.'

'Then go back to work,' Debbie said. 'She's been on the loose for two months. They can't catch her without you. Apparently.'

A staffer walked in. He didn't look at Archie. He didn't

look at anyone. He walked over to the fridge, got a box of take-out from it, and sat down two tables away. Archie recognized him – the counsellor Courtenay had stabbed.

'Are you even listening to me?' Debbie asked.

Behind her, another staffer walked through the door, pushing a mop. It was the orderly. George. Debbie turned around to see what Archie was looking at. 'What?' she said.

Archie felt the hairs on the back of his neck rise, and there was that feeling again, that he was being watched. He glanced around the room. Minutes ago, they had been alone. He tried to think back to other visits, and realized that this always happened when the kids were around – people loitering just in earshot. He was so stupid. If Gretchen were keeping an eye on him, she wouldn't just have someone in the hospital – she'd have someone in the ward.

Debbie brushed a piece of hair behind his ear and withdrew her hand. 'You need a haircut,' she said.

Archie gave her a distracted smile. 'I'm growing a pony-tail,' he said.

'If you do,' she said, 'I'll kill you myself.'

'That would only be justifiable homicide if we were still married,' Archie said.

Debbie stood up. 'I'm prepared to do time,' she said.

He watched her as she walked over to the kids and kissed them both and said goodbye. He searched the faces in the room for a reaction, some hint of too much interest.

He could use this. He could use his children as bait – see who found an excuse to get too close, to stay too long in the break room.

Debbie had walked to the door and stood there looking back at Archie. The black sundress was thin and he could see the shadow of her thigh through the cloth.

She listened for a moment and bent an ear down the hall towards Courtenay's room. 'Is that . . . ?' she asked.

'"High Hopes",' Archie said.

'They've got you guys on some good medication,' Debbie said.

Sara squealed. On *Emergency Vets*, something was going wrong on the operating table for the ferret.

Frank took Sara's hand.

'Wait,' Archie said to Debbie.

He walked to her, took her by the arm and put his face next to hers, as if to kiss her on the cheek. Instead he put his lips against her ear. 'Don't leave the kids,' he whispered.

She winced.

Archie pulled his head back, his expression neutral, his hand still on her arm.

Debbie looked at him, eyebrows lifted. Then, slowly, she glanced around at the other people in the room.

Someone else might think Archie was deluded. But Debbie knew what Gretchen was capable of.

Her gaze returned to his, and he could see a glimmer of fear in her eyes. Good. She was taking him seriously.

'Go on a trip,' he whispered.

Debbie gave him the tiniest nod, and he let her arm go.

'Your dad doesn't feel well,' she called to the kids. 'Want to see a movie?'

20

'This is Gretchen Lowell.'

Archie is sitting in his office and he looks up to see Mayor Buddy Anderson standing in the doorway with a stunning blonde. She is maybe the most beautiful woman Archie has ever seen. Her features are perfect: mouth full, nose straight and sloped, wide cheekbones, and large eyes. The long-sleeved lilac-coloured dress she is wearing rounds over her breasts, dips in deeply at the waist, and then curves around her hips to her knees. As she leans against the door jamb, she crosses her slender legs at the ankles. Her face is shaped like a heart.

'Gretchen,' Buddy says with his wolf grin. 'This is Archie Sheridan.'

'Detective,' she says, and she steps forward and offers an elegant hand.

Archie stands and leans over his desk and shakes it, suddenly conscious of the roughness of his palms. 'Nice to meet you,' he says.

'She's a psychiatrist,' Buddy explains. 'She thinks she can help catch the Beauty Killer.'

It is eleven at night. Buddy had called and asked if he could stop by. Eleven at night, and Archie is still working. Buddy, clearly, isn't. 'We already have a profiler,' Archie says.

Buddy chuckles. His cheeks are ruddy and he's not wearing his coat. His bleached white teeth are stained with red wine. 'She's not after Anne's job,' he says.

'I'm not a criminal profiler,' she explains to Archie. 'I specialize in trauma counselling.'

'She wants to help you,' Buddy says.

'Thanks,' Archie says. He sits back down and opens a crime report, hoping they'll get the message. 'But I don't need therapy.'

Buddy elbows Gretchen Lowell and winks. 'Archie Sheridan is solid as a rock. Married his college sweetheart. I don't think the guy's ever been drunk.'

'I've been drunk,' Archie says.

Buddy suddenly taps his pocket, pulls out a cell phone and frowns. He holds up a finger and slides past Gretchen out of the room. 'Hey, honey,' he says into the phone. 'I'm with Archie.'

Archie sighs.

Gretchen doesn't move. She just looks at him and smiles.

'How do you know the mayor?' Archie asks.

'I can be of use to you,' she says.

This was all he needed – the mayor's latest conquest hanging around the task force, giving pep talks. His team would never speak to him again. But the mayor allocated task-force funding. If she was sleeping with Buddy, in the end Archie probably wouldn't have any say.

'You've all been at this for what, ten years?' she asks.

'Some of us,' Archie says.

'I'm just offering coping skills. Not counselling. Just talk.' She pushes herself off the door and walks forward, her high heels making her hips swing.

She leans forward and turns around the photograph that he keeps framed on his desk. 'Your family?' she asks.

'Yes,' he says.

She turns it back to face Archie. 'They're lovely.'

'Thank you,' Archie says.

'I'm not sleeping with him,' Gretchen says.

Archie coughs. He glances out his office door for the mayor, but he is still down the hall on the phone.

'Not that it's any of your business,' she adds.

Archie shakes his head. 'No, of course not.'

She spins the open file on his desk around and picks up an autopsy photo of the Beauty Killer's latest victim. Her eyes get large. 'Who's this?' she asks.

Archie is grateful for something else to talk about. 'His name's Matthew Fowler. We found his body up at Pittock Mansion last week.'

'I heard about that,' Gretchen says. Her bottom lip quivers slightly as she examines the colour image of Matthew Fowler's open chest cavity. She shudders. 'What happened to him?'

Archie takes the photograph from her and puts it back in the file. 'I don't think you want to know,' he says gently.

Gretchen lowers her gaze at Archie. 'Try me.'

Archie sits back in his chair and looks at her. She has no

idea what he's seen. She's read the sanitized newspaper accounts and watched the true-crime shows on TV and thinks she can spend a few weeks on the case and then write a paper for some academic journal. 'He was disembowelled,' Archie says.

She lifts her hand to her mouth and turns her head away.

'This sort of work isn't for people with delicate stomachs,' Archie says.

She turns back to him and lowers her hand, straightening up a little, as if to steel her resolve. 'How?' she asks.

Maybe Archie had underestimated her. 'Disembowelled' was usually a conversation stopper. 'Transanally,' Archie says. 'With the aid of an unidentified suction device.'

Gretchen's eyelids flutter. Archie had stopped sharing crime-scene details with Debbie years ago. Those images stayed with you. The fewer you had floating around the better. He readies the *coup de grâce*.

'Then the Beauty Killer shoved a glass rod up his penis and shattered it,' Archie adds.

He can hear her breathing – short, rapid inhalations, her trepidation palpable. 'Are you trying to scare me away?' she asks.

'This isn't a hobby,' Archie says.

'I'm not a dilettante.'

'What are you?'

She perches on the front edge of his desk, sets her mouth in determination, and fans out all the photographs from the autopsy file.

Her body trembles as she scans the images, and her hand

finds the soft curve of her throat. But she keeps looking. And after a minute, she places a manicured finger on an anterior shot of Matthew Fowler's head. 'What are these marks, here?' she asks.

Archie glances down. 'Part of his scalp was surgically removed,' he says, 'and the skull beneath was shaved down.'

Her eyes are suddenly huge and animated. She grins and gives the photograph a triumphant tap. 'Amativeness,' she says. 'It's a concept in phrenology. The brain is the organ of the mind. Certain areas have specific functions, as reflected by the cranial bone.'

Archie looks at the picture. He feels the throb of her excitement. It has been months since they've had a good lead. 'Amativeness?' he says.

She takes his hand in hers, bends her head down, and lifts his hand to her head to illustrate. Her emotion – the fever of discovery – courses between them like a current. It's intoxicating. 'This spot back here,' she says, moving his fingers in her hair between her ear and neck, exploring the edge of her skull. He feels the bony lump, hard and warm beneath his fingertips. 'It's the amativeness module,' she says. 'It correlates with sexual attraction.'

Archie pulls his hand away and clears his throat.

Gretchen sweeps her hair back and lifts her head. 'All that fury,' she says, 'and you still think the Beauty Killer is a man?'

Archie looks at Gretchen Lowell, just a few feet away from him, and he knows that he can never allow her into the investigation. He will just have to tell Buddy no. It's too dangerous. But not in the way he first thought.

'Hi,' says a voice from the doorway.

Archie's heart skips. Debbie.

He turns, and there, in the doorway, stands his wife carrying a bag of takeout.

She holds it up and smiles, and then raises a quizzical eyebrow at Gretchen.

How to explain this?

'This is Gretchen Lowell,' Archie says. 'She's a psychiatrist. She's going to be consulting with us.' He pushes back his chair, gets up, walks over to his wife, and kisses her lightly on the lips. 'My wife, Debbie.'

21

It had been fifteen minutes since Archie had taken the pill.

Bedtime at Bedlam was nine o'clock. Sedatives were passed out at eight-thirty. Archie didn't need to stay up long. He just needed to stay up longer than Frank. He was hoping that the five cups of coffee he'd had since dinner would buy him some time.

Unlike regular meds, which they made you line up for, the night nurse delivered the sedatives right to the room. They didn't want you taking a sleeping pill and then falling flat on your face before they could tuck you in. It was the same every night. This time, Archie needed it to be different. Frank and Archie were in their respective beds. Frank's light was off; Archie kept his on. He usually read in bed, but he couldn't risk dozing off. Instead Archie rested on his side, listening to the sound of Frank breathing.

The pill made his blood feel warm. He had to fight it. Concentrate on blinking, prying open the lids that wanted to stay closed.

Frank shifted in his bed, sighing and chomping.

Frank, who had arrived two weeks after Archie checked himself in, and who was always around, just in earshot.

Archie's eyes closed. He liked the sedatives. It was the closest feeling to Vicodin that they allowed him. He liked the feeling of his body letting go, of giving in.

Frank took in a great rattling breath and released a slow snore.

Archie opened his eyes, glanced up at the surveillance camera in the corner of the room, and reached up and turned off the light.

With the lights off, the camera was useless.

He waited, counting Frank's snores.

When he got to ten, Archie got out of bed and felt his way around the perimeter of the room to Frank's built-in Formica dresser. Archie slid the drawers out slowly, as quietly as he could, and felt inside, running his hands along the sides of each drawer and shuffling through the clothing. He didn't know what he was looking for, but if Gretchen had managed to get a phone to Archie, maybe she had managed to get something to Frank, too.

But Archie found nothing.

He got down on the floor and ran his hand underneath Frank's bed. Frank made a garbled noise and turned over on his side. Archie froze. And waited. When Frank's snoring became rhythmic again, Archie got up, went back to his own bed, sat down, reached under the blanket and felt around until he found the phone he'd hidden there.

Gretchen had him chasing his own shadow.

Archie sat there, in the dark, for a long time. Then he

looked down at the phone, highlighted the single number in the log, and pressed call.

It picked up on the second ring.

He listened to it for a long moment. He listened for her breathing, for the catch of saliva in her throat, an involuntary sigh. Nothing. Only dead air. He could still hang up.

Next to him, Frank snored peacefully.

'Are you there?' Archie said quietly.

He heard her exhale slowly, as if she'd been holding her breath. 'Darling,' she said. 'I've been worried about you.'

It had been so long since he'd heard her voice that he had forgotten how lovely it was, her perfect enunciation and honey tones. The effects of the pill vanished. Archie lay back in bed. 'We had an agreement,' he said.

'I've been waiting for your call,' Gretchen said.

'Here I am,' Archie said.

'Are you having fun?' she asked.

It was a game to her, like tossing a ball for a dog. She was exercising him. 'I'm giving you the chance to turn yourself in,' he said.

There was a pause. 'Or what?'

Archie gritted his teeth, and his fist tightened around the phone. 'I'm coming for you.'

'Oh, goody,' she said.

She hung up and Archie rested the phone on his chest under the blanket.

It was quiet.

Frank wasn't snoring.

'Frank?' Archie said into the darkness. 'You awake?'

Frank didn't answer. Maybe he was plotting how to murder Archie in his sleep.

Archie felt the slippery warmth of the sedative take hold again. This time, he surrendered to it. His last awareness was the weight of the phone still sitting on his chest.

22

Archie sat bolt upright in bed to the sound of screaming.

He turned on the light, took a couple of breaths, and tried to order his thoughts. Frank snored softly in his bed. It was dark outside.

Life in the psych ward was basically made up of long periods of boredom punctuated by shouting.

Screaming at night? Not so unusual.

Except that this scream was not the scream of someone ranting. This was authentic terror.

Archie got up, put on his slippers, and went to the door. The patients weren't supposed to leave their rooms at night. It was the kind of thing that earned you a demerit and cost you privileges. Archie listened through the door as the conversation outside heightened. He heard the word 'police'.

He opened the door.

Courtenay's room was the fourth door on the left. A nurse was sitting on the floor just outside it being comforted by the orderly who'd tried to help Courtenay in the break room. George.

Courtenay's door was open.

Archie walked down the hallway. Other doors opened, as patients began to peer out, but none of them dared enter the corridor. Only Archie. George looked up at Archie as he approached, his hand still patting the distraught nurse. Her face was flushed, the colour of the scrubs.

Archie got to Courtenay's door and looked inside. The mattress on the floor was soaked with blood. And on top of it lay Courtenay. At first glance, she looked like she was sleeping. She was resting on her back, her arms at her sides. Her eyes were closed. Her lips slightly parted. She looked like a fairy-tale princess waiting for a kiss.

A blanket lay in a pile at the foot of the mattress. Archie could imagine what had happened. The night nurse comes in to check on Courtenay, maybe to give her more meds, thinks she's asleep, pulls back the blanket, sees the blood . . .

Once you knew, you could see it on her face – the bluish tint to her lips, the grey skin. Archie squatted next to her and touched her arm. The skin was cool. She'd been dead a few hours.

Then he noticed something about her face. You couldn't tell unless you were up close, but there was something about the shape of her profile that wasn't quite right. Archie reached over with his thumb and very gently lifted one of her eyelids.

Underneath was an empty cavern of blood and tissue.

Archie sat back on his heels and looked around the room. It didn't take him long. There, on the wall directly across, was a single heart that looked like it had been drawn with Courtenay's blood.

George was standing in the doorway.

'Lock down the ward,' Archie told him. 'No staff leaves.'

George didn't move. 'This is because of you,' he said.

'Yes,' Archie said. Courtenay was in lockdown. Frank wouldn't have been able to get in. But an orderly would have.

Archie stiffened and turned around.

This is because of you. It wasn't a question. It was a statement.

He'd been wrong about Frank.

'Where is she?' he asked George.

George smiled. 'Are you having fun yet?' he asked.

Gretchen's words.

George blinked heavily. 'Fun yet?' he repeated.

He stumbled.

Archie lunged for him.

George's smile spread wider and he lifted an unsteady hand to his forehead. Archie got to him just as he swayed backward, and managed to grab him by the shirt as he fell to the floor. George was on his knees, head back, Archie standing over him, holding him by the neck of his scrubs.

'Where is she?' Archie demanded, shaking him. George didn't respond, didn't react at all. His eyes were already shiny slits, his breathing shallow. Archie was yelling now. But it was useless. Gretchen didn't leave loose ends. Archie's shoulders heaved in a dry sob and his voice cracked. 'Where is she?'

Someone took him by the shoulders and pulled him off George. Archie sank back against the wall, just inside the door, a few feet away from where Courtenay lay. The blanket was pulled back and one of her arms was exposed. That arm, still bandaged in white gauze at the wrist, was the saddest thing Archie thought he'd ever seen. *It's down the road, not across the street.*

Archie was helpless. He just sat there, as three nurses laid George out on the floor and worked to save his life. About five chest compressions into CPR, one of the nurses stopped and looked at her hand.

'He's bleeding,' she said.

Archie sat forward to get a better view. Sure enough, the nurse had blood on the heel of her hand and a red stain had bloomed on George's chest, where the nurse had been compressing it. She pulled his shirt up, but his chest appeared uninjured.

'Check his pocket,' Archie said, sitting back against the wall.

The nurse slid a hand into the breast pocket of George's scrubs.

Archie didn't see what was in her hand when she pulled it out, but he saw her mouth open and the skin of her face stretch back in horror.

'Oh, God,' she whispered.

That kind of delicate tissue probably squashed easily.

'It's her eyes,' the nurse said.

23

When Archie woke up, he thought for a second that it had all been a dream. Then he saw Henry sitting on the plastic chair by his bed. The sun was not yet up, but the sky was a pretty shade of pale violet.

'You crawled in here and fell asleep,' Henry said. 'You've been out cold.'

Archie rubbed his face and looked over at Frank's bed. He was gone. 'It must have been the sedative,' he said. He didn't remember even coming back into his room.

'George Hay is dead,' Henry said. 'Vicodin overdose.' He glanced up at Archie. 'Nice touch, huh?'

'He must have taken more than I did,' Archie said.

Henry looked at Archie without a hint of amusement. His reading glasses were up on his forehead, and he flipped them down to his nose and glanced at the notebook open in his lap. 'We reviewed the security tapes,' he said. 'Hay went into her room at 8.49, out at 8.52.' Four minutes. That was all it took to snuff out a life. Henry continued. 'She'd been sedated at 8.30. She was lying on her stomach. The security camera in her room went out at 8.46. He must have disabled it before he went in.' Henry waved his hand in the air, not looking up. 'Apparently that happens sometimes – the camera feed goes static – which is why the nurses weren't concerned.' He scanned another page of the notebook. 'Looks like the first cut severed her spinal cord, which is why she didn't cry out. He stabbed her multiple times in the back and then must have flipped her over and covered her with the blanket. She bled out pretty quickly.'

'And then he just hung around?' Archie asked. Courtenay was dead by nine, but her body was not discovered for hours. Hay had had plenty of time to get away. But instead he was one of the first people who responded when the nurse had screamed.

Henry took the glasses off and set them on the notebook. 'Criminal genius, he wasn't,' Henry said.

Archie swung his feet to the floor and put his head in his hands. 'How did Gretchen get to him?' He tried to remember every interaction he'd had with George, and wondered at what point Gretchen had got to him.

'We're reviewing his phone records,' Henry said, 'interviewing neighbours, friends. He was recently divorced. No kids. His ex-wife said he'd started seeing someone, but she didn't know who and no one else ever saw her.'

No one ever did.

How many men had she got to kill for her? He'd seen their bodies when she was through with them. But how many of her sleeper agents were still out there, waiting, willing to do her bidding?

'She was obviously using him to keep tabs on you,' Henry continued. He looked Archie in the eye. 'Anything you want to tell me?'

Archie dropped his hands and looked up. The phone. Shit. What had he done with the phone? He remembered having it when he fell asleep. Then he must have left it when he went to Courtenay's room. What had he done with it when he got back into bed? He tried to disguise the panic that surely showed on his face and to focus on the conversation. 'When does the ex-wife think the relationship started?' he asked.

'Two months ago,' Henry said.

They thought she'd fled, that she'd left the country. But she'd been there the whole time. They'd never been safe. 'She never even left town,' Archie said.

'Why kill Courtenay Taggart?' Henry asked.

Archie looked out the window. If he hadn't talked Courtenay into giving up the shard of Formica, she'd still be alive. She wasn't going to hurt herself, not with that. She'd cut her wrists horizontally, for Christ's sake. She just wanted someone to pay attention. He had to be the hero. And it had cost Courtenay her life. 'I was nice to her,' he said softly.

'Archie,' Henry asked. 'You need to come clean right now. Has Gretchen contacted you?'

Archie glanced towards the floor, to see if the phone had fallen from the bed. It wasn't there. 'No,' he said.

Henry gnawed at his bottom lip, leaned back in the chair and crossed his arms. The plastic groaned under his weight. 'Debbie left town last night,' he said, raising an appraising eyebrow at Archie. 'She and the kids. Extended vacation. She called me from the airport.'

'She could use a vacation,' Archie said.

'Right,' Henry said. 'It's a coincidence that she took off right after she came to see you.' He hesitated and then scratched the back of his neck. 'What I don't get is, it's not all for you.' He looked up at Archie. 'Whatever she's doing out there. It doesn't connect.'

Of course. Archie had been so focused on what was happening on the ward, that he'd lost sight of the bigger picture. The rest stop. Pittock Mansion. The abandoned house. Eyeballs and old bodies. Gretchen didn't do anything without a plan. Maybe Archie was supposed to figure it out. Maybe that was the game.

'You ID the head?' Archie asked.

'Nope,' Henry said. 'Male. His eyes were removed. DNA match will take a couple of days, but the blood type matches a set from the rest stop. Robbins thinks the guy's been dead a few years. Thinks someone kept his eyes in a jar of formaldehyde.'

It didn't make sense.

'The John Doe Susan found yesterday.' Henry paused. 'Robbins called me yesterday. Someone removed his eyes, and replaced them. Apparently the ones in his sockets were a few years old.'

'Let me guess,' Archie said. 'Soaked in formaldehyde.'

'Gretchen's apparently got a little eyeball collection. Some people collect unicorns, belt buckles . . .' He spread his hands. 'You were lucky all she took was your spleen.'

'You're right,' Archie said. 'She could have taken my unicorn.'

Henry didn't laugh.

From the bed, Archie could see the sun now, a sliver of orange over the skyline. 'They want me out, don't they?' Archie said.

Henry stood. 'They're concerned about the safety of the patients. You included.' He folded his glasses closed, hooked them on the collar of his shirt, and slid his notebook into the pocket of his jeans. 'You can stay with me. Temporarily. Until we figure something else out.'

A nice padded cell in New Hampshire, maybe.

Henry stepped in front of Archie and peered down at him, his broad chest expanding with a deep sigh. 'Tell me we're not playing right into her hands,' he said.

Archie knew what he was thinking: Gretchen manipulates George into killing Courtenay, knowing that the hospital would have to ask Archie to leave.

'I'm not the one in danger,' Archie said.

'Good,' Henry said. 'Because I can't protect you.' He crossed his arms and glared down at Archie for a long moment before continuing. 'If you were in touch with Gretchen – if she had found some way to communicate with you, or you had some other information that might be of use to the investigation' – Henry lowered his chin and raised an eyebrow – 'that might allow me to reallocate some resources.'

Archie nodded. He had known Henry for fifteen years. Henry had helped nurse him back to health, had overlooked his pill popping, and had convinced him to go back to work. He'd been the one who drove Archie to the psych ward, and who'd sat with him while he was admitted. He'd put up with far more than he should have, and Archie knew it. Still, Archie didn't say anything.

Henry glanced at his watch and looked out the window for a moment. 'I've got to make some calls,' he said. 'Rosenberg's on her way to rubber-stamp your newfound mental clarity.'

Just like that. Back into the world. 'What are you doing to find Gretchen?' Archie asked.

'When you want to get over your bullshit and be a cop again, I'll be happy to brief you,' Henry said. 'Until then, you're a civilian. And your job is to stay alive.' He started to walk away, then seemed to change his mind, and turned back. 'I know you're keeping something from me,' he said.

Archie didn't move.

Henry looked at him for another moment, and then turned and walked out of the room.

The second he was gone Archie dropped to his hands and knees on the floor and looked under the bed. No phone. He got up and ran his palms along the bedding, searching for a telltale lump. Nothing.

It was gone.

Archie sank onto the floor at the foot of his bed. His one connection to Gretchen, and he'd lost it.

He was still sitting there when Frank shuffled in from the hall with a spot of egg yolk on his pyjamas.

He didn't look at Archie. Didn't say hello. Didn't

mention the fact that two people had died on the ward a few hours before.

Frank.

Archie stood up and walked past Frank's bed into the bathroom they shared. There was nothing in that bathroom but an open shower, a sink bolted to the wall, a toilet, and a metal mirror. No bathtub. Debbie would have hated it.

Archie stood in the bathroom for a minute with his hands on his hips, waiting, heart pounding. Then he looked up into the metal mirror and said to his own warped reflection, 'Hey, Frank. Come look at this.'

Frank was a big guy, heavy, but he was soft. As soon as he walked into the bathroom, Archie kicked the door shut, took him by the shoulders, and slammed him against the wall. Frank's eyes rolled towards the bathroom door.

No surveillance cameras in the bathrooms. They had a few minutes before anyone came to check on them. Maybe more.

Archie leaned in against Frank, and lowered his voice to a growl. 'Where is it?' he said.

Beads of sweat had already formed on Frank's brow. He retracted his chin an inch. 'What?' he asked.

'The phone,' Archie hissed. 'It was in my bed. And now it's gone.' He bent one elbow and pressed his forearm against the yolk stain on Frank's chest. 'What did you do with it, Frank?'

Frank's mouth opened and the tip of his tongue punched its way between his lips. 'I can't breathe,' he said.

He was authentically panicked, and Archie relented a

little. He wanted to intimidate Frank, not give the guy a seizure. Archie put his mouth right next to Frank's ear. 'I need that phone,' Archie said. 'It's important.'

Frank gave Archie a fearful look. 'I just wanted to call my sister,' he said. He waved a hand towards the bathroom door. 'It's in my bottom drawer,' he said. 'Take it.'

Archie stepped back and Frank slid away from him along the wall.

'I'm sorry,' Archie said.

He walked out of the bathroom, dug through Frank's bottom drawer, and found the phone under a stack of neatly folded underpants. Archie glanced up at the security camera. He didn't care. They wouldn't take it away from him. He was leaving anyway.

Then Archie walked back to the bathroom door.

Frank was curled up on the floor.

'Do you even have a sister, Frank?' Archie said.

Frank didn't answer.

24

Sarah Rosenberg was wearing black Lycra capri pants, flip-flops, and a long-sleeved white cotton shirt over a grey T-shirt. 'I don't approve of this,' she said.

Archie was packing. It wouldn't take long. His books alone took up half of his overnight bag. He stowed his toiletries in the outside pocket, and was now emptying the dresser into the bag, drawer by drawer.

She looked around. 'Where's Frank?' she asked.

'Morning group session,' Archie said. He scooped up an armful of socks and dumped them in his bag. The truth was he didn't know where Frank was.

'I want to check out,' Archie said to Rosenberg. Might as well make it official.

Rosenberg closed the door to the room. 'Yesterday you said you were a danger to yourself,' she said.

Archie thought of Courtenay, bleeding to death in her bed. 'It turns out I'm a danger to others,' he said.

Rosenberg sat on the edge of his bed, tucking one leg neatly under the other. 'If you still need help, you won't be turned away.'

Archie moved on to his shirt drawer. 'I don't need to be here,' he said. 'I'm well. I'm off drugs.'

'You're on different drugs,' Rosenberg said.

Archie dropped a stack of pants into his bag. 'If I stay here, she will find another way in. And she will kill someone else here. I saved Courtenay. So she killed her. You have helped me, Sarah. I like you. Gretchen will certainly have figured that out by now.'

Rosenberg's voice caught in her throat. 'What are you saying?'

'I'm saying that if I stay here, she'll go after you.'

Rosenberg paled. 'I have kids.'

'I know,' Archie said.

'There's an outpatient programme,' Rosenberg said. 'You come for meetings. For a week or so. You need to keep seeing your internist and hepatologist.' She shook her head, like even she couldn't believe what she was doing. 'You must have no contact with her.'

'I don't know where she is,' Archie said.

Rosenberg leaned forward. 'It's easy to not take Vicodin, when there isn't any,' she said. 'But if you had a few pills in front of you, what would you do then?' She let that sit between them for a minute, and then stood. 'I need to fill out some paperwork,' she said. She paused, and Archie thought he saw a glimmer of fear beneath her professional demeanour. 'All of this death – it's far from over, isn't it?'

Archie sat down in the plastic chair by the window. He could feel the phone vibrate in his pocket. 'It's just starting.'

25

Carol Littleton had been going to the Portland Rose Garden three mornings a week for forty years. She had married her husband there. He had been a Royal Rosarian. She had been the 1939 Rose Queen. They had bought a home that faced the garden, and, until her husband had died ten years before, they had routinely strolled the paved paths, past the low stone walls, through the rose archways, and along the long rows of rosebushes with their plump pungent blooms.

For the last decade, she had had a specific destination in the garden – Neville Chamberlain. All members of the Royal Rosarians were knighted under their chosen variety of rose, their 'namesake' rose, and the Neville Chamberlain had been her husband's.

The Rose Garden had rules about spreading the ashes of loved ones in the garden. Carol understood. That sort of thing piled up, and who wanted to go to a rose garden and see charred bits of people in the topsoil?

There were rules.

But you could get around them.

Carol had been secreting her husband over to the garden a few tablespoons at a time since 1997.

There were never many people in the garden at eight in the morning, so she was surprised to see the couple sitting on the bench overlooking the city. It was a nice bench. The Rose Garden was up on a hill and the bench had a nice view of downtown, and Mount Hood beyond it. Carol and her husband had sat on that same bench many times.

She walked down the path towards them, her hand around the Ziploc bag full of ashes in her pocket. She was still a good forty feet away when the stench hit her.

She didn't have much of a nose any more. Too many Lucky Strikes in her younger days. It was why she liked roses – they were one of the few flowers aromatic enough for her to appreciate.

This odour was so foul it seemed to shout at her. She didn't know how the couple on the bench were standing it. It smelled like something had died. A raccoon maybe, or a squirrel.

As she got closer, Carol lifted a handkerchief from her pocket and put it over her nose.

'Gracious,' she asked the couple. 'It smells like the devil, doesn't it?'

The two were both dressed in long coats and hats – too warm for day, but not out of the question before the sun came up. The summer nights in Portland were still chilly. But the sun had come up, and Carol could see quite clearly that the couple didn't need coats to stay warm.

The young couple were not a young couple at all.

Carol pressed the handkerchief harder against her face. For a second, a ring of black circled her vision, as her blood pressure dropped, but she took three long, deep breaths and steadied herself. *Don't faint*, she told herself.

She'd been a nurse during the war, stationed at an airbase outside London. She had seen corpses. She had even seen corpses worse than these.

Just don't faint. If you faint, you fall, if you fall, you break your hip, if you break your hip, you give up the house, you give up the walks, you give up Otis.

The bodies on the bench were mostly covered by the long coats and hats, but she could see their faces. They looked like wax dummies that had been left too close to a fire – features just beginning to melt. Their mouths were open, jaws dropped further than ever possible in life, the inside black, like they'd been drinking oil. Their noses were bent, as if the skin had slipped a little. Horrible.

She looked around the garden and saw no one. The grounds were a maze – hedges and shrubs, walls, and gates. There might be other people there, she just couldn't see.

'Hello?' she hollered. 'Is anyone out there?'

And then, as loud as an old lady could, 'Hello?'

She was alone. She wrapped her hand around the sandwich bag of ashes in her pocket, and clutched it.

A bright yellow butterfly fluttered past and alit on the hat of one of the corpses.

No human remains at the park. It was a rule.

Carol Littleton didn't have a cell phone. But she had a medical alert necklace with a panic button. Stupid thing. Her daughters had made her wear one. It was supposed to have a five-hundred-foot range.

She was a block from the house.

She looked around again, and still saw no one. A thousand feet below, the people and cars and urban kerfuffle of the city made a constant hum. Carol remembered the sound, but she could no longer hear it.

She glanced up the block, towards home. Five hundred feet. It might be close enough.

She lifted the handkerchief from her mouth, her red lipstick smeared on it like blood, found the plastic pendant with a trembling hand, and pushed the button.

26

Archie held the brass pillbox in his hand, feeling the weight of it. He had carried it in his pocket for two years. Pulled painkiller after painkiller from it. It had been the first thing he reached for in the morning, and the last thing that left his hand at night. Now it was empty. Just a relic from his past life. He looked at it for another moment, then dropped it in the bag at his feet and pulled the next item from the box of personal items that had just been returned to him at the nurses' station. His belt. A dead cell phone. Keys. Shoes.

He was threading his belt through his belt loops when Henry came around the corner, his phone in his hand. He didn't look happy. 'There's a body at the Rose Garden,' he said.

'The arena?' Archie asked. The Blazers played at an arena called the 'Rose Garden'.

'No,' Henry said. 'The actual Rose Garden. The one with the flowers.'

Gretchen had murdered a woman and left her in the Rose Garden in 2003. 'That makes two repeat locations,' Archie said. 'The Rose Garden and Pittock Mansion.' Archie buckled the belt. It buckled a notch tighter than it had the last time he'd had it on.

'I know,' Henry said.

'Just give me a second,' Archie said, dropping a shoe and slipping a foot into it.

'You're a civilian,' Henry said. 'Remember?'

Archie looked up from tying his shoe.

Henry handed him his house key. Then he looked over Archie's shoulder. 'Here comes your ride.'

Archie twisted around to see Susan Ward walking down the hall towards him. She was wearing red jeans, a white T-shirt, black boots that laced up her shins, and was carrying a giant red purse. And she'd dyed her hair purple.

'Hi,' she said, touching her hair.

Susan Ward. Archie hadn't seen her since he'd checked in. But he'd known that she was out there, in the waiting room, most mornings. He'd refused to see her. But if he allowed himself to acknowledge it, the truth was he liked knowing she was just on the other side of the wall.

'You shouldn't involve her,' he said to Henry.

Henry was checking a message on his BlackBerry. 'She's already involved,' he said.

'I'm doing a story on the murdered inmate,' Susan said.

'Patient,' Archie said with a sigh. 'Not inmate.'

Henry looked up from his BlackBerry. 'Take him to my house,' he said to Susan. 'Okay? Go inside. Lock the doors.' He turned to Archie. 'I'm sending a patrol car to sit out front.'

The way he said it, Archie wasn't sure if the patrol unit was supposed to keep Gretchen out, or Archie in.

'Did you get the pot brownies my mom sent?' Susan asked Archie.

'I didn't hear that,' Henry said, walking away.

27

It had been two months since Susan had laid eyes on Archie Sheridan. The last time she'd seen him, he'd been in a hospital bed with forty stitches in his neck and a belly full of Vicodin. He looked better than that. But there were people in hospice who looked better than that.

'So how's it going?' Susan asked lamely.

They were in her Saab, heading out of the hospital compound. Susan had no idea where Henry lived, so Archie was navigating.

They had just turned east onto Glisan, and the on-ramp to I-84 had cars backed up for half a mile. Archie squinted into the late-morning sun. 'What's all the traffic?' he asked.

No 'Hey, how are you? I missed you. Sorry for making you wait in the lobby all those mornings'? 'The freeway's jammed,' Susan said. 'People trying to get out of the city.'

They were passing the billboard advertisement for the upcoming episode of *America's Sexiest Serial Killers* starring Gretchen Lowell.

She noticed Archie's gaze linger on it as they drove by.

'What is wrong with everybody?' he asked.

Susan slid a look over at him. 'I want to write a book about it – our cultural obsession with the Beauty Killer. Maybe Henry told you?'

Archie reached down under his foot and lifted up the pink envelope. 'What's this?' he asked.

Susan rolled her eyes. She'd tossed all the crap from her in tray on the car floor. 'Some kind of dorky valentine,' she said. 'It was in my box at the *Herald*. I think it's from Derek. I mean, who gives someone a valentine in August? I guess it's sort of romantic, but Jesus, right?'

Archie flipped it over and examined the return address. Susan hadn't recognized it. Some street in Southwest Portland. He pulled the card out of the envelope.

'Are you going through my mail?' Susan asked. She didn't really care. She'd already opened it. There wasn't writing inside – just some blank, ugly old-fashioned card with two hearts connected by a gold chain.

Archie reached into the backseat and pulled his overnight bag onto his lap, dug into it, pulled out a card, and showed it to Susan.

It was the same card.

'Someone dropped this off at the hospital for me yesterday,' he said. He pointed at the return address on his card. Three-nine-seven North Fargo.

'That's where I found the body,' Susan said.

Then he pointed at the address on her card. It was in the same handwriting.

'We need to go to this address,' Archie said.

Susan shook her head. She had copy to write. She didn't have time to be murdered by Gretchen Lowell. 'You're out of your mind,' she said. 'You should call Henry.'

Archie reached back to the floor and came up with that morning's edition of the *Herald*. Susan really needed to keep her car cleaner. He pointed to the sketch on the front page. 'It's where this guy lives,' he said.

'How do you know that?' Susan asked.

'Trust me,' Archie said.

'What about Henry?' Susan asked.

'We'll call him after we check it out,' he said. 'If we tell him now, he won't let either of us go.'

Great. First the anonymous call. Now letters. Body parts all over town. It was like a scavenger hunt for psychos. Running after clues with a half-deranged, serial-killer-obsessed, recovering-addict cop was not a good idea. She knew that. Then again, the more time she spent with him, the more time she'd have to talk him into cooperating with the book.

'Okay,' she said.

'On the way, I want you to tell me everything you remember about the body in the house,' Archie said.

Susan pulled out of traffic onto a side street so they could turn around and head west. 'I dyed my hair purple,' she said.

She thought she saw Archie smile. 'I noticed,' he said.

28

A **gathering crowd** pressed against the police perimeter at the Rose Garden. There were plenty of microphones and notebooks – Henry had counted twelve news vans on his way up the hill – but mostly it was just rubberneckers.

Portland seemed divided into two groups of people these days – people who wanted to get as far away from Gretchen's crime scenes as possible, and people who wanted to rub up against her corpses.

Henry parked his car and got out and ducked under the tape. 'Whatley,' he yelled to a red-haired patrol cop. 'Get these people out of here.'

Whatley looked around helplessly at the crowd.

'Move the tape,' Henry said. 'Use pepper spray if you have to.'

Claire met him at the entrance to the park and led him to the crime scene. She was wearing a T-shirt with an image of the state of Alaska on it. Henry's third wife had bought it for him. They'd dressed quickly when the call came in about the murder at the psych ward. The T-shirt almost came down to Claire's knees. She'd scrunched it up on one side, so she could clip her gun to her waist, along with a pair of red Ray-Bans.

'How's he doing?' she asked.

'He's going to stay with me for a while,' Henry said.

'So I shouldn't leave my pantyhose hanging in the shower?' Claire asked.

'You don't wear pantyhose,' Henry said.

'I know,' she said. 'But it sounded funny.'

They cleared a hedge and Henry could see a group of cops gathered around a couple sitting on a bench.

Henry popped a piece of liquorice gum and snapped on a pair of latex gloves. 'What do we have?' he asked Claire.

They rounded the bench. The other cops stepped back. 'Meet Mr and Mrs Doe,' Claire said.

Henry took in the gruesome scene. The bodies had obviously been buried. They were practically mummified in grave wax, a sign they had been buried somewhere moist, probably sealed in something that protected them from bacteria. The features on the faces were beyond recognition, grins revealing brown teeth. That was good. That made dental records a possibility.

'Obviously not the clothes they died in,' Claire continued. 'I checked the labels and pockets. Nothing. But I did find this.' She held up an evidence bag with a tiny thread of plastic in it. 'It's one of those plastic thingies that hold tags.'

'Plastic thingies?' Henry said.

'I don't think that's the technical name,' Claire said. 'But they use them a lot at thrift stores to attach price tags. So I'm sending a few units around to some of the major stores to see if any of these lovely items seem familiar.'

'She bought them outfits and dressed them up so it would take longer for them to get noticed?' Henry said. It didn't make sense. The smell was sure to tip someone off pretty quickly.

Claire looked down at the bodies. She wasn't chewing gum. Henry had always admired that about her. She had a stomach of steel. 'You think they'll match the victim list?' she said.

Gretchen had confessed to a lot of murders, but she'd committed even more. And the task force maintained a list of people who'd gone missing during her ten-year killing spree. None of it made sense. Why would Gretchen be digging up her old victims? Unless they weren't victims.

'You have anyone checking with the cemeteries?' Henry asked.

'Already on it,' Claire said. 'So far, no one's reporting any unauthorized exhumations.'

Henry smacked his liquorice gum and leaned in close to get a look at the bodies.

It was impossible for him to tell if they'd had eyes when they were buried.

Henry heard Lorenzo Robbins's voice behind him. 'Easy, there, Quincy,' he said. 'That's my job.'

Henry stepped aside and Robbins knelt down in his white Tyvek suit next to the corpses. Robbins tied his dreads back with a rubber band that looked like it had come off a newspaper, pulled on a pair of purple latex gloves, and gave the bodies a visual once-over.

'They didn't die at the same time,' Robbins said. 'One, maybe three or four years ago, the other more like two.'

Henry squinted at the corpses. They looked the same to him. 'How do you know?' he said.

'Because I'm an ME,' Robbins said. 'And you're not.' He pulled out a penlight and shone it in the eye sockets of each body. 'Also,' he said, 'someone took their eyes out.'

Henry leaned in close to look in the eye sockets.

Robbins shooed him away. 'Go do cop stuff,' he said.

Henry turned to Claire. 'What's our time frame?'

'Park opens at seven-thirty,' Claire said. 'Not hard to get in before then. You just have to jump the gate. Grounds-keepers say they cleared the park at closing last night – nine p.m. So the bodies were set up sometime between nine and when the old lady found them just after eight. She hit her medic alert alarm. The site was pretty well trampled. She told them what she'd found and they thought she'd had a stroke. Sent fire trucks. EMTs. The whole nine yards.'

Henry looked out over the grand vista of Portland. The city skyline. The mountains. Take away the news helicopters he could see approaching from the distance, and it was something to behold. Henry ticked off the crime scenes on his hand. 'The Gorge,' he said. 'Pittock Mansion. The Rose Garden. What do all of them have in common?'

Robbins looked up. 'The letter *O*?'

Claire glanced out over the city. 'They all have great views,' she said.

'And no eyes to see them,' Henry said.

'They couldn't see anyway,' Robbins said. 'They're dead.'

'Oh, for Christ's sake,' Henry said. 'It's a metaphor.'

29

The address on Susan's card was on the other side of the river in Southwest Portland in a neighbourhood that didn't have trees or sidewalks. They'd had to take three freeways to get there. Susan peered through the windshield at the squat, ugly building. The windshield was dirty – you could trace the arcs of eyelash-sized legs and yellow juice where the wipers had ground dead bugs into the glass. That's what rain did in the summer – it just sort of smeared everything around.

'Sorry about the windshield,' she said.

Archie didn't answer. He looked at the valentine in his hand and then up at the building. 'This is it,' he said.

'Which side?' Susan asked. The square, flat-roofed 1980s duplex apartment sat at the end of a dead-end street. Nothing about the place worked. The first floor's multicoloured bricks didn't match the second storey's grey vinyl siding. There were two front doors, one grey, one blue, each with a concrete stoop. The stoop with the grey door was bare; the stoop with the blue door was lined with plants in terracotta pots. Tattered Buddhist prayer flags fluttered from the railing.

'Four-A,' Archie said.

The blue door.

He started to get out of the car.

'Wait,' Susan said. 'Don't you have a gun?'

Archie gave her a patient smile. 'The psych ward isn't really big on guns,' he said. 'Besides, I turned mine in when I took my leave of absence.'

'Well, go buy one at Wal-Mart or something,' Susan said.

Archie raised his eyebrows.

'Fine,' Susan said. 'But I'm coming with you. Someone needs to keep you from getting murdered.'

He didn't seem in the mood to argue. Susan had a special way of wearing people down like that. She got out of the car and followed him up the concrete walkway to 4A. There was no one around. A single squirrel ran across the yard and under a dying laurel hedge by the street.

Archie climbed the three steps up to the stoop and rang the doorbell. Susan heard it – an insistent buzz, like an oven timer – coming from the other side of the door. But no one answered.

'You're not going to break in, are you?' Susan asked. 'Because I've already broken in to one house this week.' She choked back a nervous laugh. Archie wouldn't break in to a house. He was a grown-up. And a cop. He'd call Henry. Any minute now.

Susan glanced back at the street. Still no one around. No cars. The squirrel was gone.

Archie dropped to his haunches. Susan's stomach knotted. He was going to break in. He was going to pick the lock.

She imagined him asking her for a hairpin. That's what they always did in the movies. She felt bad. She didn't have a hairpin. He'd have to use a credit card.

But he didn't ask for a hairpin. He flipped up the doormat. It was made of hemp fibre – she'd know it anywhere. Underneath the mat was an envelope. The corner of the envelope had been exposed, she now realized, though she hadn't noticed it.

'What is it?' Susan asked.

Archie picked up the envelope, holding it by the edges, and flipped it over so she could see it. There, in what appeared to be the same handwriting as the valentine, was Archie's name. He held the envelope up to the sky and looked at it. Then he smiled.

'Do you have a pen?' Archie asked.

Susan reached into the outside pocket of her purse and extracted a black felt tip. Archie took the pen and slid it under the flap of the envelope and worked it along the glue line until the flap lifted. Still holding the envelope by the edges, he peered inside, then turned the envelope over. A key fell out into his other palm.

Susan felt her shoulders knot. She'd played a game once like this in college. A scavenger hunt, where every location yielded another clue. But the object back then had been to find hidden yard gnomes.

Archie dropped the envelope into his jacket pocket, closed his fist around the key, and knocked on the blue door. 'It's the police,' he called. 'It's Archie Sheridan. Anyone there?'

But no one answered the door.

Archie gave Susan a shrug and pushed the key into the lock. 'Stay here,' he said.

It was dawning on Susan that Archie was a recently discharged psych patient and that they were about to open the door to who-knows-what and that they had no backup, no gun, and no one who even knew where they were. She was not used to being the voice of reason, but this was not a good idea.

'Don't you need a warrant?' she asked.

'I've been invited,' Archie said, slipping his shoes off.

'What are you doing?'

Archie lined his shoes up, heel to heel, the way someone might leave his slippers at the end of his bed. 'Trying not to contaminate a potential crime scene.'

Susan's throat constricted. 'I'm not sure this is such a good idea,' she said.

Archie stood there in his socks for a second, looking like he was deciding what to order off a menu, and then turned the doorknob and went inside, closing the door behind him. The prayer flags on the railing moved gently in the breeze. Susan didn't know what to do. Wait there, like Archie had asked her? He was crazy. Like, literally. Go inside? That was crazy, too. She glanced down at Archie's shoes, still laced, sitting side by side next to the terracotta pots that lined the stoop. The plants in the pots had hairy, clam-shaped leaves; their insides were an engorged waxy pink, like something fleshy and alive. She looked back up at the blue door, her mouth dry. 'Archie?' she called hoarsely.

Every plant, in every terracotta pot, was a Venus flytrap.

30

Photographs of Gretchen papered the wall. They were cut out of magazines, newspapers, and books, and had been tacked to the white drywall with a colourful array of plastic thumbtacks. The pictures had been cropped carefully, surgically, nothing torn or hurried. It had been done with love. The collage was in the living room. Public space. You saw it the second you entered the apartment. Archie had once tacked up a photograph of Gretchen, but at least he'd had the sense to put it on the back wall of his bedroom closet.

He made himself secure the apartment before he returned to the collage. One bedroom. Futon used as a couch. Bed unmade. A bedside table with a glass half full of water on it. A white pressboard dresser. No one hiding in the closet.

The bathroom was tiny and free of frills. No one hiding in the shower. A medicine cabinet hung above the sink and Archie opened it. No Vicodin. It was worth a shot.

He returned to the living room.

And now, at least nominally sure that no one was going to jump out and shoot him, Archie looked for clues. White electrical heating units hugged the skirting boards, shiny white venetian blinds hung over sliding vinyl windows. White walls. Grey carpet. It was the efforts at personalization that were interesting. A feather-trimmed dreamcatcher spun slowly on fishing line over the sink. Purple batik draped the couch.

The smell of peppermint filled the room. Archie could taste it in his fillings.

He stood in the centre of the living room and turned around slowly. He spotted the anatomy book on the coffee table first, one of those big full-colour hardbacks. Other medical books lined the bookshelves, next to self-help tomes by Deepak Chopra and Eckhart Tolle. On the mantel, side by side, sat a Buddha, a plaster Shiva, and one of those plastic anatomy models with removable organs. On the walls, on either side of the Gretchen collage, were laminated posters of anaemic-looking angels.

The general effect was 'New Age bookshop meets medical-student dorm room'.

It felt desperate.

It felt familiar.

He let his gaze return to the collage. Gretchen had used accomplices, men she'd seduced into killing for her. He had thought they were all dead.

Archie walked towards the pictures. There was no furniture in front of that wall. You could walk right up to the collage. The carpet was flattened there, as if someone had stood in the same spot for hours on end. Archie stood there, too, and lifted his hand up, almost touching Gretchen's face, but keeping a millimetre between them, to preserve any fingerprints the collagist might have left.

He felt the calmness settle on him.

'Hello, sweetheart,' he said.

He smiled. He could look at her image now without feeling the burning in his stomach.

'You're losing your touch,' he said.

The pictures were in black and white and in colour, on newsprint and glossy magazine stock – Gretchen lovely in every one. Archie knew them all. Gretchen's face through the back window of a squad car. Gretchen's mugshot. Gretchen smiling at the crowd that had waited through the night to catch a glimpse as she was transferred to Salem. Part of Henry's shoulder in one, as he moved her towards the idling prisoner van.

What did the collagist see when he looked at her?

Then Archie smiled. In every photograph, she was looking at the camera. She was looking at him.

The collagist liked that. A man. It had to be a man. Whoever had put up all those pictures wanted Gretchen in control. He felt weak. It was a weakness particular to a certain kind of male experience.

Archie shook his head. 'You poor fuck,' he said.

From behind him, he heard Susan ask, 'What are you doing?'

She'd let herself into the apartment. He'd been so absorbed he hadn't heard her open the door. That sort of inattention got you killed in his line of work.

'I'm talking to a collage,' he said, 'of a serial killer.'

Susan looked at him for a moment, and then let her eyes slide around the apartment. 'Who lives here?'

Archie shrugged.

'I was calling you,' Susan said.

'I don't have my phone,' Archie said. His hand went to his pocket, where the phone from Gretchen was, and then he realized that Susan had meant she'd been calling his name. His eyes went to the floor. 'Close the door,' he said.

Susan pushed the door closed behind her with her elbow. 'Those plants on the stoop?' she said. 'They're Venus flytraps. Venus was the Roman goddess of love. Known for her beauty.' She flailed an arm in the direction of the collage. 'Make you think of anyone?'

'I'm drawing a blank,' Archie said.

'Are you crazy?' Susan asked. 'Are you, like, actually crazy now?'

She started to take a step towards Archie.

'Don't move,' he said. 'Or touch anything.'

'Do you smell that?' Susan said, wrinkling her nose. She sniffed the air and grinned. 'Dr Bronner's.'

'I smell peppermint,' Archie said.

Susan shook her head. 'It's Dr Bronner's peppermint all-in-one liquid soap,' she said. 'We used it for everything when I was kid. Shampoo. Toilet cleaner . . . This guy was a clean freak.' She started walking towards the TV hutch.

'You're moving,' Archie said. 'I said no moving.'

She didn't even slow down.

'Check it out,' she said. She reached the hutch and ran

her finger along one of the wooden incense trays that lined the shelf above the television.

'That would be touching,' Archie said.

Susan lifted her finger and showed it to Archie. It was clean. 'Who wipes down their incense trays?'

There was a photograph on the shelf, too. Archie couldn't make out the image from where he was standing, just the bamboo frame. But when Susan saw it she inhaled sharply.

Archie was at her side in four steps.

'It's him,' Susan said, indicating the picture. 'That's the guy I found in the house.' She ran her hands over the goose-bumps that had appeared on her arms. 'He did live here.'

The photograph showed three young men, outdoors in the woods, squinting into the sun. They were teenagers, seventeen, eighteen, their bodies not quite formed, T-shirts and cargo shorts exposing skinny legs and soft, sunburned arms. They had posed for the shot, but they weren't smiling. The middle kid's T-shirt had an Outward Bound logo on it. The kid on the left wore the bill of his red baseball cap low enough that Archie couldn't make out his face. But the kid on the right, shaggy-haired and slight with tattoos decorating one arm, Archie recognized. He looked over at Susan to see if she'd seen the flicker of surprise on his face. She hadn't. Her attention was still fixed on the photo.

'Which one?' Archie said.

'The one in the middle,' Susan said.

'Good,' Archie said.

'Good?' Susan said.

'It's good that we've identified him.'

She turned to look at him. 'No "Are you sure it's him?"' she asked.

Archie humoured her. 'Are you sure it's him?' he said.

'He was older,' Susan said. 'Early twenties, maybe. But it's the same face.' She narrowed her eyes. 'You don't seem that surprised.'

'It makes sense,' Archie said. 'We were supposed to find out who he was. That was the idea.'

'Why not just leave a wallet in his pocket?' Susan muttered.

'There's a story,' Archie said. He looked around the apartment again. The smell of peppermint was strong and recent.

That kind of cleaning took effort. It was obsessive. But he didn't find time to make his bed? So why go to all the trouble in here? The blinds had even been dusted. The electric heaters gleamed. No coffee-cup rings on the kitchen counters; no crumbs on the coffee table. The TV screen, on the other hand, looked like it hadn't been cleaned in years.

Archie stepped to the side so he could get the right angle and then he saw it – letters where a finger had drawn in the dust. PLAY.

'People need to tell stories,' he said. He peered behind the TV and saw the tiny DV camera tucked in the corner of the hutch, a black cord snaking up to the TV's video input. 'It makes their lives seem important.'

The DV remote was on the coffee table, next to the TV

remote. Archie took a pen out of his pocket and used it to turn the remote to on and then depress the play button on the DV remote.

A cockeyed image of the room they were in appeared on the TV. A chair had been dragged in front of the collage wall. Suddenly a young man appeared on camera. He was older, his brown hair longer, his body filled out a bit, but Susan was right, he was the middle kid from the photograph.

The man fiddled with the camera for a minute, until it was level and then backed up and sat down in the chair. Grey T-shirt. Jeans. Barefoot. Beads around his neck.

'Jesus Christ,' Susan said. She dug her notebook out of her purse, opened it, sat down on the couch, and stared at the screen. Archie thought about telling her to get up, lecturing her about all the trace evidence she was getting on her pants, but he didn't really have the energy.

The dead man looked at someone off camera. 'Is it recording?' he asked. The person must have nodded, because the dead man smiled shyly at the camera. 'Okay,' he said. He crossed his legs at the knees, gripped the top knee with threaded fingers, and leaned forward. 'If you're seeing this, well, things went wrong.' He took a breath, ballooned out his cheeks, and then exhaled with a sigh. 'So, I guess I should explain,' he said. 'When I was eight my brother got sick with mono. He was twelve at the time. We didn't know he had it. He'd been complaining about a sore throat for a month, but my parents thought he had a cold. The thing about mono is that it can cause your spleen to enlarge. This is why they tell you not to engage in strenuous activities for six weeks. My brother was in a PE class when some kid ran into him. It was one of those freak things.'

Archie sat down on the couch next to Susan.

'You can live without your spleen,' the dead man said.

'That's what they do when your spleen ruptures. They just take it out. A splenectomy.

'He was in the hospital for a week. Everyone in his class made him a card.

'That's when I started thinking about it.'

One corner of the dead man's mouth lifted. 'God, that sounds crazy, doesn't it?'

'Can you pause it?' Susan asked, scrawling notes.

'No,' Archie said.

'I used to play hospital. Pretend I'd had a splenectomy, too. I wore a bandage and everything.

'Eventually, it stopped being a game. I wanted it out of me. It felt dirty. Like this foreign thing that was stuck inside of me, like a tumour. I just got really sort of obsessed with it. Listen, I know how it sounds. I've had all kinds of therapy.'

The dead man lowered a hand to his ribcage and held it over his spleen, and Archie realized that he was in the same pose, his own hand finding the scar Gretchen had left on him. Archie put his hand between his thighs and held it there.

'I found a doctor in Tijuana who said he'd do the operation,' continued the dead man. 'And after he bailed out at the last minute, I got really depressed. Then a friend hooked me up with this website, and they said they could help me. I'm sorry, Mom, Dad, everyone. I know I could die.' He licked his lips. 'But if I can just get it out of me, I'll feel better.'

The video ended and the screen went blue.

Susan was still scribbling. Archie could see the pulse throbbing rapidly in her throat.

'It wasn't Gretchen,' Archie said. 'She didn't kill him.'

'They're fans,' Susan said, not looking up. 'Wannabes.' She stopped writing, set the pen on her notebook, and turned to Archie. Her face was pale. 'They're auditioning.'

Archie shook his head. 'And you think *I'm* crazy.'

31

The tendons in Henry's neck bulged and his ears were pencil-eraser pink. Susan tried not to cringe as he towered over her and Archie, still sitting on the couch. 'Have you two lost your minds?' Henry said. Behind him, the dead guy sat frozen on the TV screen. They'd watched the video twice more since Henry had shown up. It didn't get any less weird.

Henry turned his square head towards Archie, and held his hands palms up. 'Breaking and entering?'

'I had a key,' Archie reminded him.

Henry had arrived with Claire and four patrol cops who were now poking around the apartment like boys who'd broken into a girls' dorm. They'd already found the dead guy's passport in his dresser drawer. His name was Fintan English.

'Where's *your* warrant?' Susan muttered.

Henry whipped his head around at her. 'I'm investigating a B and E,' he said. 'There's been a string of them in the last two days.' He put his hands on his hips and settled his exasperated gaze on Archie. 'How do I explain this in court?'

Archie shrugged. 'There's no crime here, Henry,' he said.

Susan pointed a finger at the TV. 'Dead guy?' she said. If her name had been Fintan English, she'd probably have snapped, too.

'He was mentally ill,' Archie said. 'He wanted his spleen out. He found some people on the Internet to do it. You can find people on the Internet to do just about anything.' He twisted his mouth. 'Haul yard debris. Cut out organs. You should be happy. This is one murder Gretchen didn't do. Maybe everyone will relax a little.'

Henry gave a heavy sigh and scratched his throat. 'So he Googled "People Who Think Gretchen Lowell Is Awesome", and ended up on your Gretchen Lowell fan site.'

'It's not *my* fan site,' Susan said flatly.

'Posted his sad-as-shit story,' continued Henry. 'And found some assholes psycho enough to be up for the job. He didn't want his spleen. They wanted to play serial killer. Match made in nutjob heaven. They used the abandoned house as their operating room. But they didn't have the practice Gretchen did. And the kid died.'

'Maybe that's what the goat spleen in the Gorge was,' Archie said. 'Practice.'

'And the head?' Henry said. 'The two bodies up at the Garden? Courtenay Taggart? You're saying this is all the work of some deranged fan club? That Gretchen is in a yurt somewhere catching up on her reading?'

Susan glanced up at the TV screen again. The pause had caught Fintan English with his eyes closed. She'd seen him dead yesterday morning, and now here he was, soon to be another morbid YouTube sensation.

'I don't know,' Archie said.

Susan looked over at him. There was one thing she was sure of: Archie Sheridan knew more than he was telling.

Henry said, 'You going to let us look at your call log now?'

There was no reason not to tell him. 'It's a dead end,' Susan said. 'I looked it up. It's a pay phone on MLK Boulevard, about a mile from where I found the body.' Good luck fingerprinting that, Susan thought.

Henry brought his fist to his mouth for a minute and pressed it against his upper lip. Then he lowered it. 'Let us make a copy of your hard drive,' he said.

'So you can track my Web-surfing history?' Susan said. 'Forget it.' The idea of Henry having access to her hard drive, with its novel-in-progress, half-baked poetry, and last month's flurry of haemorrhoid research, made her stomach drop. 'I'm working on other stories, with important sources and confidential stuff.' She looked to Archie for some support. He was a reasonable person. He understood. But he was just sitting there on the couch, looking past Henry to the already-dead-looking image of Fintan English. 'Journalists can't just give their hard drives to the police,' Susan said. 'There's a rule.'

'The crime,' Archie said to no one in particular, 'is not getting him psychiatric help. He was ill.' He looked up at Henry. 'They used him,' he said.

Something passed between them and Henry cleared his throat and then leaned over Susan, his hands on his knees. 'I told you to take him home,' Henry said.

'Sorry,' Susan said.

'I don't know what the fuck is going on,' he said to Susan. 'But he can't be here.' He looked between them. 'Take him to my house. If anyone contacts either of you with mysterious addresses, cryptic greeting cards, et cetera, ignore your natural instinct to thwart the letter of the law, and call me.'

Archie gave them a pleasant, distracted smile. 'Absolutely,' he said.

'Go,' Henry said.

Susan and Archie stood up and started walking towards the door.

'It's going to get a lot worse,' Archie called back to Henry as they left. 'They're having fun.' The door was open and he walked through it into the sunshine and onto the stoop full of Venus flytraps. Susan followed him.

32

'Oh my God,' Susan said as soon as they got in the car. 'I thought he might actually arrest us.' She left her car door open, got a fresh pack of cigarettes out of the glove compartment, lit one, and took a drag, feeling her heart rate immediately slow. 'Let me just have half of this,' she said to Archie. The car was hot, and she didn't have air conditioning. 'You can roll down your window if you want.'

Archie pulled his seat belt over his lap and buckled it. 'I need you to take me somewhere,' he said.

Susan looked over at Archie. Was he kidding? 'Henry said to take you to his house,' she said.

'I know one of the kids in the photograph,' Archie said softly. 'His sister was one of Gretchen's early victims. I want to talk to his family. See if he's involved. I owe them that.'

Susan's heart was racing again. She took another drag off the cigarette. This time, it didn't help. 'You didn't tell Henry,' she said. 'We should go back in and tell him. Right now.'

'I want to determine the extent of the boy's involvement.'

'His involvement in what?' Susan said. 'Murdering people?'

'He's a troubled kid,' Archie said. 'Like Fintan English. Only no one helped Fintan.'

Susan took one more hit off the cigarette and then tossed it in the street, closed the door, and started the car. She was supposed to be interviewing the dead orderly's neighbours right now. But fuck it, she knew what they were going to say. *He always seemed so nice.* 'This book I want to write about Gretchen's impact on pop culture,' she said. 'Will you cooperate?'

Archie sighed and rubbed his eyes with one hand. 'Why not?'

'Okay,' Susan said. She pulled forward out of the parking spot, sending a collection of pens cascading from the open glove compartment onto Archie's lap.

He gathered them up and put them back in the glovebox and closed it.

'You know, two hundred people a year choke on pens and die,' Susan said.

Archie reached under his thigh, pulled out a crushed empty cigarette box that had been on the seat and tossed it on the floor. 'How many die from smoking?'

33

Lake Oswego was where the rich people lived.

Archie wouldn't tell Susan an address. Only that it was on the lake. The town was named after the lake. The lake was where the really rich people lived. What was it with rich people and water?

Susan called Derek so the *Herald* could break the Fintan English story. He'd write it. She'd get a co-byline. The *Herald* got the scoop. Everyone was happy.

After she hung up, Archie asked to borrow her phone.

'Didn't they give you your phone back when they released you?' Susan asked him.

'"Checked out",' Archie said, taking her phone. 'Not "released". I wasn't incarcerated.' He dialled a number from memory. 'It's Archie Sheridan,' he said. 'I need to see him. Is he there?' He paused. 'Right now,' Archie said. Then he hung up.

It was all very mysterious.

They drove through First Addition. That was the old part of Lake Oswego, where you could still live on a less-than-obscene salary. There were trees and yards, and old Sears mail-order Craftsman homes, and a supermarket where you could still buy groceries on account. The town's claim to fame was that Bruce Springsteen had married local-girl-turned-model Julianne Phillips at a church there. The marriage only lasted four years, but everyone still talked about it.

'Lake No Negro,' Susan said.

Archie arched an eyebrow. 'I don't think they call it that any more.'

'I used to go to parties out here in high school,' Susan said. 'They had the best drugs.'

They were passing a newly constructed mall downtown. It had the facade of an alpine ski lodge, like something from the Swiss Pavilion at Epcot Center. 'The idle rich,' Archie said.

They drove for a while in silence with the windows rolled down. Eventually, Susan got anxious and turned the radio to the alternative rock station. She'd had a few iPods, but they were always getting stolen out of her car. That was Portland for you. Rife with pacifists and vegetarians, but if you parked your car on the street, chances were someone would jimmy the lock and sell your iPod online on craigslist.

They went over some railroad tracks and past the private drive that led to the Oswego Yacht Club, then over a quaint stone bridge. Ducks paddled on the lake. The neighbourhood got more private and quiet at this point. The homes looked like beached houseboats with docks where motorboats bobbed expectantly. As they continued around the lake, the houses got bigger and the traffic more scarce. Everyone they passed smiled and waved. The houses looked like they'd been ordered from a Pottery Barn home-furnishings catalogue and assembled from kits. The cars were all Land Rovers and Volvos and BMWs. A few Civics – but Susan was pretty sure they belonged to college-aged children home for summer break from Brown University.

Archie directed her past a plastic yellow *Herald* mailbox, up a private lane to a pair of iron gates. 'Stop here,' he said.

Susan couldn't see the house, but the gates were pretty fucking impressive.

'Who lives here?' she asked.

'His name's Jack Reynolds,' Archie said.

Susan raised her eyebrows. 'He's rich,' she said.

'He's very rich,' Archie said. There was an intercom on a pole a car length in front of the iron gates. It looked like something you might order a burger from.

Archie took his seat belt off and leaned over Susan. His sudden intrusion into her space made her stomach hurt. His dark hair, flecked with grey, was inches from her face.

When you blush, the inside of your stomach turns red, too. 'The Science of Emotions' had been Susan's first story to make the front page of the Living section.

Archie punched a button labelled TALK and said, 'It's Archie Sheridan.' There was no audible response, but a red light above the speaker turned green and the gates fanned open. Archie settled back in his seat.

'You can go in,' he said.

Susan coughed. 'Right,' she said.

They drove through the gates and onto a bridge. It wasn't

a long bridge, just twenty feet or so, constructed with big rough-hewn stones.

'It's an island,' Susan said. 'They live on a fucking island.'

'Park here,' Archie said, indicating a paved parking area where four cars already sat. There was a silver Volvo, a pair of Priuses, and a pickup truck with the name of a landscape company on the side.

Susan parked next to the pickup.

There were a limited number of ways to get island-owning rich in Oregon. Susan guessed this guy had got out of high tech just in time. Or invented Polarfleece or something. Whatever he did, he did it well. She wondered if he'd ever been profiled in the *Herald*.

'This guy's related to the kid you recognized in the photograph, how?' she asked.

'Twelve years ago, Gretchen killed his daughter,' Archie said. 'The kid in the photograph is his son.'

'Do you come out here a lot?' Susan asked.

'I used to,' Archie said. 'But it's been a couple of years.'

Two years, Susan translated. Since Gretchen had taken him captive.

Archie opened his door and got out of the car. Susan did the same. She glanced around. 'I guess I don't need to lock it,' she said.

It was not a big island. Susan guessed it was about an acre, though she really wasn't sure exactly how big an acre was. The house was old, or at least it looked old, like a movie-set version of a Tudor mansion. It was brick, with stucco and timber accents, and had steeply pitched roofs, tall windows, several chimneys, and pillared porches. Ye Olde New Money.

'There,' Archie said. But he wasn't looking at the house. He was looking to the left of the house, where a dock extended into the lake, and a man in a suit was waving.

He didn't look old enough to have a twenty-year-old kid. 'Is that him?' Susan asked.

'That's his lawyer,' Archie said.

As they got closer, Susan saw another man, hosing down the deck of a small sailboat. He was in his sixties, tanned and handsome with longish grey hair and rugged symmetrical features. He was wearing cut-offs and an old T-shirt, and he was barefoot. He saw Archie and grinned.

'Hi, Jack,' Archie said. He turned to the lawyer. 'Leo,' he said.

Leo held out a hand and Archie shook it. 'It's been too long,' Leo said. 'We sent flowers to the hospital after Gretchen was caught.'

'I remember,' Archie said. 'That was very thoughtful.' He nodded in Susan's direction. 'This is Susan Ward,' Archie said. 'She's a reporter for the *Herald*.'

'Journalist,' Susan said. 'But whatever.'

Jack Reynolds winked at her. He looked sort of like a middle-aged George Hamilton. 'Of course,' he said to Susan. 'I read your stuff. You do good work.'

Susan felt her stomach turn red.

Jack hopped off the boat with the hose and walked over to a tap and turned it off. 'Took her for a spin around the lake,' he said. He looked up at the clear sky, framed by the ridge of evergreens around the lake. 'Got to enjoy the weather while we can.'

'We need to talk about Jeremy,' Archie said.

Jack looped the hose around a nail that was driven into the dock railing. 'Is he okay?' Jack asked.

Susan suddenly felt superfluous, like she was intruding on a private conversation. She took a tiny step back. And then, feeling self-conscious about that – she was a journalist, after all – she took a tiny step forward.

Archie shot her a look and then continued. 'I think he might be involved with some people who have a dangerous interest in Gretchen Lowell.'

Jack finished winding the hose and turned around to look at Archie. The last of the water trapped in the hose leaked from the nozzle in a slow drip onto the dock.

'I'm sure you've been following the news,' Archie continued. He spoke matter-of-factly. 'We identified the body that was discovered in the abandoned house in North Portland. It was a young man named Fintan English. We were just at his house, and I saw a picture of Jeremy there. It looks like English found some people on the Internet – fans of Gretchen – to remove his spleen, and that he died in the process.'

Jack glanced over at his lawyer. 'We haven't seen Jeremy in months,' he said.

The lawyer nodded his agreement.

Archie raised an eyebrow. 'I assume you have the means to find him,' he said.

'Is he missing?' Susan asked. 'Like Costa-Gavras missing?' They ignored her.

'How is Jeremy doing?' Archie asked.

The lawyer hesitated, looking over at Susan for a moment before he continued. 'He's still hung up on Gretchen, if that's what you're asking. If anything, it's gotten worse,' he said. His gaze fell on the dock. 'He carved a heart on his chest. When she escaped' – the lawyer looked out over the lake – 'he celebrated.'

Susan realized that her mouth had fallen open. Maybe she'd misunderstood. 'Didn't Gretchen kill his sister?' she asked.

They all looked at her, a little startled, like she'd pulled down her pants. 'Sorry,' she said.

Jack looked at his boat. The fibreglass hull knocked lightly against the dock. 'Jeremy has some challenges,' Jack said. 'One of which is obsessive-compulsive disorder. Do you know much about boats?' It took Susan an instant to realize he was asking her.

'Not really,' she said. The truth was that the whole kidnapped-and-held-hostage-on-a-boat thing a few months ago had sort of soured her on watercraft in general.

'She's a sloop,' Jack said. 'Pretty, huh?'

'Sure,' Susan said.

'Jeremy was thirteen when his sister was murdered,' Jack said. 'He developed an interest in following the case.' He paused. A seagull swooped down onto the dock and squawked. 'At some point he became confused,' he continued. 'He romanticized the Beauty Killer. He drew pictures of him – always a him – what he imagined the Beauty Killer looked like, big black wings, horns. The therapists said he was attracted to the killer's strength. When Gretchen was caught, Jeremy was in love.'

'He was a fragile kid,' Archie said gently.

Jack was still gazing at his boat. 'He always worshipped you.'

The seagull flew off. The boat bobbed. 'Do you know where he is?' Archie asked.

Jack Reynolds's mouth flattened in determination. 'I can find him,' he said.

Archie took a step towards Jack. 'Find him,' he said. 'Get him out of this. But first I want to know where he is, and who he's involved with.'

Jack smiled, but his eyes flashed with something darker. 'Is there anything else I can do for you, Archie?'

'Yeah. I need a gun,' Archie said. 'And a prepaid cell phone.'

34

The gull had flown off.

It had been ten minutes since Archie had followed Jack Reynolds into the Tudor chateau, leaving Susan standing with the lawyer on the dock.

The lawyer cleared his throat. 'So, did you grow up in Oregon?' he asked her.

Susan had been giving him the silent treatment. Clearly, he wasn't getting it. 'Your client just has extra guns and prepaid cell phones lying around?'

The lawyer was wearing an expensive grey suit and a black button-down shirt, open at the collar. Susan could admire his clothes and still not like him.

The lawyer put his hands in his pockets and looked out at the lake. 'He likes to be prepared,' he said.

Right. Susan narrowed her eyes. 'What does your client do exactly?' she asked.

The lawyer shot her a reflexive smile. 'He's in real estate.'

'Uh-huh,' Susan said. She got her cigarettes out of her

purse, lit one, and took a drag. Usually, she'd have asked permission. 'He and Archie are friends?'

The lawyer paused and seemed to think about the answer. 'Archie has always been generous about keeping the family updated on the case. They've known each other for a long time.'

'How long have you worked for him?'

'He was my first client. Right out of law school.'

'Let me guess,' she said. 'Lewis and Clark?' All the lawyers in town went to Lewis and Clark. Sometimes Susan thought it must be a requirement in the state bar exam.

'Go Pioneers,' he said.

'They should have gone with Seaman,' she said.

'Excuse me?'

'They should have made the mascot Seaman. After Lewis the explorer's's Newfoundland dog. He was right there with them, blazing the Oregon Trail.'

'Is Archie in trouble?'

Susan rolled her eyes. 'Compared to . . .'

He got his wallet out, extracted an expensive-looking business card, and put it in her hand. 'You can always call me,' he said. 'I *am* a lawyer.' The corner of his mouth twitched up. 'And I'm discreet.'

Susan couldn't quite figure him out. And she didn't like that. She looked at her shoes. 'It's pretty out here.'

'As a picture.' He took the cigarette out of her hand, took a drag off it, and handed it back.

Susan looked at the cigarette.

'Thanks,' he said. 'I'm quitting. But I sneak one once in a while.'

Another gull landed on the dock and pecked at some old bait that lay baking in the sun.

'What was his daughter's name?' she asked.

The lawyer gestured to the boat. On the back, above the rudder, was a girl's name painted in glittery gold and black cursive letters. 'Isabel,' he said. 'She was my sister.' He took the cigarette out of her hand again and took another drag. 'Jack Reynolds is my father. Jeremy is my little brother.' He sucked down the rest of the cigarette, tossed it on the dock, and stepped on it. 'One big happy fucking family.'

35

'**Are we not talking?**' Archie said.

They were driving south on Highway 43, the Lake Oswego alpine shopping mall on their left, heading back towards Portland. Susan didn't answer him. A DJ on the alt rock station yammered on about LASIK surgery.

Archie shrugged. He had the gun and cell phone he'd got from Jack Reynolds on his lap. He emptied the chamber of the gun and then put the bullets in a dash cubbyhole intended for loose change, and the gun and phone in Susan's glovebox.

'What are you doing?' Susan asked.

'In case we're pulled over,' he said.

'No,' Susan said. 'In the larger sense. What the fuck are you doing?'

'I'm trying to get a lost kid out of a bad situation.'

Susan flailed a hand at the glovebox. 'You got a gun. An unregistered gun.'

'Yes,' Archie said.

'Who is that guy?'

Archie smiled. 'He's in real estate.'

Susan could feel her jaw tighten. Someday she was going to take Archie Sheridan by the shoulders and shake the truth right out of him. Until then, she'd have to rely on more subtle manipulation.

'His lawyer's cute,' she said.

She saw Archie slide her a look out of the corner of his eye. 'Don't even think about it,' he said.

'Why?'

'Leo,' Archie said slowly, 'works for Jack.'

'Doing what?' Susan said. 'Real estate contracts?'

Archie pulled at his ear. 'Jack is responsible for importing most of the heroin that comes through the West Coast.'

'You don't have to make fun of me,' Susan said.

'I'm serious.' He reached for the stereo. 'Do you mind if I change the station?'

She swatted at his hand. 'I like this song.'

Archie sighed and sat back.

They were through First Addition now and on the stretch of 43 that wound alongside the river, connecting Lake Oswego and John's Landing. 'He's a drug dealer?' Susan said.

'He's *the* drug dealer,' Archie said. 'The rectangle at the top of the org chart.'

Susan asked the obvious question. 'Why don't you arrest him?'

To the left, beyond the old-growth cedars and mountains of English ivy, were some of Portland's fanciest houses, and beyond them, up the hill, the bucolic campus of Lewis and Clark College. The truth was that Susan had applied there as an undergraduate, but hadn't got in.

'His daughter was murdered,' Archie said.

'So he gets a "Get Out of Jail Free" card?'

'He's smart,' Archie said. 'It's not like he's in Old Town palming rocks to crackheads. He's well insulated.'

Susan looked over at Archie. He was losing it.

'What?' Archie said.

'You just got a gun from a crook,' Susan said, her voice rising. 'You're trying to help his crazy son, who may or may not have been involved in cutting some poor hippie's spleen out.' Plus there were other bodies – a head, for Christ's sake. 'Possibly more.'

Archie was quiet for a moment. 'He was there,' he said softly.

Susan glanced over at him. He was facing the passenger window, looking at the river.

'Jeremy,' Archie said. 'We found him in the car. Gretchen took them both. We found him in the passenger seat. The girl was in the back seat. He was thirteen years old.'

Another secret. They'd had a witness. Someone who'd seen the Beauty Killer. Someone who could identify her, long before they even knew that the killer was a woman. And they'd covered it up. 'Why didn't she kill him?'

'Why didn't she kill me?' Archie said. 'Why does she do anything?'

The significance of all this was dawning on Susan. Archie wasn't the only one. Gretchen had let someone else live, too. 'People think you were the only one of her victims who survived.'

'We kept him out of the papers,' Archie said. 'The shrinks

said that he was in a fugue state. He didn't remember anything that happened.'

'Did she ever confess to it?' she said.

'No,' Archie said. 'It was one of the files I couldn't close.'

He glanced at the car's digital clock. It was almost
lunchtime. 'Don't you have a story due?' he asked.

36

Susan dropped Archie off at Henry's two-storey Craftsman house, and waited until he waved to the patrol cops in the car out front and went inside. Then she called Ian to check in. He was eating at his desk – something he only did when they were swamped – she could hear the wet smack of his chewing. It made her stomach growl.

'Where's the psych-ward story?' he asked.

Ian had two other reporters covering Courtenay Taggart's murder. He didn't need her interviewing the orderly's neighbours and cold-calling Taggart's family.

Susan dug under her seat for a bag of potato chips. 'I thought I could pursue the fan angle,' Susan said, opening the bag. 'Did Derek post the Fintan English story?' She put a chip in her mouth. Kettle brand salt-and-vinegar flavour. Her car was full of them. They gave them away with the sandwiches at the bakery she went to for lunch, but she always got full before she got to them. There were bags under her seat, in the back seat, in the trunk. If her car ever broke down and she was stranded in the woods, she'd feast for days, but get very thirsty. 'This is big, Ian,' Susan said. 'Gretchen Lowell might not have anything to do with this. It's her fans. That's why they're dumping bodies in places where she's already committed crimes.'

Ian paused a beat. 'Today's headline says **Beauty Killer Strikes Again**,' he said. 'We stick with that until we know something different.'

Susan sputtered and then spat out a mouthful of chips. 'You're telling me not to investigate the fan-club angle?'

Ian lowered his voice. 'I'm telling you to do your job and get me thirty inches on the psych-ward murder by the end of the day.' She heard him get up and close the door to his office. 'Gretchen sells papers. Our news-stand sales have doubled since last week.'

'Psycho copycats will sell papers,' Susan said. 'If we break the story, we'll get the paper's name all over the world. That's good for ad sales, right?'

'Psycho copycats sell papers,' Ian agreed. 'For a couple of days. Then no one cares. Psycho copycats do not have Gretchen Lowell's legs. I need a few more days of rates like we've been having. All of our jobs are on the line, Suzy.' Susan flinched at the 'Suzy'. 'But if I can show these numbers, I can save some of us,' Ian said. 'I'm talking about major layoffs. Management has a list. And you and I are both on it.'

He hung up on her.

Susan looked at her phone for a moment and then threw it in her purse.

So she was supposed to do reporter grunt work on a story

they might be getting wrong, instead of investigating the angle that might actually reveal the truth. Meanwhile, Archie Sheridan had a gun and he was going to do something. She didn't know what. But he was going to do something. He was going to help that kid.

She got out of the car, walked back to Henry's house, and knocked on the door.

Archie answered, holding a phone, like he was just about to make a call. Susan only vaguely noticed that it was not the phone that Jack Reynolds had given him.

She held out her bag of Kettle chips. 'Want a chip?' she asked.

Archie put the phone in his pocket. 'You came back to ask me that?'

'I want to help,' Susan said. 'I don't know what this means, but it's not the right address. I mean, that house shouldn't be there.'

Archie looked confused.

'Three-nine-seven North Fargo,' Susan said. 'The house where I found the body. I looked it up on Google Earth and that address doesn't exist.'

Archie glanced behind her at the patrol car. 'Get in your car and pick me up around the block. I'll go out the back.'

Susan held up her laptop. 'Or we can just go online.' She rolled her eyes and walked past him into the house. 'You are so old.'

37

Susan sat down on the couch and put the laptop on Henry's coffee table. The coffee table was made from a massive piece of driftwood that had been sanded, shellacked, and put on legs. Issues of *American Rider* magazine, *Popular Woodworking*, and *Harper's* sat on top, along with an empty bottle of Arrogant Bastard Ale. There were posters of Alaska on the wall, and framed photographs of a biplane, a fishing vessel, and Henry Sobol, looking thirty years younger, standing in a group next to Jimmy Carter.

Susan opened the laptop and checked for Wi-Fi networks, feeling only a little nervous when Archie sat down right next to her. The only network that came up was called 'northstar-warrior'. That had to be Henry. But the network listing had a padlock next to it.

'His Wi-Fi is password protected,' she said.

'Try "Lynyrd Skynyrd",' Archie said.

Susan glanced over at Archie. 'Seriously?' she said, but she typed it in anyway. Declined. 'Nope,' she said.

Susan tried a few other words: Alaska. Harley. Woodworker.

Nothing.

'Try "Claire",' Archie said.

'Oh,' Susan said. 'That's romantic.'

She typed it in.

Declined.

'Shit,' she said. 'It always looks so easy when they guess passwords in the movies. Want to go to the library?'

'I have an idea,' Archie said. He leaned back on the couch, picked up the landline from an end table, and punched in a number. Susan heard Henry's voice say hello on the other end.

'What's your Wi-Fi password?' Archie asked him.

Henry muttered something.

'Thanks,' Archie said. 'See you tonight.' He hung up the phone. 'Lynyrd Skynyrd 1,' he told Susan.

'He added a one,' Susan said. 'So it would be harder to guess.'

'He is very clever,' Archie said.

'But not as clever as we,' Susan said.

She typed in Henry's password, got online, and went to Google Earth.

'What's your plan?' Archie asked.

'The house is on the three-hundred block. I could type in every three-hundred combination and check street views until we see the house. Or I could zoom into the neighbourhood, look for the roof, click on it, and get all the information we need. There. Three-three-three North Fargo.

'You can even see the address there,' Susan said, pointing at the screen, where the numbers on the porch clearly read

333. 'Someone covered that address with a new one. Changed it to three-nine-seven. Why?'

'Because the number was important.'

'Again,' Susan said, 'I ask why.'

'Because it's not an address,' Archie said. 'It's a date. March 1997. We only found one victim that month. Isabel Reynolds.'

'She had dark hair,' Susan said. 'Like her brother Leo.'

'Yeah.'

'I think I saw her picture on one of the fan sites I was researching.' She thought for a minute, trying to recover the name.

Then she typed in: www.iheartgretchenlowell.com.

'You have got to be kidding me,' Archie said, seeing the URL.

The home page came up. A photograph of Gretchen. Click to enter. 'Just wait,' Susan said.

She clicked on the photograph and went to the menu page. The menu items included Fan Fiction, Poetry, Gallery, Merchandise, Chat Room, and Archie Sheridan.

She tried to move the cursor over the Gallery link, but Archie put his hand on her arm. 'Click on it,' he said.

She rolled the cursor over Archie's name and clicked. Photographs came up, pictures of his family. The house they had shared in Hillsboro. There were photographs of Archie's wedding day, his graduations from college and the academy, photographs of him standing at crime scenes, giving press conferences. A biography. A history of his involvement with the task force. There was even a subpage of Fan Fiction.

'What's that?' Archie asked, pointing to the fan fiction link.

Susan had been hoping he wouldn't ask. 'People write stories about what they think happened between you and Gretchen,' she said. 'When she tortured you.'

Archie scratched the back of his neck. 'How many of these sorts of websites are there?'

'I found over four hundred,' Susan said. 'Here, this is what I wanted you to see.' She clicked on Gallery, and scrolled down until she found the photograph. It was labelled 'Reynolds, Isabel'.

It had been taken at the scene. She was curled on her side in the back seat, her arms bound in front of her, her mouth gagged. Her head was bent back, and a black gash marked where her throat had been cut. She had bled onto the seat underneath her head, and the blood had dried and sealed her tangle of brown hair to the vinyl. Her eyes were half open, the lids swollen. Her grey skin was flecked with veins. She looked like something carved out of Italian marble.

She'd been dead a few days. And Jeremy Reynolds had witnessed it. How did you ever get over something like that?

'Go to the chat room,' Archie said.

Susan looked over at him. He was engaged now, sitting forward, elbows on his knees. She navigated to the chat room. There were dozens of posts, most with accompanying icons that were in some way Gretchen-related. Her picture. A cartoon heart. A scalpel.

'When the Earth Liberation Front was really active,' Archie said, 'their members communicated through chat rooms. That way they didn't have to use e-mail addresses. They just went to an agreed-upon website. And used the chat room to set up meetings.' He reached over her and began to scroll down through the posts. 'Here,' he said. He reached forward, touching the screen.

Susan read the post aloud: 'Produce. Midnight. Tonight.' She looked at him. 'Produce what?'

'*Pro*duce,' Archie said. 'As in fruit and vegetables. As in the Produce District. We found one of Gretchen's victims in the basement of a warehouse there. Good place for a Beauty Killer Elks Club meeting. Want to go?'

'Fuck, yeah,' Susan said.

38

Susan spent the rest of the day working. She even knocked on the doors of the orderly's neighbours. *He always seemed so nice.* And cold-called Courtenay Taggart's family. *She was such a lovely girl.* That night, Susan ate a vegan lasagne with her mother, waited until eleven-thirty, and then went back to pick up Archie.

He met her around the block, at the point they had arranged. She didn't know if he'd sneaked out a back window while Henry was asleep, and she didn't ask.

There was no traffic that time of night and they made it to the Produce District in fifteen minutes. Susan parked under the Morrison Street Bridge. The tangle of highways overhead made that part of town seem especially gritty and urban. There was usually more car noise, but it was late and only the occasional large truck roared past over their heads. Archie emptied his pockets, putting two cell phones in the glovebox of her car, and then untucked his shirt, tucked the gun that Jack Reynolds had given him in the back of his pants, and arranged the shirt back over it. Susan inventoried her mace. It was dark in the Produce District at night. And the wide streets and concrete loading docks made the place seem especially empty.

'This way,' Archie said. Susan followed him down the street and around the corner to an enormous old warehouse. Inner industrial Southeast Portland was full of them. But this one, at five storeys, was especially looming.

Archie hopped up onto the loading dock and went to an unmarked fire door.

'I went to a show here once in high school,' Susan said, as Archie closed the fire door behind them. 'They used to have an all-ages club upstairs.'

'Fascinating,' Archie said.

The warehouse didn't store produce any more. Instead it seemed to be filled mostly with Asian furniture, reeking of orange-oil furniture polish and tatami. A few fluorescent lights flickered overhead, illuminating great stacks of glossy ornate cabinets, Chinese lamps, trunks, Buddha statues, plant stands. Susan didn't see any security cameras. If they'd been futon thieves, there'd have been nothing to stop them.

'This way,' Archie said. He walked through another door and flipped on a light switch. A series of bare compact fluorescent bulbs stuttered to life in a hallway. The wood floors were warped, providing a facsimile of vertigo to Susan as she followed Archie down the hallway. The walls were covered with colourful airbrushed images and scrawled spray-painted signatures.

'At least the graffiti's interesting,' said Archie.

Susan took a closer look at the walls. Next to some of the

images were unmistakable round red stickers. 'It's art,' Susan said.

Archie didn't answer.

'Really,' Susan insisted. 'See the red dots? It's a gallery.'

'It's a dank hallway,' Archie said.

'Slash gallery,' Susan said. 'Low overhead. A lot of these old warehouses cater to the underground art scene.'

She thought she heard Archie sigh.

'This city really needs to start enforcing fire codes,' he said.

'You know what causes the most house fires?' Susan said. 'Cooking. It's why I don't do it.'

'Down here,' Archie said, opening another door and flipping another light switch.

The door revealed a set of wide fir stairs that led to a concrete floor and another door. Another scary basement. Of course. 'You know what I'd like to see?' Susan asked. 'More crime involving airy above-ground spaces.'

Archie started down the stairs. There was a single compact fluorescent bulb at the bottom of the stairwell that made the whole scene look like something out of a Japanese horror film.

'What makes you think this Jeremy kid will be here?' Susan said. 'Maybe he hit an earlier meeting.' Susan had a sudden vision of a group of bloodthirsty cultists sitting in a circle drinking bad coffee and sharing stories from their childhood. Like AA, but with more blood and cackling. You could hit the child-killer meeting in the morning and the support group for sexual homicide fetishists at noon.

'I don't think it works like that,' Archie said.

'Should we make a plan?' Susan asked. 'Like what's our story?' They couldn't just walk in without a story. 'Are we serial-killer enthusiasts looking for the Gretchen Lowell Fan Club meeting? Are we a nice couple who's run out of gas and wandered inside to look for lodging?' Susan looked at Archie, then down at herself. 'Never mind. No one would buy us as a couple.' She considered more options. 'I know! Let's be building inspectors.'

The door at the bottom of the stairs opened and a girl appeared. Susan and Archie froze. The fluorescent bulb made the girl's skin glow bright and blurry like television static. She was wearing black fishnets, cut-offs, a black tank top, a Goth-looking black lace-up corset over the tank top, and lace-up high-heeled pointy-toed boots that looked like they'd been salvaged from the wreck of the *Titanic*. To finish the outfit off, the girl wore a pair of antique-looking driving goggles on top of her head.

Runaway, Susan thought. Hiding out. Probably more freaked out to see them than they were to see her. The whole building-inspector cover suddenly seemed pretty weak. Susan wished she'd had her clipboard.

Archie was four steps ahead. Susan couldn't see his face. Susan willed him to say something. He didn't. 'Hi,' Susan said to the girl. 'My husband and I ran out of gas.'

The girl didn't even look at her. She was looking at Archie. Her cheeks flushed. Her stance went a little pigeon-toed, or maybe it was just the boots. And then she squeaked two words – 'Archie Sheridan' – followed by a little squeal. Like a kitten having a nightmare.

Susan had met Jack White once and reacted much the same way.

'That's me,' Archie said.

The girl had a stud in each eyebrow, and she reached up and twisted one. 'You came,' she said. 'I mean, wow.'

Archie took a step down one more stair, moving slowly, like someone approaching a wounded animal. 'I'm looking for Jeremy,' he said.

The girl nodded, but Susan wasn't sure if she was responding to what Archie had said or was just trembling with excitement.

'Do you know Jeremy?' Susan asked the girl.

The girl's pierced brows furrowed, and she shot Susan a concerned look. 'I'm not sure if you're allowed a guest,' she said to Archie.

The story of Susan's life. She couldn't even get a 'plus one' to a serial-killer sect.

Archie took another step towards the girl, all non-threatening confidence. 'I'm sure it's fine,' he said.

The cheeks deepened another shade. 'I guess,' the girl said. She shrugged and Susan noticed how bony her shoulders were. What was she? Sixteen? 'Come this way,' the girl said. She swung the door open with a self-conscious flourish that made her seem even younger. 'Everyone's waiting.'

Archie descended the final three stairs and stood face to face with the girl. She was small and seemed to shrink more in his presence. With her cinched corset, teetering boots, and brass goggles, she looked like a tiny awkward insect. Susan clomped down the stairs after them, her arms crossed.

'They're waiting,' the girl said again.

'Is Jeremy waiting?' Archie asked.

'We love Jeremy,' the girl said. She smiled and her eyes suddenly shimmered. 'Just like we love *you*, Archie.' Susan would have laughed if the whole thing hadn't been so entirely creepy. She looked for some sign from Archie, a wink or nudge, something that would reassure her that they were in on this together, but she got nothing. She clutched her purse full of mace closer.

The girl sniffed noisily, and wiped her nose with her forearm. 'You have no idea,' she said. 'We're your biggest fans.' Then, with an apologetic gesture towards a stain on the concrete floor, she stepped through the door at the base of the steps and into a dimly lit basement hallway. 'Watch the blood,' she said, wrinkling her nose. 'It's kind of slippery.'

'Blood?' Susan said.

The girl laughed. 'I'm kidding,' she said. 'God.'

39

Archie matched his gait to Susan's, so that they were side by side, a few steps behind the girl. He knew where they were going. He'd been in this basement a dozen times. He'd walked down those stairs, down this hallway, around the corner, into the old boiler room.

Seven years ago, Gretchen had killed a man here. Archie had examined the crime scene. Taken inventory of every lesion on the corpse. Watched the man split open on the ME's table. Seven years ago, Archie had notified the dead man's wife and children. He'd gone to the house, rung the doorbell in the middle of the night, and broken the news that their husband and father was dead.

Back then the main floor of the warehouse had been a used-office-furniture outfit. Metal desks, filing cabinets, stacks of steel-case cubicle components, and hundreds of pale blue and plum coloured office chairs arranged in rows three hundred feet long.

No makeshift gallery. The upper floors were empty, the windows boarded up.

'Are there still rats down here?' Archie asked the girl.

Susan stiffened.

The girl shrugged. 'You see them once in a while,' she said.

There was a persistent drip coming from a pipe some-where that echoed off the concrete. But the air down there was cool and pleasant. The ceiling was low, but looked even lower than it was, and Archie found himself reflexively hunching over a little as they walked.

The gun was tucked into his waistband, under his shirt, at the small of his back. He ordinarily wore his gun in a shoulder holster, but that was in a box in a storage unit. He could feel the gun at his back now, like someone's hand pressing him along, guiding him deeper into the basement. It would be hard to get at in a hurry, but it was there if they needed it and it was in a place that amateurs might not check. It was that or duct tape it behind his neck – he still couldn't really figure out exactly how people pulled that off on cop shows. Besides, he didn't have any duct tape.

'You guys are quiet,' the girl said.

'We're concentrating on being led to our doom,' Susan said.

They got to the boiler-room door. It was easy to spot. There was a big yellow sign on it that said BOILER ROOM in all-cap black letters. The door was grey steel. The girl knocked on it twice, then once, then twice more.

'Seriously?' Susan said, rolling her eyes at Archie. 'A secret knock?'

'They're here,' the girl called. 'Detective Sheridan and some chick friend.'

'Susan Ward,' Susan called.

The door opened.

Susan turned to Archie. 'I wonder how many people die in basements every year,' she said.

The boiler room was dark. Archie and his team had set up high-wattage lights when they were down there, illuminating every cobweb and blood spatter. Without all those high-powered bulbs defining every corner and crack, the room seemed larger, amorphous, every corner curved. The light from the hall seeped in, a warped yellow rectangle on the floor. Dust hung in the air. Water moved in pipes overhead.

The person who'd opened the door had moved back into the shadows, over by the hulking decommissioned boiler. It had taken him five steps. Archie had counted, listening for the soft shuffle of sneakers on cement. The boiler was the size of Archie's first car. Archie could make out the shapes of three people beside it.

A flashlight beam hit him in the face. He turned his head and squinted, then forced his gaze straight ahead, into the light. Susan was standing next to him, and he put his hand out and touched her wrist with his fingertips, so she'd stay close to him. He could feel the gun digging into the small of his back.

He'd thought that Gretchen had left the bodies in the park and at the mansion to get his attention, but these people had been doing it to get hers. They wanted to impress her. They wanted to get closer to her. They wanted to use him. To get to her.

'I'm here,' he said into the light. 'Now what?'

The light angled down, and a man stepped forward. It took a moment for Archie, blinded by the sudden darkness, to blink the dark spots from his vision. The man was in his twenties or thirties, with a soft untrimmed beard and plugs the size of bottle caps in his earlobes. He looked like he should be bagging groceries at a natural-foods store.

He smiled at Archie, revealing a mouthful of teeth that had been filed into sharp points. 'We weren't sure you'd come,' he said.

Susan's fingers folded around Archie's hand.

'It's been a while since I was down here,' Archie said.

The teeth were good. The teeth meant they were going to be able to find out who this guy was. Cops loved body modification. Tattoos? Half the world had those. You couldn't throw a hackee sack at the University of Oregon without hitting a sorority girl with a butterfly on her ankle. But file your pearly whites into shark fangs and you were special. People remembered you.

Archie smiled.

Shark Boy's face faltered. 'What?' he said.

'You're not in charge, are you?' Archie asked.

Susan squeezed his hand. He glanced over at her and she nodded towards the boiler, where one of the shapes had stepped forward.

'The rest of the fan club?' Archie said.

'We're more of a collective,' Shark Boy said.

The girl laughed.

Archie squinted at the shape that had stepped forward: tall, male, but Archie couldn't make out more than that. 'Jeremy?' he said.

The shape didn't move.

'I don't think that's Jeremy,' Susan said quietly.

Archie didn't like where this was going. He turned to the girl. 'There still a bloodstain?' he asked.

Shark Boy lifted his flashlight beam to the floor near the opposite wall. 'Over there,' he said.

Archie pretended not to see it. 'Turn on the light,' he said. 'The mood is great. Very *Nightmare on Elm Street*. But if you turn on the light, I can show you what happened.'

Archie kept his focus on Shark Boy, watching as his gaze flicked over to the man by the boiler, looking for permission. The man must have nodded, because Shark Boy said, 'Okay.'

Someone turned on the lights. Nothing fancy. Three bulbs. No one had bothered to install compact fluorescents down here. Maybe they were waiting for these to burn out first.

Archie turned back towards the boiler. The man was still standing there. He wore black pants and a grey T-shirt and a nylon stocking over his head. He was relaxed. His hands were in his pockets. Behind him were two young men in their twenties. No masks.

'There you are,' Archie said.

'Start talking,' the man in the mask said.

Archie turned his attention to the bloodstain. Susan

unfolded her hand from his. 'Go ahead,' she whispered, and Archie took a step away from her.

It had been seven years, but it was still there, much as he remembered it: a bathmat-sized stain, a human body's length from the wall. Someone had lovingly swept the dust off it.

Seven years. But it was hard to get blood off concrete. You had to work at it. Sandblast it. Use flame. Grind. Scab. Plane. Scour. Douse with chemicals. No reason to waste the effort in an old boiler room. Who was ever going to see it?

He hesitated for a second. Susan didn't need to hear what he was going to say. He looked over at her.

'Go ahead,' she whispered again.

'She taped him to a chair,' Archie said. He looked around the room. He wasn't looking at the people. He was looking for the chair. It was gone. Someone had had the decency, at least, to get rid of that. 'An office chair. From a shop upstairs. It was pale blue.' He didn't know why, but that detail had always struck him, the powder-blue cloth of the chair, dated even then, like something out of a dentist's waiting room. 'She used an entire roll of duct tape.' One hundred and eighty feet. One of the crime techs had measured it. It had taken them forty minutes to peel it off him before he could be sent to the morgue. 'Mummified him from his ankles to his neck.' He glanced over at Susan. Her face was a mask of journalistic objectivity. Good girl, Archie thought. And then he mentally kicked himself for being condescending.

He reached up and touched his chest, feeling the thick scars under the cloth of his shirt. 'She had carved up his chest. She always did that. But the incisions on this one were unusually passionate.' He shot Shark Boy a wicked grin. 'The duct tape stopped him from bleeding out.' The girl had taken a step closer to Shark Boy and was working the stud in her eyebrow again. 'Duct tape's good for that,' he said. 'Among other things.' Shark Boy was smiling, but it was a put-on smile, another kind of mask.

The man in the mask was perfectly still.

Archie needed to make it worse. Much worse.

'Then she sliced open his chin,' Archie continued. 'About an inch below his bottom lip, a two-inch-wide opening.' He walked over to the girl. She was the one. If he could get to any of them, it would be her. He lifted his hand and brushed his thumb along her bottom lip. She was stock-still, but she didn't shrink from him. She held her ground. Archie pressed his thumb into her chin. 'And she pulled his tongue through the incision.' He let that image sink in for all of them. 'And then she pushed piercing needles through the part of the tongue that was exposed.' He moved his hand up the girl's face and tapped one of the studs that pierced her eyebrows. 'Two-inch hollow piercing needles,' he said. 'Three of them. She left two of the needles in, so he couldn't pull his tongue back through the hole. And then she removed the third needle.'

The girl turned her head. Not much, but enough that she pulled away from Archie's hand. He looked at it there in mid-air and then closed his fist and dropped it to his side. She was just a kid.

He turned to Shark Boy and the others.

'There's a pretty big vein in the tongue that apparently

bleeds a lot,' he said. He paused. Susan's face was still impenetrable, but she'd crossed her arms tightly across her chest. A black sludge dripped from the rusty joint of a sewer pipe overhead.

'It took him sixteen hours to die. He lost five quarts of blood. But in the end, he died of suffocation. His tongue swelled up, and he choked on it.' He looked back at the girl. Uncle Archie. Scaring them straight. 'Still having fun?' he asked.

The girl took another small step back. She had goose-bumps on her arms, but it might have just been because the basement was chilly.

'We found him four days later,' Archie continued. 'Sitting in here in the dark, taped to the chair, his eggplant of a tongue engorged, drool, blood everywhere. Strange to see someone's tongue coming out of the wrong orifice like that, blue lips, mouth open above it.'

'What about his eyes?' the masked man asked. Archie thought he detected a smile behind the mask, but the man's features were so flattened by the nylon, he couldn't be sure.

The details about the eyes had not been made public. 'She'd pushed a needle through each of his pupils,' Archie said.

'Jesus Christ,' Susan said softly.

'Such is our reward for those in sin,' the masked man said.

One of the young men behind him smirked.

Archie lowered the timbre of his voice. It was time to get serious. 'This ends now,' he said. 'Whatever *this* is. Go home to your parents,' he said to the girl. 'Your halfway houses,' he added to Shark Boy. 'I don't give a shit where you go. Gretchen Lowell is a psychopath. She is not some sort of anti-hero. This is real life.' He addressed them all. 'This man, his name was Can Giang. He came here from Vietnam with his wife. They ran a convenience store downtown. After he died, his teenage son dropped out of high school to keep the place afloat. He was a human being.'

The girl pulled at the white fringe of her cut-offs. 'He wanted to,' she said.

'Shut up,' the masked man snapped.

'Fintan wanted us to do it,' the girl said. 'He begged us. We didn't know he'd die.'

'Shut up, Pearl,' the masked man said again.

The girl was wavering. Archie had reached her. It had worked. 'Where's Jeremy?' Archie asked her.

'Jeremy's part of our family,' Shark Boy said.

'Jeremy is the only person besides you who survived Gretchen Lowell,' the masked man said, walking towards Archie. 'Jeremy is special.' He tapped Archie on the centre of his chest. 'Like you.'

'Jeremy was a kid,' Archie said. 'He doesn't remember.'

'Yes he does,' the masked man said. He motioned to Shark Boy. 'Show him.'

Shark Boy lifted his shirt and bared his shark teeth in a frightening smile. Archie felt a shiver run down his back. Gretchen didn't have an MO. She did whatever crazy shit she felt like in the moment. But it usually involved, at some point, carving into the person's torso. Archie had come to know the marks and abrasions on her victims' chests like a curator would know a collection of paintings. Every stroke was exact. Each victim was painted differently.

He remembered Isabel Reynolds's wounds. Sixteen vertical slices stacked up on the left ribcage, a latticework of tiny hash marks on her belly, and below her left clavicle, carved with a scalpel, a thinly rendered heart. Even more unique, Gretchen had carved a pattern of triangles across her right ribcage, something she had done to no other victims.

Shark Boy's chest bore the same marks.

'Jeremy did it for me,' he said. 'How does it look?'

The shiver turned into a cold chill. The morgue photos were sealed. If Jeremy had carved those marks into Shark Boy's chest, it meant that he did remember. He knew what had happened. He was a witness. With his testimony they might be able to close the case. Archie cleared his throat. 'I need to talk to him,' he said.

The man in the mask put his nylon face right in front of Archie's. Archie could make out short brown hair beneath the stocking. 'Starting to take us seriously?' the masked man asked.

Archie had heard of scarification, of cutting, but this? He pulled Shark Boy's shirt back down. 'You think this would amuse her?' Archie said. 'That she'd take it as some sort of deranged compliment?'

'I know why she's here,' the man in the mask said, jabbing a thumb at Susan. 'She wants a story. But why are you here?' He turned to Susan, addressing her for the first time. 'You wonder that, too?'

'I'm wondering why you're the only one wearing a mask,' Susan said.

There was a slight adjustment in the masked man's stance, like a boxer inhaling before a blow. Archie, still over by the bloodstain, was too far away. He took a step closer to Susan, and tried to refocus the masked man's attention. 'I came for Jeremy,' Archie said.

But things had already been set in motion.

Shark Boy stepped behind Susan and wrapped his arms around her, pinning her arms to her sides. Her mouth opened, more out of surprise than fear, and she struggled for something in her purse, but Shark Boy pulled the purse off her arm and threw it across the room.

Archie could see it happening, see the man in the mask lift something sharp and silver to Susan's face – a piercing needle. Shark Boy tightened his grip. Susan struggled but the masked man held the sharp needle against the smooth flushed flesh of her cheek, and she froze.

The masked man's featureless face was pointed at Archie. 'I think you came for something else,' he said.

Nobody moved. The needle was nearly touching Susan's face, so close that if she flinched, it would pierce the skin. Susan's eyes widened.

'The major vessels of the lingual artery go through the tongue,' the masked man continued. 'That's that big vein you were talking about. Ever had Manchego cheese? That's what pushing a needle through a tongue feels like. Like slicing a knife through Manchego cheese. Cartilage makes a popping, squashy sound, like poking through the skin of a baked acorn squash.'

'Let me guess,' Susan said. 'You work in food service?'

Shark Boy put a hand on Susan's forehead and snapped her head back, securing the back of her skull against his shoulder.

She didn't know what was happening yet, but Archie did. He couldn't stop it. 'It's going to be okay,' he said.

The masked man slid one end of the needle into Susan's cheek. It went in effortlessly, like a thumbtack into corkboard. The skin tented on the other side for a moment and then the tip of the needle popped through, just under her eye. It happened in an instant. Susan barely had time to cry out. Then it was over. The two-inch needle was left threaded through her cheek.

The gun pressed insistently into Archie's back. He could recover it, but it was under his shirt, and he would have to fumble for it. It would take seconds. So would they hurt her more in the panic of those few seconds, or if Archie did nothing?

Susan's eyes were wild with anger and disbelief. She fought to lift her hands up, but Shark Boy held her tight.

'Jesus fuck!' Susan screamed. 'You pierced my fucking face!' She looked at Archie, her eyes pleading with him to do something. She knew he had a gun. It was not unthinkable that she would wonder why the hell he wasn't using it.

'Flesh,' the man in the mask said, producing another needle, 'is more like a frozen grape.' He moved the needle down just below Susan's bottom lip. 'Is this about where Gretchen cut your noble immigrant?'

Susan stopped struggling and squeezed her eyes shut. A tiny rivulet of blood made a trail down her chin and neck, and under the collar of her white shirt.

Archie summoned all the calm in his body and focused on Susan. 'Susan,' he said. 'Look at me.'

He half expected her to ignore him. He'd brought her down here, into this. No backup. No badge. And a masked madman had just put a needle through her face. Trust was probably not high on her emotional agenda right now.

But she opened her eyes.

Archie tried to exude confidence, to project mettle into her gaze. 'It's going to be okay,' he told her.

She nodded. It was a tiny movement. Archie might have imagined it.

Without taking his eyes off Susan, he asked the masked man, 'What do you want?'

Archie needed to get Susan out of this.

'I want you to do me a favour,' the man in the mask said.

'I'm not going to help you move,' Archie said.

'I want you to cut me.'

His words floated in the air like dust. Everyone waited. Archie could hear Susan breathing.

Shark Boy started rummaging around in a pocket and then they heard the snap of a case opening. Archie refused to unlock his eyes from Susan's. He refused to look away. He could do that, at least, for her. He could keep her calm.

Susan caught sight of what Shark Boy had in his hands a split second before Archie did. He saw the fear register in her eyes. But Archie already knew what it was. He knew it from the word 'cut'. So when Shark Boy lifted the tempered steel blade to Susan's throat, Archie did not react at all.

Resolve.

Susan's breathing now came in short little bursts. Archie worried she was going to hyperventilate. He needed her thinking straight.

He reached forward with his left hand, took her right hand, and squeezed it. Her hand was cold to the touch. He could feel her pulse through his palm.

But she looked at him. And she squeezed his hand back.

Archie had a plan.

He held his right hand out for the scalpel. Shark Boy set it in his palm. It was larger than the scalpel that Gretchen had used to carve into Archie's chest, but not as pretty. This one was disposable, plastic and steel. Gretchen's was top-of-the-line.

Archie folded his hand around the plastic handle.

'Where?' he asked the masked man.

He could smell the sour stink of the masked man's breath; hear Shark Boy's teeth clicking; feel Susan's pulse beat against his fingers.

If someone had walked in, they would have thought that the four of them were having an intimate discussion – the masked man pressed next to Susan, Shark Boy behind her, Archie facing Susan, gripping her hand.

'Lift up my shirt,' the masked man said.

Archie gave Susan's hand a firm squeeze and then released it.

He took a step forward. He was so close to Susan now that his right shoulder touched her bare left shoulder just above where Shark Boy's arm wrapped around her. He could feel the rise and fall of her chest against his shirt. Archie untucked the masked man's T-shirt from the front of his pants and lifted it up. He waited a moment to look down. He knew what he'd see.

The masked man's chest was a mass of scar tissue.

The scars were more healed than Shark Boy's. There were dozens of them. They'd been done over time – the oldest ones looked to be at least a year old. The freshest were still red and raw.

'I did it myself,' the masked man said. 'I want you to do it better. I want it to look like yours.'

'I see you've waxed,' Archie said.

Susan started to smile, but winced as the needle moved in her cheek.

The masked man lowered his chin at the scalpel in Archie's hand. 'Go ahead,' he said. 'Cut me.'

Archie held up the scalpel and wiggled it. 'Let her go,' he said.

No one moved.

Archie adjusted his grip on the scalpel. 'This is the Palmar grip,' he said, holding the handle with his second through fourth fingers, the base of his thumb along the side of the handle securing it, his index finger extended along the top rear of the blade. 'It's also called "dinner knife" grip.' He sawed at something imaginary in the air. 'You can see why.' He looked at the scalpel. Even in the low light, it glittered. Even the sight of the blade made his stomach tighten, but he wouldn't let them see it. 'This grip is best for initial incisions and larger cuts,' he said.

He adjusted his grip again, this time holding the scalpel with the tips of his first and second fingers and the tip of his thumb, so that the plastic handle was resting on the crook between his index finger and thumb. He wrote something imaginary in the air. 'The pencil grip,' Archie said. 'You've got to be careful with this one not to let the handle rest too far along the index finger. Don't want your hand cramping up.' Archie looked at the blade and frowned. 'Better for smaller blades.

'Gretchen preferred the Palmar,' he said. 'Most medical professionals do.' He leaned close to the masked man. So close he could see the colour of his eyes through the nylon – blue. 'Let her go,' Archie said. 'And I'll do what you want.'

The masked man lifted the second needle away from Susan's chin and with the same hand grabbed hold of the end of the needle piercing her cheek. With a smooth movement of his elbow, he snapped it out of her face.

'Fuck,' she yelled. This time Shark Boy let her lift her hands to her face and she cupped both to her bleeding cheek.

'Get out of here,' the masked man told her softly.

She drew her head back in rage. 'No,' she said.

Archie lowered the scalpel and leaned in to Susan. He

kissed the hand that covered her cheek. 'Trust me,' he whispered.

She glared at all of them for a moment and then took a step towards her purse, which still lay on the floor by the wall.

'No,' the masked man said. 'Leave it.'

She looked at Archie questioningly and he nodded, and then she turned and ran, her hand still on her face.

The man in the mask nodded at Archie. 'Let me see yours,' he said.

Archie smiled. 'Sure,' he said.

He reached up with his left hand and began unbuttoning his shirt. The girl appeared at the masked man's shoulder and then the two other men from over by the boiler joined her. Shark Boy licked his lips. They all wanted to see Gretchen's work in person.

When Archie had unbuttoned his shirt and opened it, he reached out and lifted the masked man's shirt again. He compared the damage.

'It's not so different,' he said.

The man in the mask wasn't even looking at Archie's face any more. His entire focus was on Archie's chest. Hands trembling, he reached out and brushed his fingertips across the topography of Archie's scars.

As he did, Archie moved his right hand to his waist, dropped the scalpel, and pulled the gun from the back of his pants.

The scalpel made a metallic crack as it hit the concrete

floor and the masked man and Shark Boy and the girl and the two other men all looked down reflexively. When they looked back up, Archie had his gun trained at the masked man's sternum.

'I'm arresting you for assault with a deadly weapon,' he said. 'At least.' He paused. 'Thank you. You've all made me feel very sane.'

Archie saw the flash of light an instant before the electrical jolt hit his body. The wave of pain blasted through every sensation. He had been tasered once before, during academy training. It didn't help. It wasn't something you got used to. All of his muscles tightened, and he dropped to the floor unable to move. Information came in stuttering chunks. He'd lost the gun. It was the girl. She'd got him from behind, below his ribcage. She tasered him again in the same spot. He curled on the floor, overcome by the pulsing charge, every cell vibrating. The girl. She was a kid. Like Jeremy.

How old? Sixteen?

She tasered him again. His body jerked involuntarily, causing a tiny dust storm to rise off the cement floor. The yellow bulb on the ceiling got smaller, like it was getting further away.

They'd named the taser after an old kids' adventure book: *Tom Swift and His Electric Rifle*. They'd added the *A*. It was the kind of useless trivia that Susan would want to know.

He felt bad he'd never told her.

40

'How long do we have?' Gretchen asks.

Archie takes his jacket off and lays it on the back of the chair. 'An hour,' he says.

They are in her home office, where she sees patients. It is grey outside. The rain falls in steady cold sheets against the window behind Gretchen's desk. Through the window Archie can see the plum trees in Gretchen's backyard bend, their purple leaves trembling in the downpour.

Gretchen walks to the window and pulls the velvet curtains closed. 'That long?' she says, walking back to him.

It is ten in the morning, and Archie has been up for six hours, most of it spent standing outside in the rain. He has left his muddy shoes inside the front door and is standing in his wet brown socks.

She stops a step in front of him and leans her head against his chest, like she's listening for a heartbeat. The smell of her hair slows everything down. When he is with her he can almost forget the death that surrounds him. It's one of the ways he justifies coming here. She keeps him sane. He can do his job better. Moral relativism.

Archie holds up the folder at his side. 'I told Henry I was getting a consultation,' he says. He tosses the folder on her desk.

She lifts her head and reaches up to touch his wet hair. 'What happened to you?' she asks.

'I came from a crime scene,' he says. It was the third body in four weeks.

Her eyes soften and fill with tenderness. 'I'm sorry,' she says. 'I hate that you have to see that.' She kisses him on the cheek and then takes him by the hand and guides him to a chair. He sits down and Gretchen sinks to the floor in front of him. She takes one of his feet in her hands and peels off a wet sock.

She runs a finger down the top of his naked foot, to the tip of his toe. 'You have beautiful feet,' she says.

He knows she's lying – his feet are pale and calloused, with bunions the size of marbles.

'Anne thinks you're right,' he says. 'About the possibility of the killer being a woman.' Even at a time like this, his mind returns to work. 'If it is a woman, Anne thinks she might have help. She says that dominant serial killers will sometimes take on partners with less powerful personalities.'

'Not partners,' Gretchen says, peeling off his other sock. 'I've read the literature.' She drops the sock on the floor. 'They're more like apprentices.'

Archie shrugs. 'Henry thinks it's bullshit,' he says. 'It challenges everything we know about serial killers. They're supposed to be pudgy forty-year-old white guys with mother issues and panel vans.'

'Maybe they're just the ones who get caught,' Gretchen says, climbing into Archie's lap. She is settling in when she suddenly looks down and smiles. 'You came ready to go,' she says, arching a teasing eyebrow.

'That's my gun,' Archie says.

'Your gun,' Gretchen says, reaching to his right side and patting the leather gun holster on his belt, 'is over here.'

She unclips the holster, lifts it off his pants, and sets it on the end table next to the chair.

Then she reaches into his pants pocket and pulls out his cell phone, his keys, and his small field notebook, setting them all next to the gun.

After sliding her hand in the other pocket, she comes out with a pair of latex gloves.

'They're for handling evidence,' Archie explains.

'Uh-huh,' she says. She tosses the gloves on the table with the rest, then unbuckles his belt, slides it out of the loops, holds it off to the side and drops it on the floor.

The belt had been a gift from Debbie.

What was he doing here?

Archie takes Gretchen's face lightly in his hands. His voice cracks with despair. 'We need to talk,' he says. 'I can't keep doing this.'

She moves his knees apart and eases down between them, back onto the floor in front of him. He doesn't stop her. They have done this before. But it still mesmerizes him. He can't believe his luck, to be wanted by a woman like her.

She unbuttons and unzips his pants and her face disappears in a tangle of blonde hair as she lowers her head to his lap.

The rain stops. Archie leans his head back and closes his eyes.

41

Someone had turned the lights out. When she'd fled into the hallway she had been met with a wall of inky black. Susan had never experienced darkness like that. She froze for a second, unsure of what to do. Then she ran to her left, tracing her hand along the concrete wall. It was cool to the touch and pitted where pieces of concrete had crumbled off over the years. She concentrated on that. It kept her from being enveloped by the darkness.

In all that black, noise overwhelmed her. Pipes knocking. Water gurgling. The slap of her boots on the concrete. She could hear her heart beat and her face throb. She had never breathed so loud in her entire life. Every sound was someone coming up behind her, someone ready to lay a hand on her shoulder, drive her head back, and slice open her throat.

She heard her little voice in her head. The voice sounded a lot like Archie's.

Just keep moving.
Don't panic.

Get out. Call for help.

Her phone was in her purse back in the boiler room, along with her mace. But Archie had put his phone in her glovebox.

Susan closed her eyes and concentrated on her hand moving along the wall. There was a comfort to the dark canvas of her eyelids. *Her* darkness. *Her* control. She forced herself to clear her senses, to ignore the building's noises and the beating of her heart, and to remember only the route they'd taken to get there – the route that, if reversed, would get her out.

She felt some pipes she remembered passing. She was close. Then her hand brushed against something. She stopped and ran both hands along the wall. Then she found it – a lever-style doorknob. The stairwell. She turned the knob, pushed the door in with her shoulder, slipped through, and pulled it closed behind her.

The quality of the dark was different. Susan could make out the shape of her body, the angle of the stairs, and at the top of the stairs, another door. This door was not entirely airtight, and through the broken seals of its perimeter shone ribbons of bright, milky, marvellous light. There were lights on. There were lights on in the hall upstairs.

She ran up the stairs, into the fluorescent-lit expanse of lacquered coffee tables, cabinets, and geisha screens. She didn't stop. She kept running. Out the door, and into the night and down the dead-quiet middle of the street, and all the way to the car.

It was only then that she realized she didn't have her keys.

She was locked out. And she couldn't help but think that fate was punishing her for buying that fucking Beauty Killer key chain.

She rested her head against the top of the Saab, and fought back tears.

He's counting on you.

She did a story on a car thief once. He'd stolen two hundred cars by the time he was sixteen. She stood up and started walking around the car, searching for something that would help her get inside.

To break into a car you need a rubber doorstop, a wire hanger, and a rubber band. You straighten the hanger, and bend a ninety-degree angle about a half-inch from one end. Wrap the rubber band around the tip. Jam the doorstop into the gap where the car door meets the body, so you have room to slide the wire in. If the doorstop doesn't seem to work – jam a smaller plastic wedge in first, and then the doorstop. Insert the wire and use the rubber tip to hit the unlock button inside the door.

You learned a lot writing features for a newspaper.

Most of it was useless.

Susan picked up a piece of an angled-parking kerb that had broken off and hurled it through her car's passenger-side window.

The window shattered, sending beads of auto glass all over the inside of the car. Susan reached in, unlocked the car, opened the glovebox, and got out the phone that Jack Reynolds had given Archie.

She called 911.

And she called Henry.

This time she didn't call the paper.

42

Susan sank down low in the driver's seat of her car, and waited, like Henry had told her to. She had cleared most of the glass off her seat, and shaken a few stray pieces off the front of her shirt. It was dark under the bridge. Susan wished she'd parked near a streetlight. The car shook as trucks passed overhead. She was almost grateful for the wailing of approaching sirens. It turns out that when you call 911 for help in the middle of the night they get anxious and go all *Hill Street Blues*.

Susan peeked her head up. Cops were descending on the warehouse like shoppers at a Wal-Mart the day after Thanksgiving. They went in through every door.

She sank back down until her face was next to the gearstick. There was an old Burgerville napkin that had been on her car floor for two weeks and she grabbed it and held it to her cheek. It smelled like ketchup.

More sirens were arriving. Her rearview mirror reflected the red, white, and blue lights, filling the car with stutters of colour.

'Go to your car and stay there until I get there,' Henry had said. 'Promise me.'

Susan fiddled with the door handle.

But all those cops didn't know where Archie was. She did.

So, what? She just runs up and explains the whole thing? She tried to imagine the scenario. It ended with both her and Archie getting arrested for trespassing. What if Archie had ended up cutting the guy? How would they explain that?

Fuck.

She glanced down at the phone in her hands. She had called the cops from a phone that Archie had got from a drug dealer.

Maybe not the smartest move.

She reached back over to the glovebox and dug out the other phone she'd seen Archie stow in there.

Its red message light was blinking. Why did Archie need two phones? Maybe it wasn't Archie's. Maybe he was holding it for someone. She was always accidentally stealing people's phones. There were probably three or four phones floating around the back seat. There were probably old rotary phones in her back seat. It had been that long since she'd cleaned out her car.

She hit the phone's answer button and a text message sprang up.

'How are you feeling, darling?'

Susan's throat tightened.

She could barely steady her thumb enough to scroll down through the text history.

There were hundreds of texts. All from the same 'number'. All the same message.

'How are you feeling, darling?'

'How are you feeling, darling?'

'How are you feeling, darling?'

Darling. That's what Gretchen called Archie.

She was trying to contact him.

She looked at the call log. There was an outgoing call to the number that had sent the texts. He had called her.

There was a tap on the car window and Susan almost dropped the phone. She looked up to see Henry.

She slipped the phone into her pocket.

'I waited in the car,' Susan said.

'Show me where he is,' Henry said.

Susan got out of the car and slammed the door behind her. Henry was already five steps ahead of her and she had to catch up as they headed towards the warehouse. The streets in the Produce District were wide and scarred with old train tracks. Another patrol car zoomed up and skidded to a halt at an angle.

'When you call nine-one-one, they really send in the army,' Susan said.

'I called in backup,' Henry said. 'Not to disillusion you, but the nine-one-one operator who took your call did not consider your report of a crazed masked piercer very reliable.'

It had been a poor choice of words. But she'd been panicked. 'Oh.'

Claire came jogging up. 'They've searched the basement,' she said. 'Couldn't find anyone. But they found this.' She held up an evidence bag with a gun in it. 'And this.' She held up Susan's red purse.

Susan took the purse.

Henry slid her a suspicious look. 'You seen that gun before?' he asked.

It was the gun Archie had got from Jack Reynolds. Susan was certain of it. 'I don't know a lot about guns,' she said. She turned to Claire. 'What do you mean they couldn't find anyone?'

'They found the gun in the room you said to go to – the old boiler room,' Claire said. 'But there's no one in there. They're continuing to search the basement. Then we'll take it floor by floor. We've sealed off the building so if anyone's still in there, they're not getting out.'

'You see anyone leave?' Henry asked Susan.

'I was hiding in my car,' she said. She was furious with herself. She should have kept an eye on the building. Henry had said to wait in her car – he didn't say to cower in the car. Gretchen's sicko fans knew she was going to go for help. Of course they ran.

'Susan,' Henry said. He took her by the shoulders. 'This is important.' She could see him trying to formulate the right words. 'Did he go off with them?' he said finally. 'Or did they take him?'

It was a fair question. Archie had a history of going off with lunatics. But he'd got her out of there. He knew they were dangerous. 'I don't know,' Susan said. She didn't know what Archie was capable of any more.

'Either way,' Henry said, 'I'm keeping Archie out of this for now.'

'He might have gone with them,' Susan said. 'If they'd said they'd take him to Jeremy.'

'Jeremy?' Henry said.

'Jeremy Reynolds,' Susan said.

Henry took a deep breath and exchanged a look with Claire. 'Jeremy Reynolds is involved in this?'

'Archie saw his picture at Fintan English's apartment,' Susan said.

Henry was shaking his head. 'He went to see Jack Reynolds,' he said.

Susan gave a non-committal shrug.

'Are Archie's prints going to be on that gun?' Henry asked.

Susan looked at her feet and nodded.

If Henry had been a cartoon character, steam would have come out his ears.

Claire lowered her voice. 'Go to your happy place,' she said to Henry.

He put his hands on his hips and gazed up at the night sky.

Susan figured she might as well spill everything. 'The cult people,' she said. 'They said that Jeremy remembers what happened. You know, with Gretchen.'

Henry whipped his head toward her. 'That's bullshit.'

'Archie didn't think so,' Susan said. 'One of the guys had these scars on his chest. Cut marks. A heart. And this weird triangle pattern. He said that Jeremy had carved them.'

'How would he know about the triangles?' Henry said to no one in particular.

A red-haired patrol cop with a badge that read WHATLEY appeared at Henry's shoulder. 'I'm sorry, Detective,' he said. 'What crime are we investigating here?'

Henry tilted his head towards Susan. 'Assault,' he said.

Whatley gave Susan a slow look. She'd left the Burgerville napkin back in the car. She reached up and touched her cheek. It wasn't even bleeding any more. She felt bad. Like she was a disappointment.

'You must be a bigwig,' Whatley said, scratching his chin. 'This is a lot to throw at an assault investigation.'

Susan shot him a sparkling smile. 'It's really comforting that our police force is so responsive,' she said.

'Get back to work, Officer,' Claire said.

'Okey-dokey,' Whatley said, and he turned around and walked back inside the warehouse.

Henry leaned close to Susan. He hadn't shaved and his head and chin had the same five o'clock shadow. 'Everywhere I've gone today,' he said, 'I have found you, up to your purple hair, in peril.'

'They wanted Archie and me involved,' Susan said. 'They orchestrated this.'

Henry lifted his hands in frustration. 'Gretchen is out there, murdering people. Right now I don't give a fuck about Fintan English or Jeremy Reynolds. And neither should you.'

'What if it's connected?' Susan said.

'You've got blood on your chin,' he said.

Susan wiped the spot with her finger, looked at it, and put her finger in her mouth. It was tart and sweet. 'Ketchup,' she said.

43

When Archie woke up he was floating. He could see the floor a few feet below, parallel to his body. His neck was stiff, his head hurt, and his back and legs felt like they were on fire. His arms were extended, his fingertips just above the floor. He lifted them. The effort made his head swim. The floor moved. Only it wasn't, he realized, the floor that was moving – it was him. He was swinging. The motion ripped at his body, and fierce flesh-opening pain washed over him a moment before he settled back into blackness.

When he woke up again, the pain had settled into a dull burn. He was still suspended over the floor. He slowly moved an arm up, and reached over his shoulder blade. The skin over his scapula was taut like a drum, stretched three or four inches straight up in a tent. Archie moved his hand to the top of his stretched flesh and found something metal and curved piercing his skin. A hook. He tried to roll over, to turn his head back to see if he could wrench it out, but he couldn't move without more brutal pain.

The masked man put his face next to Archie's. He was

squatting next to him, wearing a ratty grey robe, nylon still pulled over his face. Who knows how long he'd been there. Archie was barely aware of the room around him. The light was low. The floor was concrete. He'd been moved. Archie lifted his head to look around, but he didn't see anyone else, just a large empty room. Ducts ran overhead and rusty fittings for long-gone equipment were still affixed to the ceiling.

'Don't make such a funeral face,' the masked man said.

'What have you done to me?' Archie asked.

'Body suspension,' the masked man said. He stood up and walked slowly around Archie, bending over to touch the spots where hooks pierced Archie's flesh. 'Six hooks in your back, two on each leg.' He gave Archie a little push and he swung, and Archie fought the urge to vomit. 'The trick is to distribute the weight evenly,' the masked man went on. 'Or your skin will split open.'

Archie could feel him checking the rigging. His body burned with every touch.

'The hooks are attached to nylon ropes,' the masked man said. He came around the front again. Archie could see his bare feet. 'The ropes are attached to a pulley system, which I control.' Archie was lifted a few more inches off the floor. The pain of gravity fighting the hooks for his body was startling. It overwhelmed him. 'I had to take your clothes off,' the masked man said. 'For the hooks. Sorry.'

Archie grimaced through the pain. 'You're starting to piss me off,' he said.

The masked man reached out and put a hand on Archie's

shoulder and steadied him. 'Exhale,' he said gently. 'If you relax, I think you'll like it.'

'You didn't get this from Gretchen's strategy book,' Archie said.

'I'm improvising.'

'Let me see Jeremy,' Archie said.

The masked man squatted down next to Archie's head again. 'He understands you,' he said, his nylon-smashed features nodding thoughtfully. 'I think he can help you if you let him.'

'I was thinking more the other way around,' Archie said.

He fiddled with some of the rigging above Archie's head. 'You have a lot in common.'

'Let me see him,' Archie said. Archie had always liked Jeremy. He was a weird kid. A quiet kid. He'd been kid-napped by Gretchen Lowell. He'd most likely witnessed his sister's torture and murder. Archie had always believed Jeremy's claims that he didn't remember what had hap-pened, because Archie had hoped Jeremy didn't remember, because remembering something like that, remembering Gretchen, that would fuck you up epically. 'Take off your mask and let me see you, Jeremy.'

Jeremy peeled off the nylon stocking and dropped it on the concrete floor.

'You're in a shitload of trouble, kiddo,' Archie said.

44

Susan took a gulp of lukewarm coffee out of a cracked Ziggy mug and clicked through another set of booking shots on the computer.

'Anything?' Claire asked.

'Do you have any pictures of just their teeth?' Susan said.

'Believe me, if that guy's in the system, the teeth will pop up as an identifying characteristic.'

The Beauty Killer Task Force offices were in an old bank that the city had provided when Archie Sheridan had come off medical leave to hunt the After-School Strangler. The last time Susan had been there, it was because Gretchen had escaped from prison, taking Archie with her.

It was two in the morning, but you'd never know it from the activity level. They were all there, every detective on the force, even the front-desk receptionist. International maps papered the walls, with pushpins marking every sighting, every crime that could possibly be related to Gretchen.

The task force at the *Herald* might have grown bored and

dark-witted over the last few months, but the real Beauty Killer Task Force was hard at work.

There were three photographs tacked on top of the maps. All three appeared to be booking photos – one was of a young woman, two were of middle-aged men.

'Who are they?' Susan asked.

'Our victims,' Claire said. 'All three were homeless. The man on the left was named Abe Farley.' She stood up and walked over to the photographs. Abe Farley had a long salt-and-pepper beard and a weathered, haggard face. 'Fifty-six,' she said. 'Last seen December 2004. That was his head rolling around at Pittock Mansion.' She touched the middle photograph. This man had shoulder-length light-coloured hair and a long, regal face. 'Jackson Beathe,' she said. 'Last seen March 2005. Sort of handsome, huh?' Claire took a step to her right. 'The woman with him on the Rose Garden bench was named Braids Williams.' Slender and dark-skinned, she smiled from her photo. 'She disappeared in 2006. Cause of death is still pending, but it looks like the two on the bench were stabbed.'

Susan looked at the three faces, lives reduced to snap-shots. 'How did you identify them?'

'They were missed,' Claire said. 'Family. Friends. Social workers. Missing-person reports were filed. We had dental records.' She turned back to face the photographs and raised a hand to tenderly brush against the face of Braids Williams. 'Someone stabbed them, removed their eyes, buried them for a few years, and then dug them up. The eyes they kept in a jar of formaldehyde.' She lowered her hand and turned back to Susan. 'Braids Williams's eyes went into Fintan English. The others were dumped in the rest-stop toilet.'

Henry stood in the doorway. His sleeves were rolled up and he carried a stack of papers in his hands. 'Gretchen didn't kill the homeless,' he said. 'It wasn't near scary enough.'

'So it wasn't Gretchen,' Susan said.

'I'm not ready to rule out anything yet,' Henry said.

'We're going through his computer records now to see if Hay – the orderly – was visiting any Gretchen-related sites,' Claire said. 'Could be he's involved in this group.'

Susan's face ached. The EMTs had irrigated the hole in her cheek and bandaged it up, but no one had offered her any painkillers. She reached up and gingerly touched the white gauze.

'Try www.iheartgretchenlowell.com,' Susan said. 'That's the site the freaks at the warehouse were using.'

Claire exhaled. 'Good,' she said. 'Thank you.' She turned to Henry. 'I'm going to get that to Martin,' she said. She glanced back at Susan. 'Take care of yourself,' she said, and she left the room.

Henry fanned the papers out on the table in front of Susan. 'Here are photos of runaways that have been reported in the last year,' he said.

Susan knew her instantly. She laid her hand on one of the pictures. 'That's her.'

'You sure?' Henry asked.

Susan took a closer look at the picture. The name over the image was Margaux Clinton. 'They called her "Pearl",' Susan said.

Henry turned the picture around and looked at it. 'Maybe it's a street name,' he said. 'She's from Eugene. I'll have someone down there go talk to the mother. And I'll put out a broadcast for her.'

'How old is she?' Susan asked.

Henry glanced back down at the report. 'Sixteen.'

There was a knock on the door and a uniformed cop came in, followed by Leo Reynolds. He was wearing a beautifully cut suit, no tie, crisp white shirt open at the neck, and his dark hair was still wet from a shower. Four in the morning, and he'd taken the time to put on cufflinks.

Henry's upper lip tightened, and he looked from Susan to Leo and back again. 'What's this?' Henry said, between gritted teeth.

'I called him,' Susan said. 'He's my lawyer.'

Henry raised an eyebrow at Susan. He was even better at issuing disapproving gazes than her mother.

Susan shrank down in her chair a little.

'Where's your crazy little brother?' Henry asked Leo.

'I don't know,' Leo said. 'I want him out of this. Believe me, if I knew where he was, I'd tell you.'

Henry took a step towards Leo. 'We need to talk to Jeremy,' he said. 'He knows who these people are.' He waited a beat. 'I also need to talk to your father.'

Leo's voice was soft and reasonable, but firm. 'My father is dedicating his considerable community organization to locating Jeremy right now,' he said. 'It might be better to delay an interview.'

'Archie trusts Jack,' Susan piped in. She wasn't sure that

was true. But she needed Jack and Leo Reynolds right now. And Archie needed them, too.

Henry rubbed his face with a meaty hand. When he brought it down the skin had reddened. He put both his palms on the table and leaned in close to Susan. 'Archie feels bad for Jack because Gretchen carved up and murdered his daughter,' he said. 'Archie operates on guilt.' His blue eyes were hard and threaded with red veins. 'If you haven't figured that out yet, then you haven't figured out anything.'

'We'll find them,' Leo said. 'All of them.'

He said it with such casual confidence that Susan almost believed him.

Leo reached into his suit pocket, withdrew a neatly folded piece of paper and held it out to Henry. 'It's a hotel downtown,' Leo said. 'Jeremy was staying there up until three days ago. I paid the bill through tonight, so if you want to go look around his room, you have until noon tomorrow before they clean out his personal possessions.'

Henry took the piece of paper and looked at it. He blinked a few times. 'Okay,' he said.

Susan looked up at the three faces on the wall. 'You don't actually think Archie would go off with these people?' she said.

'You don't know what he went through,' Henry said.

She didn't. But Jeremy Reynolds did.

'You could waste time getting a warrant, or I, as the person who has paid the bill, could let you in Jeremy's hotel room.'

'What's the catch?' Henry said.

Leo smiled. 'Company,' he said.

45

The Joyce Hotel was a seedy joint in Downtown Portland near what used to be called 'Vaseline Alley', due to its many gay bars. It was four storeys with a dirty ivory-coloured brick frontage, and an aged forest-green awning.

Henry, Claire, Leo, and Susan entered through the hotel's metal-framed glass doors. A sign listed room rates at twenty-five to thirty-five dollars per night. A toothless man behind the check-in counter yawned as they walked by.

'Room four-twenty-six,' Leo said to them.

They walked through the dingy lobby area, and up the brown-carpeted staircase. The walls had once been white, but were now mottled beige. The handrails and moulding were painted forest green.

Four-twenty-six was on the fourth floor, just down the hall from the stairwell. A sticker on the door read KIDS NEED BOTH PARENTS! Leo inserted the key, pushed the door, and they all went inside. There was a double bed, a small nightstand, a dresser, and an old Zenith TV, with the hotel's name scratched on the side, in case someone got the idea of stealing it.

'Well,' Claire said, pulling on a pair of latex gloves. 'Let's take a look.'

'You don't touch anything,' Henry growled to Susan and Leo, as he pulled on his own set of gloves.

Susan wandered around the room. The bed was made, and two white towels, bleached so many times they looked like they would crack if anyone ever touched them, were folded and set on the bedspread, as were a plastic cup still encased in its clear wrapping and two matchbox-sized bars of soap.

'He's neat,' Susan said. No one answered. Henry was going through the dresser. Claire was going through the nightstand. Leo was staring out a window that looked like it had been reinforced with chicken wire.

Susan walked over and opened the closet. Nothing was hung up. There were just three plastic hangers – one red, one white, and one blue. And dozens and dozens of photographs of Gretchen Lowell.

'Guys,' Susan said.

Henry stepped behind her.

She recognized the collagist. The perfectly cut edges. It was the same person who'd done the Gretchen wall collage at Fintan English's house.

'Told you he was OCD,' Leo said, from the window.

'You weren't kidding,' Henry said.

'Check this out,' Claire said.

Susan and Henry spun around. Claire was standing at the bedside table, reading a beat-up blue spiral-bound notebook.

'Tell me that's a diary,' Henry said.

Claire widened her eyes and shook her head. 'I don't know what it is,' she said. She flipped a page. 'Ranting, mostly. Letters to Gretchen. And this.' She held up a page with pencil-written paragraphs and a childlike drawing of a woman's face. 'It's a mockup for a Match.com page. A woman in her mid-thirties. Blonde. Psychiatrist.'

'The orderly,' Susan said. 'George Hay. His friends said he'd started dating someone.'

'Maybe he never met her,' Claire said slowly.

'Gretchen didn't kill Courtenay, either,' Susan said. 'Jeremy manufactured an identity and used it to manipulate Hay into committing murder.' She felt light-headed. It all seemed so clear. 'Jeremy was the one in the mask.'

Henry turned slowly to Leo. 'How crazy is your brother?' Henry asked.

Leo stood at the chicken-wire window, not looking back. 'Pretty crazy,' he said.

46

Susan sat in her car outside the Joyce Hotel and drummed her fingers on her sheepskin-covered steering wheel. She needed to find Jeremy and she needed to find him fast, before he did something terrible to Archie.

She glanced over at her purse on the passenger seat. Inside it was the phone Gretchen had been using to text Archie. She reached over and pulled it open, so she could see the phones she'd slipped inside. The one Archie had got from Jack Reynolds. And the one he'd got, somehow, from Gretchen Lowell. The number that the texts had been sent from was stored in the call log. Which meant that Susan had a way to contact Gretchen.

She dug into the purse, pulled out the phone, and looked at the screen. There were twenty-four missed calls and fifteen new texts.

'*Where are you, darling?*'

'*Where are you, darling?*'

'*Where are you, darling?*'

Gretchen was looking for Archie, too. Which meant that

she wasn't involved in this. These lunatics had killed five people. She traced her finger over the phone's buttons. It was a stupid idea.

But Archie had already called her. It was right there, in the log. They were already communicating.

Susan didn't know exactly what Archie's relationship with Gretchen was – not the extent of it anyway. Gretchen was a psychopath. She was a killer. And she was just plain mean. But she *had* saved Archie's life. Twice.

Maybe she would do it again.

Susan typed in a text.

'Archie is in trouble.'

And she hit send.

Susan looked down at the phone in her hands as the hourglass turned and then blipped out of sight. She had a nagging feeling that she'd just done exactly what Gretchen would have wanted.

Across the street, she saw Leo Reynolds just getting into a silver Volvo. She grabbed her purse, got out of her car, ran to his window and knocked on it.

He looked up, startled, and rolled the window down.

'You're not going home, are you?' Susan said.

'He's my brother,' Leo said. 'He's my responsibility.'

'I want to come with you,' Susan said. Henry and Claire had called in the crime techs to go over Jeremy's room. Susan was on her own. But she didn't know where to start.

Leo hesitated.

'Archie's my friend,' Susan said. 'He saved my life. That makes him my responsibility.'

Susan could see him sizing her up, his face blue from the glow of the dash lights. 'Okay,' he said. He hit a button on his door and she heard the car unlock. She ran behind the car to the passenger side and got in.

'Where are we going?' she asked.

'It's time to rely on the kindness of lesser elements,' Leo said.

Susan looked at him blankly.

He shrugged. 'I've got friends in low places.'

I bet you do, thought Susan.

47

'It's called the "Superman position",' Jeremy explained. 'It's the least painful. And I thought it was fitting. Archie Sheridan. Superhero cop.'

If this was the least painful, Archie was glad he wasn't being introduced to any of the alternatives. His head was killing him, probably from the enthusiastic tasering. But his muscles, which were also reeling from the massive dose of electric current, had at least relaxed a little. He couldn't lift his head far enough to see much in the room, so he hung there and looked at the floor. And he tried to keep Jeremy talking.

'They have names for all of the suspensions,' Jeremy continued. 'You can hang flat, facing up, with the hooks in your chest and legs. That's called the "Coma". Like from the movie. You know, that scene where they find all the people hanging from the ceiling? Or you can suspend yourself from your shoulder blades so you're hanging upright – they call that one the "Suicide", because if you do it right it looks like you've hung yourself.'

He untied his robe and let it hang open. He was naked underneath, his crotch at Archie's eye level. He'd shaved his pubic area and his scrotum was cuffed in a metal ring, stretched a good ten inches. It made Archie's solar plexus hurt just to look at it.

Jeremy let the robe drop to the floor and put a hand under his testicles, lifting them for Archie to see.

'It started my first night home,' he explained. 'I wanted to feel the pain. So I tied my balls to my bedpost and bent over backwards. Later, I saw some pictures on the Internet, and I started experimenting with stretching. Ropes, then with a wooden block, and finally metal rings.' He motioned to the one currently encircling his scrotum. 'I wear this one all the time,' he said.

'It's not your fault,' Archie said. 'Surviving. You couldn't have done anything to save your sister.'

'It's important to warm up before any session,' Jeremy said. 'To relax.' He picked up a tub of Vaseline off the floor and scooped some out with his fingers and began to rub it on his balls and up the shaft of his penis. Archie looked away. 'I'm showing you this because I think it will help you understand,' Jeremy explained. 'Please watch me.'

Archie lifted his head again. Jeremy was partially aroused. There was a sturdy-looking pipe overhead. Two ropes dangled from it. Jeremy stepped on a child's plastic step stool, attached the ring around his testicles to a hook at the end of one rope, took the other rope in his hands to control the weight, and then kicked back, so that he was dangling from his genitals. His testicles stretched eight inches and Jeremy slowly leaned back, letting go of the safety rope. He dangled there, hung from his groin, red-faced, his back arched so that his head and feet were at the same level.

'There are easier ways to punish yourself, Jeremy.'

After a few minutes, Jeremy reached up and took hold of the rope he was hanging from, and used it to sit up enough to grab onto the safe rope. He swung his feet back down to the step stool, unhooked his testicles, sank to the floor, curled on his side, and started masturbating. He did not seem to be aware of Archie any more, did not seem to care that he was there. He was neither performing for him, nor being exactly discreet.

When he came, his body shuddered and the ejaculate shot several feet forward, before it landed, a milky glop on the concrete floor.

This kid was more fucked-up than Archie thought.

Jeremy laughed. 'You should try it,' he said. He rolled onto his back and wiped his hands on his bare thighs. 'You've never felt anything like it.'

Gretchen had done a number on Archie. But she'd outdone herself with Jeremy Reynolds.

'When did you start to remember?' Archie asked him.

Jeremy stared up at the ceiling. 'When she took you,' he said. He waved a hand in the air. 'All the press. It brought back memories. Flashes at first. But they filled in.'

'That must have been horrible,' Archie said.

Jeremy rolled his head over and looked at Archie. 'You understand, right?'

He did understand. At least he was in a unique position

to imagine. But then again, Archie thought, you don't see me hanging by my scrotum.

'She killed your sister,' Archie said. 'You need help. There are people who can help you. I've been helped.'

Jeremy stood up and lifted the robe back over his shoulders. 'You can help me,' he said. 'And I can help you. Because we know, don't we?' He put his lips next to Archie's ear. 'We know her. We know pain and pleasure. The whole universe is just an immense, inexorable torture-garden. Blood everywhere.'

'O-kay,' Archie said.

Jeremy gave Archie a little push, and he swung forward and back. 'How do you feel?' Jeremy asked.

'Like a marionette,' said Archie.

Jeremy reached above him and pulled the rigging, wrenching Archie upward.

Archie steeled himself, balling his fists against the pain. And then it settled.

'Exhale,' Jeremy said.

And Archie did.

Jeremy moved his mouth to Archie's ear again. 'Do you know what I think about?' he asked. 'When I'm hanging there and my balls feel like they're going to explode?'

Archie had the feeling it was a rhetorical question.

'I think about you fucking her,' Jeremy said. 'I think about her hurting you, making you do things, and then I think about you on top of her forcing her, fucking the shit out of her, so that when you come, it's so hot and hard it's like a fist inside her.'

Jeremy's eyes were closed. It was all fantasy. He couldn't possibly know that Archie and Gretchen had had an affair.

'Doesn't being upside down like that make the blood rush to your head?' Archie asked, changing the subject.

'You get used to it,' Jeremy said.

48

Leo Reynolds pulled his Volvo into the parking lot of a club called George's Dancin' Bare, directly across from a thirty-one-foot-tall painted plaster statue of Paul Bunyan in the Kenton neighbourhood of North Portland.

The statue had been erected in 1959 to greet visitors to the Oregon Centennial Exposition and International Trade Fair. He was dressed in belted and cuffed dungarees, six-foot-tall black boots, and a black and red chequered shirt, and he was leaning on a giant axe.

The sun was coming up and the peach sky made the Dancin' Bare's plain tan facade look especially forlorn. Paul Bunyan leered at them from across the street.

Archie was with Jeremy and she was going to a titty bar.

Susan looked sceptically at her phone. It was 5 a.m. No bar was open this late.

'Private party,' Leo said, getting out of the car and heading for the club's front door.

Susan followed him. An orange and black plastic sign very clearly announced that the club was closed. Susan was just about to say something like 'See? I told you so,' when Leo pulled out his BlackBerry and punched in a number.

'It's me,' he said. 'I'm outside.'

The door opened almost immediately and a man stepped halfway out, his hand on the inside door handle. He was huge and bearded and wore a chequered flannel shirt. Susan turned around and glanced back at Paul Bunyan. Then back at the man.

'I get that a lot,' the man said to Susan. He smiled, revealing a gold front tooth, then put a meaty hand on Leo's shoulder. 'How ya doing, Leo?' he said, and he opened the door and gestured them inside.

The door opened onto a narrow wood-panelled entryway. Posters for amateur night and offers to meet this girl or that girl 'up close' plastered the walls. Paul Bunyan stayed behind, taking a seat next to the door and going back to reading a library copy of *The Sheltering Sky*.

Like every strip club Susan had ever been to, it smelled like sweat and cigarettes and beer. The carpet was a ratty brown. The walls were stained with decades of cigarette smoke. There were only a few patrons – two middle-aged guys in sweatshirts at the bar, and two more at a small stage, where a woman danced in a pair of black flouncy knickers. She had massive breasts and huge wine-coloured nipples. Her nipples were bigger than Susan's entire breasts. They lunged and swayed as she moved. Susan was fascinated. The song 'Milk-shake' was blasting over the speakers. A busted subwoofer made the bass notes tremble. No one seemed very happy. For a private party, it didn't seem to be a very festive event.

Leo didn't stop. He took her hand and led her past the bar, past several tables, to another part of the club. This was where the real action was, apparently. There was a big stage, complete with a brass pole and a fully naked woman. Several men sat smoking at the stage's rack. A waitress in short-shorts and a yellow T-shirt leaned up against a wall.

She smiled when she saw Leo.

Just beyond the big stage was a third stage, near the back of the bar. This one had a rack all the way around it, but only one patron, a twentysomething black man who sat, looking gangsta, with a stack of banknotes and a beer in front of him.

The dancer on this stage was completely naked. Her breasts were of a more normal proportion, her body was lean and firm, and she'd been fully and effectively waxed. The hair on top of her head was so blonde and so long and lush and gently curled that Susan thought it might be a wig. There was a brass pole at the centre of the stage, and the dancer leaped, straddling it four feet off the ground, and spun, back arched, one knee bent, painted toes pointed, her hair flying out behind her, her breasts sitting to attention on her chest. Ha, Susan thought. Implants.

'You're staring,' Leo said.

Susan coloured. 'I like her hair,' she said.

Leo led Susan over to the stage. She tried to stand up straight, so that she'd seem taller, and arched her back so her 34As would poke out a bit. When they got to the rack, Leo dropped her hand and tapped the gangsta kid on the shoulder.

He glanced up at Leo and widened his bleary eyes. 'Hey, man,' he said. 'What gives?'

Upon closer look, Susan realized that he wasn't very gangsta at all. More like a college kid trying to look gangsta. Big pants. Athletic jacket. Blazers basketball top. But his affect wasn't urban. This kid hadn't grown up in Detroit or Compton or even North Portland. This kid probably played basketball for Lake Oswego High. Susan would have bet her life on it.

The dancer leaped up and did another spin on the pole. She had a tattoo of a star on the top of her pubic bone. She was so close to them that Susan had to step back to avoid getting a face full of her hair as she twirled by them.

'Can I have a word?' Leo said.

The black guy frowned and then shrugged. 'Sure, Cuz,' he said. He got up, adjusted his pants, then remembered his beer and turned and got it.

The dancer sank into jazz splits in front of them and tossed her hair. She was pretty. Susan had hoped she would be ugly. It would have been more fair if she'd had a hot body and a pockmarked, hollow face.

'Hi, Leo,' the dancer said.

'Hi, Star,' Leo said.

Susan searched Star for imperfections. She had a tiny bit of cellulite under her butt cheeks. It would have to do.

Susan and the not-very-gangsta gangster followed Leo over to a table between the two stages and sat down. Susan lit a cigarette, took a drag, and set it in the black plastic Camel-logo ashtray in the middle of the table.

'This is Susan,' Leo said to the black man. The music was loud, and he had to speak forcefully to be heard, but he somehow made it seem like he wasn't raising his voice. 'She's a reporter for the *Herald*.' He turned to Susan. 'You can call him "Cousin",' Leo said.

'You're cousins?' Susan said.

'I'm adopted,' the black man said.

Leo picked the cigarette up out of the ashtray and took a drag of it. 'This is off the record.' He looked at Susan. 'Right, Susan?'

She nodded. She had no idea what he was up to. 'Deep background,' she said. 'Anonymous sources. Totally.'

Cousin looked at them both like they were out of their minds. He took a sip of beer and set the glass on the table.

'I'm looking for some people,' Leo continued. 'Jeremy's caught up in something. I want to find him. And I want to find the people he's with. This will be in the news tomorrow. The cops are releasing his picture, and the girl's picture, and sketches of the rest of them.'

Cousin blinked at him. 'You want me to help the cops find your brother?'

'Susan,' Leo said, 'describe Jeremy's friends to my associate here.'

Susan dug in her bag and got out her reporter's notebook. 'I'll write it down for you,' she said, and she described the pointy-teethed guy and the masked piercer and the two big dudes, taking notes as she talked. Then she tore the page off the spiral notebook and handed it to Cousin.

'Sound familiar?' Leo asked.

Cousin took the paper and looked at it. 'They junkies?'

Leo took another drag off Susan's cigarette. 'I'm guessing they move in that circle.'

Susan set the tip of her pen on the fresh page of her notebook and leaned forward. 'Are you a drug dealer?' she asked Cousin.

He backed up an inch. '"Deep background", you said. "Anonymous sources".'

Susan shrugged and closed the notebook. 'I'm curious.'

Cousin slugged his last sip of beer and motioned to the waitress who had returned to sulking against the wall. 'Middle management,' he said.

'What do you deal?' Susan asked.

Leo sighed and dropped his head in his hands.

Cousin smiled. 'Cocaine,' he said with a shrug. 'Hard, not soft. I used to move soft, but man, everyone starts calling you when the bars close and you never get any sleep.' He put his finger in the air for emphasis. 'Crackheads are in bed by eleven.'

He reached into the pocket of his Adidas warm-up jacket and took out a plastic bag and dumped some white powder on the table. 'You want some?' he asked.

Susan tried to look blasé. 'No,' she said.

Cousin was busy cutting himself a fat line. 'Leo?' he said, not looking up.

'No,' Leo said.

'Your call, Cuz,' Cousin said. He had a green plastic straw

that had been cut about the length of a pinkie finger, and he snorted the line and then put his head back for a second and plugged his nose.

When he put his head back down, his eyes were wet and he had a big grin on his face. He wiggled the straw at Susan. 'You sure?'

'Fuck it,' Susan said. She hadn't done coke since college. She was tired. She wasn't going to be going to bed anytime soon.

She took the straw from him, and he laughed and cut a line.

'You sure you want to do that?' Leo asked.

Susan bent over the table, held a nostril closed and inhaled. It burned and she squeezed her eyes shut and wrinkled her face. Her sinuses felt like they were on fire, like she'd just snorted bleach. The back of her throat filled with a sludge of foul, bitter mucus. It took her a moment to identify the taste – gasoline. She forced herself to swallow a couple of times and pressed her nostrils closed. 'Ow,' she said.

'It's pretty pure,' Leo said softly.

When she opened her eyes, Cousin was still rocking back and forth in his chair. She felt a surge of energy. The burning stopped. The bad taste in her mouth subsided. Her face and arms tingled.

It was better than what she remembered from college.

'Is that what crack's like?' Susan asked him.

Cousin stopped laughing. 'You think I've used crack?' he said. 'Shit, girl. I don't touch the stuff. You go near that, your life is ruined.'

Leo put out Susan's cigarette in the Camel ashtray. 'Find these people,' he said to Cousin. 'It's important to the old man. Put the word out. I want them to know we're looking for them.' He turned to Susan. 'Let's go,' he said. 'Before you get us all arrested.'

They stood up and Susan followed him towards the door. She left her half-drunk coffee on the table.

'You have interesting friends,' she said to Leo.

'My job involves a lot of community outreach,' Leo said.

They took a few more steps.

'Star?' Susan said.

Leo's eyes fell away from her and he made a non-committal motion with his hand. 'We slept together once or twice,' he said.

Susan felt a ball of disappointment in her stomach. It was stupid. So he'd had sex with a hot stripper with implants. She had other things to worry about besides another inappropriate crush. She had to focus on finding Archie.

They passed the dancers' dressing-room door. A green street sign over the door read STRIPPER ALLEY.

Susan's mind was going a mile a minute.

Leo Reynolds didn't know she existed. Not that way. She had purple hair and the body of a ten-year-old boy. He slept with strippers and was, apparently, some sort of drug lawyer. His sister had been murdered. His brother was part of some fucked-up Gretchen Lowell Love Club killing spree. And his father was a drug kingpin.

Leo had led the police to Jeremy's room. He'd been there. He knew about the collage, about the notebook. Now everyone would know. Jeremy's face, his story, his family, would be all over the news. It would not be good for business.

Something wasn't right.

They walked past Paul-Bunyan-the-doorman and out into the early morning light. The entire sky glowed tangerine, bathing the Paul Bunyan statue across the street in a fiery light that made him look even more like an axe murderer.

It was almost six. Archie had been missing for over five hours.

As they walked to the car, Leo handed her a perfectly folded white handkerchief. 'Your nose is running,' he said.

Susan sniffled and wiped her nose with the handkerchief, then handed it back to him. He raised an eyebrow at the snotty handkerchief, but folded it and put it back in his pocket.

When they got to the car, he opened the door for her, and she got in. 'Does your father know you're helping the police?' Susan asked him.

He closed her door, walked around the back of the car, and got in the driver's seat. He looked at her. 'Yep,' he said.

'Do you do anything without your father's approval?' Susan said.

Leo started the car. 'He would not approve of you.'

49

The coke had worn off and Susan had to will herself to look passably alert. Ian had started holding the editorial meetings in his office instead of the conference room, so he could sit behind his desk and make everyone else gaze in awe at his authority. There were only two extra chairs in Ian's office and there were six reporters who had to come to the meeting, which meant that four of them had to stand or sit on the floor.

Susan usually came early to get one of the chairs. But she'd come straight here after Leo had dropped her at her car, and there was only space left on the floor.

'So,' Ian was saying. 'Apparently what we have on our hands here is a serial-killer cult. These are all people of interest in all of the recent murders we've been attributing to the Beauty Killer. Two have been identified.' Ian had a dry-erase board he'd hauled in from the conference room and propped behind his desk so he could write down story ides and then cross them out or circle them, and he'd taped pictures of Jeremy and Pearl on it. 'Jeremy Reynolds.

From Lake Oswego. His father's a bigwig in real estate and
venture capital. Margaux Clinton. Sixteen. Runaway from
Eugene.' He held his pen frozen in mid-air. 'Who are they?
What led them astray? We've also got three victims.' He
didn't have their pictures on his board. 'Let's wrap them into
a story about the victimization of the homeless – bum fights,
violence against transients, et cetera.

'And, obviously, I think the time has come to examine
our cultural obsession with Gretchen Lowell.'

Susan looked around the room. It was neat by newspaper-
office standards. A New York Yankees pennant on the wall.
An *Absence of Malice* poster. A framed copy of the *Oregon
Herald* from the day Ian was born (1963 – God, he was old).
And two waist-high stacks of newspapers. On a bulletin
board on the wall, next to a five-year-old press release
announcing his Pulitzer win, Ian had tacked up a quote that
he'd scrawled on a piece of copy paper. 'Millions saw the
apple fall, but Newton asked why' – Bernard Baruch. Next
to that was a cartoon from *The New Yorker* of a guy who
was supposed to be Archie Sheridan sitting at a bar. The
bartender was handing him a drink and saying, 'Gretchen
Lowell wants to buy you a beer.'

'I know the answer,' Susan said.

Ian, who had been going on about the role of the anti-
hero in society, stopped talking and looked down at her,
annoyed.

'I know the answer,' Susan said again.

'Excuse me?' Ian said.

'We're the ones who did it,' Susan said. 'It was us.' The

walls at the *Herald* were paper-thin, and everyone could hear everything anyone said over a whisper. She didn't care. 'We glamorized Gretchen Lowell,' Susan said. 'We made her into a celebrity.'

Ian remained perfectly motionless, pen still aloft. He was always perfectly motionless when he was pissed off. Susan didn't care. She had a hole in her cheek and Archie was missing and she was at a stupid story meeting and they were all going to be laid off anyway. 'There are people out there who think she's a hero,' she said. She looked around at all of them. Sitting on the floor, leaning awkwardly against the wall. Derek sat in one of the chairs. Derek almost never got a chair. Susan could only imagine how early he'd got there to get one. And why? No one wanted to be there. This was a joke.

Susan uncrossed her legs and stood up. 'They maintain fan sites,' she said. 'They update her Wikipedia page. They write fan fiction about her. The audio of the nine-one-one call she made when she turned herself in? Someone remixed it and made a music video. You can watch it on YouTube. There are T-shirts with her face on them that say "I 'heart' the Beauty Killer".' She got her foot in one boot, and then pulled on the other one. 'Not just T-shirts. Babygros. *Esquire* magazine put her in their "Women We Love" issue last year. I put her name into eBay and I found someone selling a set of scalpels they claimed Gretchen had used to slice someone up. The bidding was up to nine hundred dollars.'

She stood there, nose running, bandage on her cheek. She was so fired. She was beyond fired. She would be blacklisted. But she couldn't stop herself. It all just came blubbering out. 'We put all that out there,' she said, flailing a hand. 'Story after story after story. The same stale crap. Anything to have an excuse to run her picture, because everyone knows that her picture increases the news-stand pickup by twenty-five per cent. So when there wasn't news, we found other reasons to write about her. "How to Make a Gretchen Lowell Halloween Costume".' She forced a laugh and wiped her nose with her wrist. 'I wrote that one.'

Ian capped his pen and set it on his desk. He did it with a little too much emphasis, and it rolled across the desk and off the front of it and dropped to the carpet. No one made a move to pick it up for him. No one moved at all.

'We are in the business of selling ads,' Ian said. 'We can charge more for our ads if we sell more papers. Gretchen Lowell sells papers. The *Baltimore Sun*. The *Chicago Trib*. The *L.A. Times*. Their newsrooms have been gutted. You want to take a redundancy package? Or do you want to write a story lots of people will read so the ad department can go to Starbucks and talk them into running quarter-page ads in our dying little medium? Because you can either sell Frappuccino ads, or you can sell Frappuccinos. So do you want to be a newspaper reporter, or do you want to be a barista?'

'I want to be a journalist,' Susan said. It sounded absurd even as she said it. Someone leaning against the wall smirked.

'Then write me a story about why you were treated for a puncture wound in the Produce District at two a.m. this morning. Then write me seventy-five inches on our cultural obsession with Gretchen Lowell. You can put in everything you just said.'

'Seventy-five inches?' Susan said.

'Do you think you can fill it?' Ian asked.

'Absolutely,' Susan said.

'Then go, get out of here,' Ian said.

She looked at Ian. Maybe he wasn't a total asshole, after all.

One of the other reporters raised his hand. 'Can I go?' he said.

'Don't even think about it,' Ian said.

Susan backed out of the room and closed the door behind her before Ian could change his mind.

50

Anne Boyd was the best criminal profiler that Henry knew. She'd been the third one the FBI had sent to work on the Beauty Killer Task Force, and had spent months at a time in Portland, away from her husband and two boys. Henry called her from a table outside Taco Del Mar on Martin Luther King Jr. Boulevard. The taco stand was in an old gas station. Everything in Portland was in an old something. The task force offices were in an old bank. You could get a burger and see a movie inside an old elementary school. Even the old Henry Weinhard's brewery downtown had been turned into green certified apartment complexes. Everything was repurposed. Portlanders loved to recycle.

It was 11 a.m. PST. Two o'clock in Virginia.

Henry punched in Anne's number.

She picked up right away.

'Henry,' she said. 'Did they catch her?'

'No,' Henry said. 'No.'

He could hear the bustle of food preparation and teenage

boys in the background. 'Well,' she said, 'you're not calling to ask for fashion tips.'

'What do you remember about Jeremy Reynolds?' Henry asked.

'Hold on,' Anne said. Henry heard a door close and it got quiet. 'Want to let me in on what's going on?' she said.

'Archie checked himself out of the hospital,' Henry said.

'He can do that, Henry,' Anne said. 'He was there voluntarily.'

A woman came out of the taco place with a burrito, looked around at the outdoor seating options, and took the spot furthest from Henry. 'There's this group of, I don't know . . .' He rested his forehead on his hand. It was hot and he wasn't wearing a jacket and he could feel sweat forming under his shoulder holster. 'It's sort of a Gretchen Lowell fan club.' Fuck, the world was getting weird. 'They got ahold of this poor fuck who'd been fantasizing about getting his spleen removed.'

'Body integrity identity disorder,' Anne said with a whistle. 'I've never heard of an organ focus before.'

Henry waved his hand. 'Whatever. They found each other over the Internet. They took out his spleen for him. Only he died. Because, you know, they're not fucking doctors.' The woman with the burrito was pretending to read an issue of the *Portland Mercury*, but she kept stealing looks at him. 'Susan Ward found the body, courtesy of an anonymous tip. Archie found out who the kid was, courtesy of an anonymous tip.'

'That's an interesting confluence of anonymous tips,' Anne said softly.

'I was going to say that,' Henry said, 'but not so fancy.'

'Go on,' Anne said.

'Turns out the dead kid was a friend of Jeremy Reynolds's.'

'The brother of Isabel Reynolds.'

Henry nodded even though Anne couldn't see him. 'Apparently he's part of the fan club. Yesterday Archie checks himself out of the hospital, goes out to see Papa Jack and tells him to find Jeremy, and also gets a gun. And then last night he and Susan go to a club meeting, or whatever the fuck.'

'They were expecting them,' Anne said.

'Of course they were expecting them.' Henry slammed his hand on the table. 'They'd anonymous-tipped them right there. Susan got herself pierced in the face.'

'Pierced in the face?' Anne said.

'Like with a piercing needle,' Henry said. The woman with the burrito had put down the *Mercury* and now sat staring at him openly. 'The group's leader, who is wearing – get this – a nylon footy over his head, wants Archie to cut him. At least two of these assholes have carved up their own torsos, Gretchen style. Archie agrees, if they let Susan go. Susan runs. She thinks she hears Archie cry out, but it could have been anyone. She calls me. But when we get there, everyone's cleared out, Archie's gone. Gun's on the floor.'

'And you think Archie went off with them, of his own accord?'

'I don't know,' Henry said. 'I thought he was recovering. But it's a Gretchen Lowell fan club. He's like an honorary lifetime member. And if he wants to get Jeremy Reynolds out of this, he'd do whatever it takes. You know him.'

'He always seemed very protective of Jeremy,' Anne said.

'The kid saw his sister murdered. I would imagine he's a little scarred.' The woman with the burrito picked it up and went inside. Henry shot at her with his finger when she went by. 'So now we've got reason to believe these people are involved in the recent killings out here. That they're copycat murders.'

Anne paused. 'I'm going to tell you something completely unprofessional,' she said.

'I'm on the edge of my seat,' said Henry.

'Jeremy Reynolds is dangerous,' Anne said.

'No shit,' Henry said.

Anne sighed deeply. 'He suffered a dissociative fugue. He survived a life-altering event. He was sure to be traumatized, which is why I never drew darker conclusions in any of my reports.'

Henry was no shrink, but he'd seen enough violence to know that it did a number on people. 'He'd just seen his sister murdered,' he said.

'His affect was off,' Anne said. She hesitated. 'And this is not my professional opinion. My opinion as a psychologist was in the reports: dissociative fugue. My opinion as a mother? Jeremy Reynolds is dangerous.'

'Susan said his memory's come back,' Henry said. He told Anne what Susan had said about the chest carvings apparently matching the marks on Isabel's torso.

'In a kid like Jeremy,' Anne said, 'without the proper

support, that could send him reeling. He'd look for alternative support structures. Like the Internet, the fan club. And he'd look for people he could talk to.'

Henry finished the thought. 'Like Archie. The one person who understands.' Archie had left the hospital and gone into that basement looking for Jeremy. Someone had to know the connection he and Jeremy had shared. Someone had to figure that Archie, knowing what Jeremy had gone through, would do almost anything to save him.

'Susan thinks Jeremy was the man in the mask,' Henry said.

'Well, duh,' Anne said.

51

After a while, Archie found that the pain from the hooks became a sort of physical white noise. He relaxed his body, letting his arms dangle, fingertips almost brushing the floor, and he took slow, deep breaths. The weightlessness was disorientating and he was getting dizzier and increasingly light-headed. His mind skittered. When he tried to focus on the floor, his vision blurred.

His blood pressure was dropping.

At this rate, he wouldn't be conscious much longer.

'I can let you down now,' Jeremy said.

Archie lifted his head. The room spun. 'I think that would be an excellent idea,' he said.

Jeremy pulled at a mechanism Archie couldn't see and after a painful jerk, he was lowered blissfully to the concrete. Archie lay on his belly, his arms under his torso, his cheek on the floor. The concrete was cool. Jeremy lifted his head and held a sports bottle to his lips. 'It's sugar water,' he said. 'To get your glucose up.'

Archie parted his lips and Jeremy pressed the nozzle into

his mouth and squeezed the bottle. The sugar water was room temperature and sweet, like flat cola, but Archie suckled at it feverishly, his mind clearing as the fluid found its way down his throat. When Jeremy pulled the bottle away, Archie managed to sit up, his bare knees pulled to his chest. 'Take the hooks out,' he said.

Jeremy knelt behind him. 'I have to do it fast,' Jeremy said. 'The faster you take them out, the less it hurts.' Archie could feel him working, feel the pressure as Jeremy held a cloth to his skin to stop the bleeding, but he didn't feel any pain. He knew each hook was out only because of the sound it made as Jeremy dropped it into an empty Nancy's Yogurt container.

'I'm going to massage the air out of your skin,' Jeremy said. 'To help prevent infection. It's going to hurt a little.' Jeremy pushed around the puncture wounds, with a circular motion. It was more unsettling than painful, like Rice Krispies popping under his skin. The air made a burping sound as it exited his flesh, and warm blood spurted from the wounds, splattering and running down Archie's back. Archie rested his forehead against his knees and hugged his shins.

Then he felt Jeremy rub something cool on his back.

'Antibacterial solution,' Jeremy said. He cleaned up the blood and then continued to massage Archie's back, working up his spine and rubbing his neck and shoulders, rubbing his fingers up the back of Archie's skull through his hair.

'Did Gretchen touch you like this . . . ?' Jeremy asked softly.

'Yes,' Archie said. 'The carvings you made on the guy with the teeth, you remember Gretchen doing that to Isabel?'

'I watched her do it.'

'Do you want to tell me what happened, Jeremy?'

'Yes,' Jeremy said. 'But I want to get the scalpel first.'

52

Henry would've been happy to go years before seeing the inside of the Providence psych ward again. He didn't like the way it smelled. He didn't like the security cameras and locked doors. He didn't like the nurses. And he didn't like the fact that his best friend had spent two months there.

'This better be good,' Henry said to Claire. He was standing with Claire next to Archie's psychologist, Sarah Rosenberg, in the hall. They were looking into the activities room, where a department shrink sat across the table from Archie's old room-mate, Frank. The shrink was interviewing all the mental patients about Courtenay Taggart's death. The hospital would only approve professional crazy wranglers to wrangle its crazies.

Henry thought it was all bullshit.

'Frank doesn't have a sister,' Rosenberg said.

Henry let that soak in. 'Fuck,' he said.

'Your psychiatrist saw it in his file,' Rosenberg said, looking through the glass at Frank. 'No one ever thought to check.'

Claire stood with her arms crossed. Henry could see the

concern tightening the corners of her mouth. They both knew what this meant.

'It's her,' Claire said.

Henry turned to Rosenberg. 'Take me in there,' he said.

'He won't admit it,' Rosenberg said. 'He's adamant.'

Henry looked through the glass at Frank. He was slumped over the table, his patient scrubs too big, white tube socks pushed down around his ankles. He was weak and vulnerable. Just the kind of man Gretchen preyed on. 'Let me talk to him,' Henry said.

Rosenberg looked at him for a moment and then nodded. 'I'll take you in,' she said. She hesitated. 'He is a patient,' she said. 'If you cause him any trauma at all, I will lose my position here.'

'I won't use the boiling oil,' Henry said.

'Be nice,' Claire said.

'I'm always nice,' Henry said, following Rosenberg into the room.

Frank looked up immediately and waved. 'Hi, Henry,' he said.

Henry put on a big fake grin. 'Hey, buddy,' Henry said. He pulled up a chair and sat down next to Frank. Rosenberg sat in a chair next to the other shrink. That was good. It was Henry and Frank against the doctors. That would create an alliance. Just friendly old Henry and his buddy Frank against the big bad medical establishment.

The department shrink – a middle-aged man in a golf shirt and pleated shorts – shifted uncomfortably in his plastic chair.

'I missed you this morning,' Henry said to Frank. 'I missed visiting my buddy Frank.'

'Archie's gone,' Frank said.

'Yeah,' Henry said. 'But hey, I can still visit you, right? I can still visit my buddy Frank.'

Frank smiled shyly. 'Okay.'

'But I bet you get lots of visitors, right, Frank?' Henry said. 'I bet your sister's here all the time.'

Frank's face faltered.

'No?' Henry said.

Frank looked away. 'She gets busy,' he said.

Henry folded his hands in his lap and smiled. 'Do you have a sister, Frank?'

Frank's forehead wrinkled and he swatted at the air with his hand. 'Stop asking me that,' he said.

Henry saw Rosenberg lay a palm down on the table.

'Who else has asked you that?' Henry said.

'Him,' Frank said, pointing at the golf-shirted shrink. 'And Archie.'

Henry tried to keep his voice even, his demeanour neutral. 'When did Archie ask you that?'

'After I took his phone,' Frank said. He shook his head sadly. 'I didn't mean to. I heard it.' He covered his ears. 'Buzz. Buzz.' He let his hands drop. 'I found it in his dresser. He was so mad. He made me give it back. That's when he asked me. "Do you even have a sister, Frank?"' He sank down in his chair, shoulders hunched. 'He was so mad,' he said again.

'Did you talk to anyone on that phone?' Henry asked.

'No,' Frank said. 'I was going to call my sister, but I couldn't remember her number.' He bit his lip. 'I think she's mad, too. She stopped calling.'

'What's your sister's name, Frank?'

Frank turned away, hunching further down in his chair. 'I don't want to talk to you any more,' he said.

'When was the last time she called?' Henry asked.

Frank covered his ears again. 'Buzz, buzz, buzz.'

Rosenberg stood. 'We're done,' she said.

53

There were three elevators at the *Herald*. Only two of them ever worked at one time. Today, the elevator on the far right was broken, so Susan stood waiting near the other two.

No sleep and five hours in front of the computer had left her grainy-eyed and exhausted, even with the hour-long nap she'd managed to take in the lunchroom. She'd got her seventy-five inches in, though. It was the best piece of newspaper work she'd ever done. She only wished that Quentin Parker was around to see it.

With the story in, she was going to go home and take a nap. Leo Reynolds was not returning her calls, which either meant that his low-placed friends had turned up nothing, or they had turned up something and he'd decided not to tell her about it.

A few hours of sleep, and she would try him again.

The elevator was taking forever and Susan leaned her head against the wall next to it, and rested her eyes.

She awoke, with a sudden start, when the elevator doors

opened. She blinked, still groggy. There, in the elevator, stood Henry Sobol.

He held the elevator door open and beckoned her inside. 'We need to talk,' he said. 'What floor?'

Susan moved her purse – with Archie's cell phone in it – to her other shoulder. There hadn't been a single call since she'd sent her text. 'Lobby,' she said.

Henry pushed the 'L' button.

Just as the doors started to close, Derek Rogers slipped into the elevator with them.

'You're Dick, right?' Henry said.

'Derek,' Derek said.

'Over seventeen thousand people a year in the US are seriously injured in incidents involving elevators and escalators,' Susan said.

Henry did not look remotely amused. His mouth was drawn tight and there were no laugh lines around his eyes. In the elevator light, Susan could see tiny spider veins blooming along his jawline.

'So we finished interviewing the psych-ward inmates this afternoon,' he said.

'Patients,' Susan corrected him.

He ignored her. 'You ever meet Archie's room-mate?' Henry said. 'Name's Frank. Depressive. A little slow. Gets a lot of calls from his sister, talks about her constantly. Only it turns out he doesn't have a sister.'

It wasn't making very much sense to Susan. But then she was so tired, she wasn't sure that simple arithmetic would make much sense. 'So he lied about having a sister,' she said.

Henry hit the elevator emergency stop button. The elevator ground to a halt.

Susan looked up at the floor lights above the doors. Both the two and the three were lit up. They were stuck between floors. She was suddenly feeling more awake.

'You can't do that,' Derek said, his voice rising. 'There are only two working elevators. What if there's a fire?'

Henry took a step right up against Derek. 'If there's a fire,' he said between gritted teeth, 'you're supposed to take the stairs.'

Derek backed against the wall. 'Okay, sir,' he said.

Susan's mind was clearing.

Henry leaned back on the elevator wall next to Derek. 'I'll tell you what I think,' he said to Derek, giving him a tap on the upper arm. 'I think that Gretchen pretended to be Frank's sister. I think that she was keeping tabs on Archie through Frank. Frank won't admit to any of this.' He waved a hand in the air. 'Swears on the Bible that he has a sister, who loves him very much.' He held up a single finger. 'But he did tell me about a phone,' Henry said. 'A cell phone. Frank took it out of Archie's dresser drawer and Archie got mad. What do you think, Susan?'

Susan was having trouble breathing.

'You know anything about a cell phone?' Henry asked.

'No,' Susan said.

'I'll tell you what I think,' Henry said. 'I think Gretchen is in town.' He shrugged. 'I don't know. Maybe she never left. So this Beauty Killer fan club, or cult, or whatever the fuck, may be responsible for much of our city's recent mayhem. But I can't find any evidence that our homicidal orderly ever used an Internet dating service. We've searched his computer at home. We've searched the computers he had access to at work. We've even searched the computers at his local library branch, which I can assure you is not easy. Nothing. Jeremy Reynolds didn't manipulate our orderly into killing Courtenay Taggart. Gretchen Lowell did. I think she used the orderly to get Archie a phone. And then I think she had him kill a patient on the ward because she knew it would get Archie out of there. And if I find out that you knew about this phone, I will rain holy hell on you.'

'I think I found Pearl Clinton,' Derek said. 'I got a call from a woman who runs a store on Hawthorne: From the Earth to the Moon. She said that Pearl used to work for her. I'm supposed to meet her there. You can check it out. If you want.'

No one said anything for a moment.

Finally, Susan broke the silence. 'Pearl could lead us to Archie,' she said to Henry.

Henry hit the emergency button with the heel of his fist and the elevator strained for a moment and then started to move.

54

From the Earth to the Moon was on Hawthorne Boulevard in between a coffee shop and a free-trade store. Susan knew the place. It had been there about a year, replacing a Goth store, which had replaced a head shop.

If you had a subculture, Portland had a store for you.

'Here,' Susan said.

Henry pulled over in a loading zone directly in front of the store. Sometimes Susan wished she were a cop. Or at least had a car with cop plates.

'What is with this place?' Henry asked.

'It's steampunk.'

'Steampunk?'

'It's a subculture,' Susan said. 'Sort of Victorian. Sort of sci-fi. The world as imagined by Jules Verne.'

Henry looked at her blankly.

'Have you ever read *The League of Extraordinary Gentlemen*?'

'Is it a baseball book?' Henry said.

'Never mind,' Susan said. 'Pearl was wearing a corset and

a pair of goggles. This place sells that kind of thing. It makes sense that she worked here.'

They got out of the car and went inside the store.

It was like a jewel box. The walls were painted sea-serpent green, the wood floors were painted black, the cashier's counter was covered in red velvet, and the light fixtures appeared to be made of old brass watch parts. Brass pipes hung on chains from the ceiling, adorned with gowns, corsets, petticoats, and bustles; gentlemen's suits with waistcoats, coats, and spats; old-fashioned military uniforms. Antique dark wood shelving displayed quirky pocket watches, old-fashioned parasols, goggles, and ray guns.

The woman standing behind the red velvet counter was wearing a black Edwardian gown under a black leather corset. Around her neck was a magnifying glass and, in a glass relic locket, what looked to be a human tooth. She was wearing a leather gun belt with a Flash Gordon ray gun in each holster.

'I'm with the *Herald*,' Susan said. 'Derek Rogers sent me.'

'Good for you,' she said.

'You called him earlier today,' Susan said. 'We're looking for Margaux Clinton. Goes by "Pearl". Sixteen. About five feet four. Skinny. Short dark hair. Goggles' – she pointed to the goggles displayed on the shelf – 'like those. You told Derek Rogers that she used to work here.'

'I don't know anyone named Derek Rogers,' the woman said. 'And I don't read the *Herald*.'

'You didn't call the *Herald* today?'

'No. But Pearl did work here. I fired her for shoplifting

about a month ago.' The woman slid a glance at Henry, and then back at Susan. 'She a runaway?' she asked.

'She's wanted in connection with several murders,' Henry said.

The woman gave Henry a disapproving look. 'He the father?' she asked Susan.

'I'm a cop,' Henry said.

'She's involved with some bad people,' Susan explained. She got a business card out of her wallet and set it on the counter. 'Journalist,' she said. As if that might help cancel out the cop thing.

'If she ran away,' the woman said, 'she probably had a reason.'

Henry looked around the store. 'Maybe her parents wanted her to dress like a normal person,' he said.

The woman gave Henry a once-over. He was wearing black jeans and a sweat-stained, faded black T-shirt. She seemed unimpressed. 'People look at you, they frown,' the woman said to Henry. She posed, *Vogue*-style, and fluttered her eyelashes. 'They look at me, they smile.'

Henry stepped in front of her, drawing to his full, barrel-chested height. 'Look at me,' he said. 'I don't give a shit if you smile. I don't give a shit if you wear dumb-ass goggles. What I care about is finding Pearl Clinton.' His shaved head was beaded with sweat. 'And I'm going to give you ten seconds to tell us where she is.'

55

The intersection of Thirty-eighth Avenue and Hawthorne Boulevard was a prime area for begging in the street, and according to the manager of From the Earth to the Moon, Pearl had been a regular, hitting up Hawthorne shoppers for cash.

'Jesus, watch out,' Susan said, as Henry barely avoided sideswiping a cyclist.

Henry grumbled something under his breath and then did a double take out the windshield. 'There,' he said.

Pearl was just rounding the corner onto Thirty-eighth.

'Hold on,' Henry said. He screeched the car to a halt halfway up on the kerb, opened the door, and lunged out after her.

Susan braced herself on the dashboard, and then got out and sprinted after Henry.

By the time she got there, Henry already had Pearl by the arm.

'I want a lawyer,' Pearl said.

Henry gripped her arm tighter, and the muscles in his

bare upper arm bulged. 'If I take you in and dial you up a lawyer,' he said, 'it will mean calling your parents and child services. Still want one?'

A small crowd had gathered. There was always plenty of foot traffic on Hawthorne. A couple of other street kids had come up, a few people with shopping bags, a couple of bicyclists who had stopped and were standing with their helmets on – all watching. Some of them were taking cell-phone video.

'Ordinary citizen, here,' Pearl cried, 'getting harassed by the fuzz.'

'Henry,' Susan said.

Henry let go of Pearl's arm. She rubbed the spot where he'd been holding her and then crossed her arms defiantly.

'This isn't a game,' Henry said. 'Tell me where Archie Sheridan is.'

'I haven't done anything wrong,' Pearl said, loud enough that the bystanders could hear.

Henry blinked in disbelief. 'Nothing wrong? You're part of a serial-killer fan club.'

Pearl shrugged. 'So? I was into Wicca in junior high. It doesn't mean anything.'

'Where's Jeremy Reynolds?' Henry demanded.

Pearl just glared at him.

'Let me talk to her,' Susan said.

Henry pointed a finger at Pearl's nose. 'There's a foster family with your name on it,' he said.

'Go fuck yourself,' Pearl said.

Henry's face reddened and Susan wedged between him

and Pearl. 'How long have you been a part of the Beauty Killer . . .' – she looked for the right word – 'group?'

Pearl rolled her eyes and sighed. 'I met Jeremy at the Country Fair in Eugene,' she said. 'He invited me to join. It sounded fun. You hook up in the middle of the night in some scary spot and try to scare the shit out of each other.'

'They scar themselves to look like murder victims,' Henry said behind Susan.

'I didn't know that until last night,' Pearl said.

'Tell me about last night,' Susan said.

Pearl stabbed at the sidewalk with one of her pointy shoes. 'Look, last night went too far. I didn't know the guys were going to pull that shit with the needle.' Her voice got small. 'I thought they were just trying to mess with you.'

'Jeremy's not who you thought he was,' Susan said softly. 'Is he?'

Teenage girls didn't join clubs because they sounded fun. They joined them because of boys.

Pearl nodded, and her eyes filled with tears. 'After you left, Sheridan pulled a gun,' she said. 'Wanted to know where Jeremy was. Which was, you know, freaky, because Jeremy was right there.' She wiped her nose. 'And then he got tasered. Kind of a lot. He might have passed out.'

'And then?' Henry said.

'I don't know,' Pearl said, sniffing. 'I ran. I ran out of the building and up to Grand and then caught the number fourteen bus up Hawthorne.'

Henry turned around and threaded his hands behind his head.

'Those murders,' Susan said. 'The bodies up at the Rose Garden. The head at Pittock Mansion. Gretchen Lowell didn't kill those people. Jeremy did.'

Pearl's mouth got small and she frowned and dropped her head. 'I thought he liked me,' she said.

Susan patted her on the arm. 'I know, sweetie.' She let Pearl meditate on her unfortunate love life for a moment, and then Susan leaned in, and in her best big-sister voice, asked, 'Did he ever take you anywhere?'

56

Jeremy had covered Archie's wounds with gauze and given him a towel to sit on. Archie sat naked, cross-legged, across from Jeremy, who sat naked in the same position. A scalpel case was open on the floor between them.

'Any chance I can put my clothes back on?' Archie asked.

'I need to see you,' Jeremy said.

He picked up the scalpel and held it the way that Archie had shown him in the basement, dinner-knife style, and with his other hand he reached across and ran his fingers over the heart-shaped scar on Archie's chest.

Jeremy's chest was brutalized. Some of the scar tissue looked quite old, pale and stretched, like he'd been cutting himself like this for years. Hash marks climbed his ribs, dashed his belly, and one thin scar ran along his lower rib line on the right side – where a splenectomy incision might be. It wasn't thick enough to be anything but a surface laceration. Jeremy had cut himself to look like he'd had his spleen removed. To look like Archie.

And up and down his arms and the inside of his thighs

was the same triangular pattern they'd found on Isabel, carved over and over again. Some of the scars were barely discernible, some were recent. He'd been self-mutilating for a long time.

Jeremy's fingers moved away from Archie's heart and traced the five-inch scar that ran up his midsection. 'What's this one?' Jeremy asked.

It was the only scar that Gretchen hadn't carved on him, a functional bold line, different from the other scars, like someone else's handwriting. 'I was bleeding internally when they brought me to the hospital,' Archie said. 'They had to go back in and clean up the damage from when she took out my spleen.' It was the scar Archie felt most disconnected from, because unlike the scars Gretchen had left, he had no memory of getting it.

'Fintan would have done it anyway,' Jeremy said. 'He would have done it himself.'

Archie glanced down at the scalpel in Jeremy's hand. He needed to stall. 'You met Fintan English at camp,' he said.

Jeremy's face was slack, his eyes distant. 'We were in high school,' he said. 'Fintan was as fucked-up as me.' He moved his free hand to his upper arm, and absent-mindedly rubbed the triangle-shaped scars, as if they were the source of an old itch. He still held the scalpel in his other hand, wrist resting on his knee. 'He wanted his spleen out,' Jeremy said. 'It was all he talked about. No one took him seriously. Except for me. I read some books. And looked on the Internet. I printed out instructions.'

Archie thought about the goat spleen that had been left in the rest-stop toilet. 'You practised on goats.'

'Their spleens are about the same size,' Jeremy said. 'I read that on the Internet, too.'

'How'd the goats do?' Archie asked.

'They all died,' Jeremy said. He leaned forward, so close to Archie that Archie could feel Jeremy's breath on his face, and he put his mouth near Archie's ear. 'I wanted to know what it was like to be her,' he said. 'To be Gretchen Lowell.' His lips brushed Archie's ear. 'And I liked it. I liked cutting into him. Reaching into his body. I liked the smell of it.' Jeremy paused. 'It reminded me of Isabel.'

Archie tried hard not to react. Jeremy was testing him.

Jeremy sat back and looked at Archie for a long moment. 'You can leave,' he said.

Archie nodded. 'I know.'

'But you're still here,' Jeremy said.

'Because I'm interested in you, Jeremy.'

Jeremy looked down at the scalpel. 'You were nice to me when I was a kid,' he said. 'My father and brother – I just reminded them of what had happened to Isabel. I could see it when they looked at me.'

Jeremy's upper lip started to twitch, and Archie could see the kid he'd met so long ago in the young man sitting in front of him. Lost, damaged, angry. Jeremy's eyes narrowed with accusation. 'I wanted you to take me away,' he said. The corners of his mouth went down and his lips trembled, as he fought back tears. 'You know what they do.' His voice rose. 'They're criminals.' His face was so full of pain, it broke Archie's heart. 'Why didn't you take me away?'

Archie had never thought about it. He'd been so focused

on catching the Beauty Killer, on solving Isabel's murder, on protecting Jeremy from Gretchen and from the press, that he'd never really thought about protecting him from his father. 'I'm sorry,' Archie said. It was really all he could think of to say.

Jeremy started to cry. He cried like a child, body rocking, nose running, face pink and ugly. Gretchen had fucked Archie up, but she had broken Jeremy Reynolds.

Jeremy took several gasping breaths, sat perfectly still for a moment, and then calmly lifted the scalpel and pressed it into his chest below his left nipple.

'Don't,' Archie said. 'Please.' He watched as Jeremy dragged the blade over the heart scar that was there, in an effort to more approximate the scar on Archie's own chest. But Jeremy was pushing too hard, and the skin split and spread apart, blood oozing from the fatty gash.

Archie put his hand around Jeremy's wrist. 'It's too deep, Jeremy,' he said. Jeremy was trembling, his face feverish, the scalpel still sliding through flesh and muscle. Archie had to get the scalpel out of Jeremy's hand. 'Why don't you let me cut myself to look like you?' Archie said.

Jeremy froze and glanced up. It was the first time that Archie saw something clear and solid in his gaze. It wasn't too late.

Archie held his hand out, palm up. 'Give it to me,' he said.

Jeremy lifted the scalpel out of his flesh and looked at it, blinking. Then he wiped the bloody blade on a corner of the towel he was sitting on, and handed the scalpel to Archie.

And waited.

'Okay,' Archie said.

Jeremy was close. Archie felt like he had won his trust. Passed his tests. Now he could do this. Archie had survived ten days of torture at the hands of Gretchen Lowell. What were a few more scars?

He looked at Jeremy's arms and thighs, the triangle-shaped scars, the scars that Gretchen had carved on Isabel and none of her other victims.

He lowered the blade to his thigh, on the inside, just above his left knee, and he pulled the scalpel over his skin. It was easy. The blade was sharp and it didn't hurt. An inch-long line of blood formed instantly.

'She had a sock with a brick in it and she'd hit Isabel in the head,' Jeremy said.

Archie looked up.

Jeremy did remember.

And although Archie knew he should be thinking about Jeremy's fragile psyche, about closing the case, about gathering more evidence against Gretchen, all he could think was: I am not alone.

And he was glad. It was what he was after, wasn't it? He wanted Jeremy to remember because it would mean that there was someone else who knew. Someone else who had survived. Someone else as damaged as Archie was.

He didn't want to be alone.

Neither of them did.

Jeremy was staring past him. The half-carved heart on his chest was still bleeding, and Jeremy must have got blood on his hands, because it was smeared on his face and arm.

'She swung it hard,' he said. 'It hit her here.' He touched his scalp, behind the left ear. Archie remembered Isabel's autopsy reports. It matched the site of a small fracture the ME had found on her skull. 'Then she tied her up.'

Jeremy stopped and looked at Archie, his gaze flickering down to the small cut Archie had managed on his leg.

Archie lifted the scalpel again and drew another line of blood in his thigh. He did it slowly this time. He had to be careful. If he used anything but the lightest touch, the scalpel would cut too deep.

Jeremy continued. 'Isabel was in the back seat. I was in the passenger seat. She didn't tie me up. We didn't talk. She drove us to the woods.' His voice was flat now, dissociative, like someone reporting the details of a dream. Archie wiped his blood off the scalpel onto the towel.

'It must have been a timber road,' Jeremy said. 'She had to get out and open one of those Forest Service gates. We drove for a long time. She didn't say anything. Isabel woke up and was crying in the back seat. I could hear her, but I was too afraid to turn around or say anything.'

Archie pressed the blade to his flesh again. There were four children listed as presumed Beauty Killer victims, all subjected to torture and found with Gretchen's signature heart carved on their chests. Archie could never get Gretchen to confess to any of them. She lorded them over him, the final prize, just out of reach.

'We parked at the side of the road,' Jeremy said. 'And Gretchen got in the back seat with my sister.'

Archie pressed the blade in harder. He wanted to feel it.

He deserved to feel it. Gretchen had dangled the children like confections. But Archie had never wanted her to confess, because he would have had to hear her confession, to listen to what she had done to them, and to correlate that with all the nights he thought of her, his dick in his hand. *Feel it.*

'She cut her with an X-Acto blade,' Jeremy said. 'She had a package of blades, and when one got dull she'd replace it with a new one. Isabel cried. She looked so afraid. Gretchen cut off one of her breasts. She said that Amazons used to cut off one of their breasts to make it easier to shoot a bow. When she'd freed the flesh from the muscle she threw it out the window and said, "Now she's an Amazon."'

Archie felt something. But it wasn't pain – it was loathing. And for the first time in years, it wasn't directed inward. He loathed her. He wanted Jeremy to keep going. He wanted to hear every gory detail. Because every horror she committed just made him hate her more. The rage moved through his veins like endorphins.

'I don't know how long it lasted,' Jeremy said. 'Hours. After a while Isabel's eyes glazed over and she got really pale and limp. Gretchen put a new blade in and cut her throat. She showed me how to do it. She said that it was something everyone should know. Little bloody bubbles came out of her neck. After she was dead, Gretchen carved a heart on her. It was only then that I knew who she was. The Beauty Killer. I'd seen some of the stories on the news. We sat there for a long time. It got dark. I started to cry, and Gretchen held me and stroked my hair. She didn't say anything after that. I thought she was mad at me. We sat in the car the whole next day and night. I got out to pee. And then I got back in. She got out sometimes, too. On the second day I said I was hungry, and she started the car and drove back into town. Then she parked and got out and walked away. I didn't know if she was coming back. I didn't know if I was supposed to follow her. So I waited. And after a while I fell asleep again.'

Archie set the bloody scalpel back on the tray.

Jeremy sat shaking his head. 'Why didn't she kill me?'

'I don't know,' Archie said.

'She took care of me.'

'She tortured you, as much as she tortured your sister,' Archie said gently. 'Only you've had to live with it. There was no reason.' He was talking to himself now as much as Jeremy. 'She didn't care about you. You don't owe her anything.'

Jeremy started to sob. 'I'm sorry,' he gasped. 'I killed those people. I killed a man I found sleeping in a park and a girl I picked up hitchhiking. I tricked another man into getting into my car, by offering him work. I killed them and I kept their eyes. Because their eyes reminded me of Isabel's. Dead eyes, like hers.'

'You put them at Gretchen's crime scenes.'

'I wanted her to notice me.'

Archie looked at Jeremy, wasted, wrecked – the garbage Gretchen had thrown to the kerb – and he promised himself that he would do everything he could for him. 'You're in trouble,' Archie said. 'People are dead. You stabbed a journalist.' Archie could have gone on, but Jeremy didn't seem to be in the state of mind to discuss the practising-medicine-without-a-licence charge.

'Help me,' Jeremy pleaded.

'Your dad will get you a good criminal lawyer,' Archie said. They were both damaged goods. Face to face, with their ravaged torsos exposed, Archie felt like he was looking in the mirror. 'You'll be okay,' Archie said. 'You're going to be okay. You'll get help. We're going to be okay.'

The lights flickered.

Archie looked up. Something was wrong.

The ceiling seemed to bend toward him, and Archie shook his head and looked at Jeremy to see if he had seen it, too. But Jeremy wasn't looking at the ceiling. He was looking at Archie, a soft smile on his lips.

'We should get out of here,' Archie said. He felt warm, his head muddy. Maybe his blood pressure was still off from the suspension. He tried to stand but his stomach lurched, like the floor had elevated and dropped, or they had hit a swell on a boat, and he fell to his knees.

He looked to Jeremy, to see if he'd felt it that time, but Jeremy hadn't moved. He still sat there, monk-like, watching. Then Archie saw Jeremy's eyes drift to the sports bottle of sugar water.

'What did you do?' Archie said. A warm tingle gnawed up his spine and down his arms, and he tried again to stand, but his legs were useless.

It was all sickeningly familiar.

Archie tried to lift a dead arm, to reach out to Jeremy,

but the aperture of his vision was already closing and his head swam. He fell forward into Jeremy's arms. He heard a fleshy smack and it took a moment to realize it was the sound of his own jaw hitting Jeremy's bony shoulder. Archie's face slid a few inches and came to a stop pressed against Jeremy's hairless and scar-ravaged chest. Archie could taste the blood from Jeremy's wound mixed with his own saliva, hear Jeremy's heart beat, as Archie's own pulse unnaturally slowed. It took all of his energy just to speak one word. It came out in a thick, barely perceptible rasp: 'Phentobomine.'

'Yes,' Jeremy said. He held Archie, rocking him. Archie couldn't feel it, couldn't feel anything any more, but he could sense the motion through a pinhole vision of colour and light. 'It's what Gretchen drugged you with when she took you captive,' Jeremy said. 'I read it in *The Last Victim.*' He slipped out from under Archie's weight and gently rolled him over onto his back on the floor. 'It will wear off in the next half-hour,' Jeremy said. He seemed genuinely sorry. Which did not in the least make up for being left drugged and naked on a concrete floor.

'Don't leave,' Archie said. But it came out 'doneeeiliv'.

Jeremy stepped away, into the darkness. 'I don't want to go to jail,' Archie heard him say in the black. 'They won't let me bring my toys.'

Archie tried again to speak. But his tongue was too huge, too thick, his mouth too dry, and Jeremy was gone into the dark.

It was only one sentence. Three words. But he couldn't form them in his mouth.

Turn me over.

Gretchen Lowell had been a nurse. She knew how to use Phentobomine. Jeremy had probably ordered it on the Internet. He was a kid. He was scared. He didn't know.

He didn't know that he shouldn't leave Archie on his back. That he couldn't move. That he couldn't clear the saliva that was pooling in his throat.

The lights flickered, as Archie listened to the rattling of his laboured breaths. He tried to expand his lungs slowly, to draw in as much oxygen as he could. But his body was betraying him. His heart rate increased. He focused on that, counting beats, trying to stay alive another twenty beats, another ten. His lungs ached. The rattle turned to an ugly hum. Every cell of his body wanted to take a great gasp of air, and he could do nothing but lie there, drowning in his own spit.

A pleasant black whirlpool enveloped him, as his lungs surrendered their last store of oxygen.

Archie fought it. He willed his body to breathe, to stay alive just a few minutes more. He struggled and strained and raged, and forced his lungs to draw in a thin thread of air.

As he did, a pair of hands pressed against his body and rolled him over on his side.

57

Susan clutched her purse on her lap. Mace, to be most effective, should be held upright and sprayed in short half-second bursts at the assailant's face. Eyes and noses are especially good targets. Range is ten to twelve feet (more or less, depending on canister pressure and wind conditions). Spray and move. Then spray again. If you keep moving, you lessen the likelihood of being a victim of your own chemical attack. Done right, mace causes immediate capillary dilation, temporary blindness, and instant inflammation of the breathing-tube tissues. It also burns like a motherfucker.

Henry slid her a look. 'You're staying in the car,' he said.

Fuck that, Susan thought, gripping her purse full of self-defence sprays a little tighter. 'Right,' she said.

Jeremy's squat was in Portland's Northwest Industrial District. Years ago it had been a swamp. Then someone had got the fine idea to put in a great big rail yard, and after that folks from the Lewis and Clark Exposition of 1905 saw the land and they thought it would be just perfect for their fair, waist-high stagnant water notwithstanding. The fair was a big success, and folks from all around came to Portland for the pavilions, and stayed for the cheap beer and strapping lumberjacks. The fairgrounds' structures rotted away. The lumberjacks went back to the woods, and the area was built up with light industrial businesses that didn't make anything, but made parts for a lot of things.

'That's it,' Pearl said from the back seat. Henry slid the car in front of it and parked. The building was blue, one storey, with no windows. The remnants of a hand-painted sign of some long-dead business still hung above the old office.

Pearl pointed to a banger parked on the street. 'That's Jeremy's car,' she said.

Henry's mouth flattened and he snatched the radio receiver off the dash console and called for backup.

Goosebumps rose on Susan's arms. Wheat-pasted along the entire length of the building's buckling loading dock were posters for the upcoming Gretchen Lowell episode of *America's Sexiest Serial Killers*.

Henry hung up the radio, and looked over at Susan. 'Let me go in first. Stay in the car with the doors locked. Don't touch anything.' And then, as if anticipating her protest, he threw a glance back at Pearl. 'You need to stay with the girl.'

Susan held her purse tighter and looked out the window at the building, Gretchen's face on the posters, the axe on the old sign. If Archie was in there, he needed help. There wasn't time to argue.

She bit her lip and nodded.

Henry unholstered his gun, treated her to one last stern look, and then got out of the car.

She didn't take her eyes off Henry as he walked towards the building in a low crouch, gun angled at the ground in front of him. The loading-bay door was open a foot and she watched as Henry pounded on it and shouted something and then, with one last glance back at the car, slipped inside.

They were alone. A trickle of fear inched down Susan's arms and she reached into her bag and got out one of the spray cans and pushed the purse on the floor in front of her.

Susan glanced in the car's rearview mirror, looking for telltale flashing blue and red lights. There would be sirens any minute. There were probably dozens of cop cars headed to that intersection.

Henry would secure the situation. You could count on Henry for that – securing situations. Jeremy didn't stand a chance. She almost smiled. She'd like to see him try to pierce Henry.

'Jeremy has a gun,' Pearl said from the back seat.

Susan snapped her head around. 'What?'

Pearl sat, cross-armed, slumped in the back, her goggles on the top of her head like a pair of sunglasses. 'I just thought of it,' she said. 'He showed it to me once. Said he got it from his father.'

Susan lifted her hand over her mouth and sank into her seat, unsure what to do. Henry had gone inside. Did she roll down the window and yell? Get out of the car? Did she call him on his cell phone? Figure out how the fuck to use the radio?

She twisted around and looked out the back windshield. Where was the backup?

Then she heard it.

If she'd been walking by, she would not have known it was a gunshot. It was a dull pop – the kind of thing that could be easily explained away by a car backfire or a fire-cracker.

But it wasn't either of those things.

Someone inside had been shot, or someone had tried to shoot someone.

'Shit,' she said.

'Was that a gun?' Pearl asked, suddenly sounding her age.

Susan needed to go inside.

There was no choice now. Henry could be shot, lying in there, bleeding. She grabbed her purse off the floor and tossed it back to Pearl. 'Stay in the car. When backup gets here, tell them what's happening. There's mace in the bag if you need it. Don't touch anything else in my purse.'

Pearl looked pale. 'Okay,' she said.

Susan started walking to the loading-bay door. She moved quickly, the spray can in one hand, thumb on the nozzle. Her entire focus was on the door. Get to the door. Go inside. Don't get shot.

Four people were killed every hour in the US by guns. It made her feel better. What were the odds one of them would be Henry? Archie? I mean, *four people.* It was a big country. Over 300 million people. There were people shooting at each other right this minute in much bigger cities – spurned lovers, crazed high school students, bank robbers, you name it.

She got to the door. It was still open a crack, but it was dark inside and she couldn't see anything. 'Henry?' she croaked. 'Are you okay?'

No one answered.

She lifted the spray can and went inside. She was getting to be an expert at entering dirty, unlit rooms, and she paused for a moment just inside the door to let her eyes adjust. There were some broken windows that let in shards of light, and once her pupils dilated, Susan could actually make out quite a bit. Pieces of rotting wooden pallets scattered the floor. Whatever they had made there had once been stored in boxes in this room, then loaded through the door onto trucks and shipped off to long-dead customers.

She stood perfectly still and listened. Every hair on her body lifted.

Someone coughed. It was Archie. Susan didn't know how she knew. She didn't question it. It was Archie's cough. She was certain of it.

Susan searched for the origin of the sound and identified a door that stood open on the opposite wall. She hurried to it, not even trying to dodge the splintered two-by-fours in her path.

From outside, one siren wailed its approach, and then there seemed to be a thousand all at once.

But Susan had crossed the room then.

The next room was bigger, the old manufacturing floor. A single light hung from an extension cord in the centre of the room. Archie was naked, on his hands and knees, trying to stand. He looked up and saw her and she ran to him.

As she got closer she saw the bandages on his back, the white already soaked through with blood. He tried again to stand, putting his hands on his knees for leverage, and he managed to get unsteadily to his feet. His leg was lacerated and bleeding. He was buck naked. But this was not what shocked Susan. What shocked her were the scars. Susan had read the case files, the newspaper clippings – she'd even read *The Last Victim*. She knew what Gretchen had done to him. She knew about the basement splenectomy. She knew that Gretchen had driven nails into his chest, broken his ribs, played doctor on him with an X-Acto knife and scalpel. She knew she'd cut a heart into his chest.

But she had never seen the aftermath. His torso was brutalized, webbed with scar tissue; the slight brown hair grew in patches, around slick white new skin. There wasn't a square inch on his chest that hadn't been marked by her. The largest scar, the one that split him in two up the midsection, was a knotty pink rope, umbilical-like. But the one that her eyes fell to, that she had to force herself not to stare at, was the heart-shaped scar below his left scapula. Two years old, and it still looked raw, like he had spent months picking at it.

She stepped close to him, lifted one of his arms around her shoulder, and wrapped her arm around his waist, the spray can still clutched in her hand. He cringed from her touch, and she saw the deep purple bruise on his side where he must have been tasered, and she adjusted her hand lower on his hip. He swayed and his weight shifted and it was all she could do to hold him up. But his eyes were clear and focused. 'I heard a shot,' he said.

'Henry came in first,' Susan said.

'I didn't see him,' Archie said. He nodded, like he was trying to make sense of things. 'My legs aren't working yet.' He looked over at Susan. 'Can you get us out of here?'

A police megaphone crackled to life outside and Susan could hear someone shouting orders, but she couldn't make out what they were saying.

She kept her focus on the door. Archie could barely walk, and it took all her effort to guide him, step by step, towards the exit. 'Will they come in?' she asked.

'They need to secure the perimeter,' Archie said. 'Determine hostages. They won't come in unless they hear another shot.'

To the left of their path, just at the edge of the circle of light, sat a massive pockmarked anvil. It was the only manufacturing tool they'd left in the place, like they'd cleaned out the building and decided it was too heavy to move.

'What was this place?' Susan asked.

'They made axes,' Archie said.

She saw the glint of it before she saw the weapon itself. The steel head was orange with rust and the wooden handle had faded to a soft grey. Jeremy was moving fast, and the axe was held high. He came at them, a blur. Susan thought Jeremy screamed, but it was so loud in her head, the scream might have been coming from her.

She untangled her arm from Archie's waist, held the spray can high, squeezed her eyes shut and pushed down on the nozzle.

Spray. Move.

She couldn't move. She tried, but she was rooted to the floor, bracing for the blow from the axe. She could still hear the screaming.

> Lizzie Borden took an axe.
> And gave her mother forty whacks.
> And when she saw what she had done.
> She gave her father forty-one.

Lizzie Borden had murdered her stepmother, not her mother. And she'd done it with just nineteen whacks.

Archie threw her to the ground. How he did that, since he could barely walk, she didn't know. Maybe he just stopped trying to stand and took her with him when he fell.

She opened her eyes just as the axe hit the concrete by her head. The floor shook and sparks exploded from the blade.

The axe lifted again and she covered her head with her hands.

And then there was another gunshot – this one much, much closer – and then the thud of a body hitting concrete along with the metallic slap of an axe head.

Susan did a quick mental inventory of limbs. No blinding pain. Her head still seemed attached to her neck.

She opened her eyes and lifted her head. She was panting. Archie was on top of her, shielding her from the axe blow. He rolled off her and sat up.

Henry was moving towards them, his gun still trained on Jeremy, who now lay facedown on the floor.

Cops rushed in from everywhere – impressive, because as

far as Susan could tell, there were only two doors. They had their guns drawn and it seemed as if all of them were shouting, only Susan's head was spinning so hard she still couldn't absorb any of the content.

'It's okay,' Henry yelled at no one in particular. He put his gun down and lifted his arms. 'We're okay.' He lowered his gaze at Susan. 'I told you to wait for me.'

Susan, for once, didn't have a comeback.

'She doesn't do that,' Archie said. He crawled over to where Jeremy lay facedown on the floor. 'She doesn't wait.'

'Is Jeremy dead?' Susan asked.

'It's not Jeremy,' Archie said.

Claire burst through a foursome of anxious-looking patrol cops who were standing, guns still at the ready, on the edge of the light. She stopped in her tracks at the sight before her and then said something to the patrol cops that made them lower their weapons.

Then she moved to the body.

Susan crawled closer, too, next to Archie, so she could get a better look at the man who'd nearly chopped her up. His head was twisted to the side, eyes open blankly, and his lips fallen apart, revealing a set of sharply filed teeth. The bullet had hit him in the back of the neck. He was definitely dead.

Archie glanced up at Henry. 'Jeremy left,' he said. 'About a half-hour ago. I don't know when Shark Boy got here.'

Susan saw Henry's face falter. He looked down at the man he'd just killed and cleared his throat. 'It's not Jeremy?'

'He was swinging an axe,' Claire said. 'It was justifiable force.'

Henry's face was slack for a moment and then he snapped back into action. 'Suspect's still at large,' he barked to everyone who'd assembled. 'His car's still out front. So he may be on foot. Fan out. He's got a half-hour on us.'

Someone hit a light switch and fifty caged industrial fluorescents sprang to life overhead, illuminating everything, and everybody. Susan's eyes stung. Archie lifted a hand to wipe a smear of blood off his forehead. 'Would you mind helping me find my pants?' he said.

58

Archie's task force office was exactly as he'd left it two months earlier. His cherry-veneer desk, left over from the bank manager who'd had the office before him, was stacked with files. A faint layer of dust covered his computer keyboard. The office was small, just big enough for the desk, a bookshelf behind it, and two cheaply upholstered armchairs in front. The blinds were closed over the small window that looked out over the street. Henry, who'd run the place since he'd left, had locked it and led the manhunt for Gretchen from his own desk in the main room.

Archie leaned back in his chair, and was instantly reminded of the wounds on his back. He flinched and then eased back slowly. He was bandaged and back in his clothes; he'd washed his face; he'd given his statement; he'd let the EMTs re-dress his wounds.

A photograph of Debbie and the kids still sat propped by his desk lamp. Archie ran a finger along the top of the frame, lifting up the dust – Debbie with her mouth open, saying something, an arm around each kid. He realized, sadly, that he wouldn't tell her about today. She didn't need to know. She would never see the new scars.

Looking at the picture, he noticed for the first time that there was a picnic bench in the background. Archie picked up the photograph and squinted at it. *They had stopped at a rest stop on their way up to Timberline Lodge.* He chuckled darkly with recognition. His smiling family portrait – the only evidence of the only vacation they'd taken that year, and it was taken at the rest stop where Jeremy Reynolds would later spew his carnage.

Fucking perfect.

Archie pulled his top left desk drawer open. He reached in and felt around for the bottle of Vicodin he'd kept in there, but it was gone.

The office was *almost* exactly as Archie had left it.

Henry appeared in the doorway. He'd been in the conference room with Internal Affairs for the last two hours and he looked tired. Archie slid the drawer back closed.

'You know Frank doesn't have a sister,' Henry said.

'I had an inkling,' Archie said.

'A woman called the *Herald*, claiming to be the owner of a shop on Hawthorne,' Henry said. 'Said Pearl worked for her. But when Susan and I went there, the owner said she'd never made the call. But she did lead us to Pearl, which is how we found you.'

Archie leaned back in his chair. 'You think Gretchen is my guardian angel now?'

Henry put his palms on the desk and looked, for a second,

like he might push the thing through the floor. 'Do you have a phone from her?' he asked.

Archie looked him right in the eye. 'Nope,' he said.

He wasn't lying. As far as he knew, it was still in Susan's car.

Henry took a step back and sat down in one of the armchairs. 'Claire said you refused medical care.'

'I refused to go to the hospital,' Archie said. 'I let them treat me at the scene. Don't worry. I have an appointment with Rosenberg in the morning. And a schedule for Narcotics Anonymous in my bag.'

Henry folded his hands in his lap and looked at them. 'What did he do to you?' he said gruffly.

Archie had been tempted to omit some details. By the time he had recovered enough movement to lift his head the suspension gear was gone. He wasn't sure he wanted them to know what had gone on between him and Jeremy. But he was tired of keeping secrets.

'I gave Claire a statement,' Archie said. 'Go ahead and read it. But I'm not pressing charges.'

Henry lifted his head and glanced up at the ceiling as if for guidance. 'What is it with you and psychopaths?'

'Jeremy confessed,' Archie said. 'He took responsibility for the rest stop, and Fintan English, and the other three. You have him for four murders – everyone but Courtenay. You don't need me.' Archie sat forward and folded his hands on his desk. 'He remembers his sister's murder. He told me everything.'

'You buy it?' Henry asked.

'He knew about the triangles, the contusions,' Archie said. 'He remembers. He watched Gretchen kill her. He spent almost two days in that car.' He wanted Henry to see what this meant, to know that everything had changed. 'She made him what he is.'

'You went through worse, and you've managed not to carve anyone's eyes out.'

Archie shook his head. 'I didn't go through worse,' he said. Jeremy had watched Gretchen torture his sister. Archie had survived his own torture. But Jeremy had been innocent. Archie had brought it on himself. 'It was just a different kind of bad.'

'No,' Henry said. 'You aren't like him.'

Jeremy had committed murder. Archie had merely killed his marriage, his sense of self, his job. All without firing his weapon. He couldn't imagine what it would feel like, to actually do it, to take someone's life, what might drive a person to cross that line.

He couldn't imagine. But Henry could.

'Are you okay?' Archie asked him.

A faint smile crossed Henry's lips. 'That's a switch. You asking me that.'

Shark Boy had swung at Henry when he'd come in, and Henry had fired at him and given chase. 'He was going to kill us,' Archie said.

Henry stared into space for a moment, then frowned. 'I'm on desk duty, pending official clearance,' he said. 'But it's a formality.' He scratched the back of his neck. 'They identified him. His name was Troy Lipton. Twenty-seven. Worked as a fry cook at a roadhouse out in Sherwood. He's got a record in Idaho. Robbery. Assault.' Henry coughed and stood up. 'You should go back to the house,' he said, waving a hand in Archie's direction. 'Get some rest.'

Archie looked down at his wrinkled clothes, the shirt spotted with blood. 'I could use a shower.'

'I'm sending someone with you,' Henry said. 'Gretchen's still out there, and now Jeremy.'

'Agreed.'

Henry took a step and stopped in the doorway, his back to Archie, head down. 'I've killed people before,' he said.

59

Archie stood in Henry's shower, eyes closed, letting the hot water run down his back. The bandages had come off in the water and circled the drain of the tub. Archie turned up the hot water. He stayed like that for another few minutes, until his skin burned and the steam was thick enough that he could barely breathe, and then he opened his eyes and took a step out of the shower stream. He opened the plastic curtain a few inches, to let in some fresh air, and he examined his wounds. The taser had left a vicious-looking bruise on his side. It was the size of a handprint, hard and tender to the touch, with two dark red circles, like teeth marks, where the electrical current had entered his body.

His back and legs still stung from the hooks, but he wasn't bleeding any more. He lifted his foot and put it on the edge of the tub so he could examine the triangle he'd cut into his thigh. The sliced skin hadn't required stitches. He rubbed his hand on a bar of soap in the tub's soap dish and then moved his fingers over the cuts in his skin. Triangles. Isabel had been the only victim Gretchen had ever carved that shape into. Strange that it would be what captured Jeremy's attention. That he would carve it on his own body so many times. He had not seen the wounds on her other victims. He would have no way of knowing that it was special.

Archie brushed a tiny scab off one of the cuts and it started to bleed, mixing with the water and sending a pale pink stream down his thigh and around the back of his knee.

Triangles.

He sank to the bottom of the tub and sat there. The bathroom was filled with steam. The mirror was fogged. Archie reached forward and turned off the water. The wound on his leg wasn't very deep, but it had started to throb.

Archie pulled himself up, climbed out of the tub, dried off, and wrapped a towel around his waist. Then wiped the condensation off the mirror so he could see himself. His hollow reflection gave him a start. He put his hand on the edge of the mirror and waited a minute, and then opened the medicine cabinet and scanned the shelves. He didn't see what he wanted. He looked under the sink. No pills there. He wondered if Henry really didn't have any painkillers or if he'd just hidden them.

Archie was walking through the living room on his way to search Henry's kitchen cabinets when he heard her voice.

'I'm glad you're all right,' Gretchen said.

He turned around and saw her sitting in Henry's chair. She was holding one of Henry's cats in her lap – a grey tabby he'd saved from a crime scene. Her hair was red and pulled back. She was wearing a black sleeveless cotton dress, bare legs crossed. She looked tanned. He had seen her so many times in his head that it took a minute to sink in that it was really her.

He wished that he could take that part of himself – the part that remembered her, was connected to her, the part that wanted her – and cut it out and bury it.

He laughed. 'I wish I'd killed you,' Archie said.

The cat rubbed its head against her hand and purred. 'I'd imagine.'

'There was no reason,' Archie said. 'I've been looking for a reason why you kept me alive. Some humanity in you. But there was no reason.'

Gretchen frowned thoughtfully. 'Maybe it was love.'

Archie smiled. He beckoned her over with a finger. 'I want to show you something,' he said.

She didn't hesitate. She nudged the cat off her lap onto the floor, stood and walked over. She was wearing high heels and her hips swung as she stepped. When she was a few feet away, he dropped the towel.

'No hard-on,' he said.

He followed her eyes down to his flaccid cock, and he marvelled happily at it. 'Do you know how long it's been since I was in the same room with you, without getting hard?' he said. 'Jesus, I couldn't even look at your picture, think your name, without getting a fucking erection.' He touched it, moving it a little to prove it wasn't stiff. 'I could fill a bathtub with the semen I've spilled in your honour.'

Gretchen reached out and put a hand behind his head and pulled his lips to hers. He let her do it. But he kept his arms at his sides. She kissed him, pushing her tongue into his mouth. And he felt: nothing.

He laughed again.

She pulled away, took a step back, and smoothed her hair. 'The therapy is paying off,' she said. 'You've been a good patient. I've been very pleased. '

'Stop calling Frank,' Archie said. 'You've got him believing that you're actually his sister.'

She smiled and arched a sculpted eyebrow. 'Maybe I am.'

Henry and Claire were at the task force offices, not due back for hours. 'How did you know I was here?' Archie asked. Henry kept an extra gun in a box in the closet. Archie would have to get to it, open the box, and load it.

Gretchen leaned her elbows on Henry's sideboard. 'Where else would you go? Vancouver?' She ran her eyes over him and he realized he was still standing there, naked. 'I think Debbie's had enough of your wandering eye.' She ran a fingertip along the top of the sideboard and looked at it. 'I can see Claire's influence,' she said. 'It's much neater.' She was fucking with him. She'd never been in Henry's house before.

Archie picked up the towel and tucked it around his waist. 'Why are you here?' he asked.

She smiled her movie-star smile. 'I came to save you.'

He had hoped it wasn't true. 'You called the *Herald* with the tip about Pearl.'

'How is Jeremy Reynolds?' Gretchen said. 'I see he's introduced you to body suspension.'

'He's what you made him,' Archie said.

'I'm thinking of suing for trademark infringement. I don't like being copied.'

'Yet you had George Hay gouge out Courtenay Taggart's eyes.'

'I was copying Jeremy copying me. That's not copyright infringement. It's sampling.'

Henry would have the gun loaded. He didn't have kids. He didn't need to worry about that. Boxed, in a closet like that, the gun would be loaded.

Gretchen glanced down the hall. 'Where is it?' she said. 'The gun you're thinking about using. There? You'd never get there in time.' She stepped in front of him and took one of his hands in hers and lifted it to her neck. 'You could use your hands,' she said. She held it there for a moment and he could feel the thump thump of her pulse. Then she lowered it and kissed his palm.

'You're so confident I won't do it,' Archie said.

She smiled and turned away from him. 'You're close, darling. Don't worry. You'll get there. But first you want to ask me about Isabel Reynolds. What is it that's nagging at you? The triangles?' She touched the towel over his thigh, where he had cut himself for Jeremy.

'Okay,' he said. 'I'll play. Did you kill Isabel Reynolds?'

Gretchen lifted her finger to her chin thoughtfully and seemed to consider the question. Then she shook her head. 'No,' she said. 'I don't kill children.'

'Fuck you,' he said.

'There you go,' Gretchen said. 'That's what you need. Anger. The psych ward took some of your edge, didn't it? We need to get that back.'

'You think I won't kill you? I daydream about killing you.'

She stepped away from the sideboard. 'It's in the drawer,' she said. 'Go ahead. I put it there for you.'

Archie went to the drawer and pulled it open. There, lying on a stack of cloth Christmas napkins, was Henry's gun.

Archie picked it up and pointed it at Gretchen.

She smiled.

'Did you kill Isabel Reynolds?' Archie said.

Gretchen looked him in the eyes. 'I don't kill children,' she said.

She was lying. There were three children on the Beauty Killer victim list besides Isabel Reynolds. All tortured and left with hearts carved on their chests. 'I saw the bodies,' Archie said.

'I had an apprentice,' Gretchen said with a dismissive motion of her hand. 'His name is Ryan Motley. I couldn't control him. When he left my orbit he embraced his own work.'

Archie didn't believe her. Sometimes he wondered if everything out of her mouth was a lie.

'You're saying he killed Isabel?' Archie said.

'No,' Gretchen said. 'He didn't kill Isabel Reynolds.'

'Who did?' Archie asked. And even as he said it, his gut twisted, because somehow, deep down, he already knew.

'I always assumed it was the brother,' Gretchen said.

She'd had access to the confidential case files when she'd

infiltrated the case as a psychiatrist. She could have read everything they had on Jeremy, even his psych reports.

'He killed her,' she continued, 'and carved a heart on her and then screamed Beauty Killer. I don't mind usually when I get credit for other people's work. But Jeremy Reynolds was a psycho little shit who killed his sister and got away with it.'

Archie fought it. He shook his head. 'No,' he said. 'No.' She was fucking with him. She was manipulating him. She was trying to take Jeremy away from him.

'Why now?' Archie asked. 'You've let us think you killed those children. Why deny it now? You expect me to believe there's some moral line you won't cross? That you have rules?'

'You know I'm telling the truth. Because if I did kill children, you know – in your heart – that I'd have killed yours.'

Archie pulled the trigger. The hammer came down harmlessly. The chamber was empty.

'That was fun, wasn't it?' Gretchen said.

Archie snapped. He lunged for her, knotted his fist in her hair, and pushed her against the wall. She laughed at him, and it fuelled his rage. He used his body as leverage against hers, pinning her. Then he placed his free hand on her throat and pushed. She didn't struggle. She just looked at him. Her face reddened and she gasped involuntarily against his grasp. Saliva pooled at the corners of her mouth. Her eyes widened.

He could smell her, the sweet stink of their sweat intermingled. Her dress was torn at the shoulder from when he'd grabbed her. Her hair was messed.

She didn't look so beautiful any more.

His chest heaved and she arched her back, pressing her breasts into him. He lifted her up off her feet, sliding her up against the wall, until they were face to face. Her lips parted and her hands lifted and wrapped around his wrists. He knew those hands.

It had not been Jeremy who had saved him from choking, it had been Gretchen. Her hands. She had been there. She had rolled him over. She had been watching over him. Jeremy had left Archie to die.

Archie hated her for that, and he pushed harder into her, feeling her body letting go, sinking into his, her life evaporating.

And it made him hard.

The sensation of desire at that moment was so disorientating that Archie nearly vomited.

He let Gretchen drop to the floor and stumbled back away from her, gathering the towel around his waist.

She lifted a hand to her neck and coughed, and the red drained from her face. There was merriment in her blue eyes when she looked up at him. She wiped her mouth with the back of her hand and laughed. 'Don't worry,' she said, flicking her amused gaze to his groin. 'It happens to everyone.'

She smoothed her hair and got up. She took a step, stumbled, then straightened up, walked over, and picked her purse up off the couch. Then she walked over to him and stuck him with something below his ribcage.

His body jerked and seized and he fell to the ground. He choked with laughter as his muscles jerked. She'd fucking tasered him.

'I'm going to go now,' she said. She tossed him a black pouch. 'Here's a package. A few special presents, plus a flash drive on the table with everything I know about Ryan Motley on it. You might want to do something about him.' She took a few steps towards the door and then turned back. 'You thought you had a little friend, didn't you, darling?'

She knelt down next to him, the smell and heat of her again filling his senses. 'Here's something to remember him by,' she said, and she put something wet and slippery in Archie's clawed hand.

He continued to jerk and twitch as she slid her fingernail up his arm, across his shoulder, and down his spine to his tailbone, and then he couldn't feel her any more.

The back door opened and closed.

Archie rolled onto his back and the cat padded over and started licking his face. It took Archie several minutes to force his muscles to relax enough to open his hand, revealing her parting gift to him – two white orbs the colour of spoiled milk, threaded with red vessels and slippery with blood.

He reflexively pulled his hand back and Jeremy's eyeballs rolled out of his palm and onto the floor.

The cat cocked its head.

Archie struggled to his feet, and backed away from them, looking at his hand, smeared with Jeremy's blood. Then he turned, went to the front window, pulled back the curtain, and searched for the patrol unit Henry had stationed in front of the house. The car was there. The dome light was on and the officer was inside. Alive.

Archie leaned his head against the glass, caught his

breath, then stumbled into the bathroom and held his hand under the tap, the water as hot as he could stand it.

Had Jeremy killed Isabel?

Or was this just another one of Gretchen's lies?

He had to know. Archie was calm now, his heart rate settled. Twin red bite marks already showed on his side where the taser's projectiles had made contact. A purple bruise would rise soon, matching the opposite side.

Archie turned the water off and dried his hands. Then, moving slowly and painfully, he put on clean clothes. By the time he was done, he had stopped shaking.

He went back out into the living room. One of the eyes was gone. So was the cat. Archie scooped up the keys to Claire's car off the sideboard, picked the empty gun up off the floor, and made a call on Henry's landline.

'It's me,' Archie said. 'I need to see you.'

Archie could hear the beat of club music in the background. 'You know where I am,' Leo Reynolds said.

Archie hung up and picked the phone up again. This time he dialled Henry. He carried the receiver into Henry's bedroom and opened the closet.

'Jeremy's dead,' Archie said when Henry picked up.

'Where are you?' Henry asked.

Archie scanned the closet shelf, looking for the box the gun would have been in. 'At your house. Gretchen was here. You'll find Jeremy's eyes on your living-room floor.' He paused, remembering the cat. 'Or under the couch.' He saw a box and dumped the contents out on the floor. Photographs. 'Where do you keep the bullets to your gun?' he asked.

'Stay there,' Henry said. 'I'm on my way.'

Archie moved to Henry's dresser and starting pulling open drawers. He had to get out of there, before Henry sent in the cop out front. 'Goddamn, Henry. Where are the fucking bullets?'

'Night table,' Henry said quietly. 'Top drawer.'

'Thank you,' Archie said. He hung up the phone and tossed it on the bed, and then went to Henry's bedside table and opened the drawer. The bullets were in a box next to a pair of reading glasses. Archie loaded the gun and kept a handful of extra bullets. He needed something to keep them in, so he went back to the bathroom, to his overnight bag from the hospital, and dug out the brass pillbox he had kept his painkillers in. He'd missed it.

He opened the pillbox, dropped the bullets in, and went out the back door.

He was never going to let Gretchen catch him unarmed again.

60

The bouncer at George's Dancin' Bare had his nose in a book. Behind him, pinned on the wall, was a flyer advertising a Gretchen Lowell lookalike stripper contest.

'I'm looking for Leo,' Archie said.

'Room three,' the bouncer said, not looking up.

The club was busier than Archie remembered it, and louder. He tried to stand up straight, to not favour the side where Gretchen's taser bruise still burned. Cigarette smoke choked the air. Portland was going to ban smoking in bars in the new year, and it seemed like everyone was trying to suck down as much nicotine as possible while they still could.

Archie moved like a hunchback, but no one noticed. There were a dozen men collected around the first stage, where a half-dressed woman was working on disassembling the rest of her nurse's ensemble. Behind the stage was the club's trademark sign, a dancing bear, crossed out, above a drawing of a naked woman, reclined, legs extended in front of her. Beside that sign was another sign that read GIRLS, UP CLOSE, with an arrow pointing right.

Archie followed it down a hall where there were four doors, all quilted with brown fake-leather fabric held in place in a harlequin pattern with brass furniture tacks. Archie went to the door marked '3' and knocked. 'It's me,' he said. If Leo was in there, Archie wasn't sure he could hear him over the club's main speakers.

He tried the door.

It wasn't locked.

He opened the door a tiny crack and peered in.

The room was mirrored. Mirrored walls, mirrored ceiling. If they could have figured out a way to make the floor mirrored, they would have. A cherry-red vinyl sofa went around the perimeter.

Leo looked up and waved Archie in. He was sitting back on the red sofa, knees apart, arms resting on his thighs. Grey suit pants, white shirt unbuttoned midway down his chest. There was a glass of something dark on the sofa next to him.

A blonde well-toned stripper with a star tattoo danced around a pole in the middle of the room.

The stripper looked up as Archie entered. She had one long leg wrapped around the pole and the other in a stiletto pump on the floor, and she was bending back, breasts high in the air, so that her hair piled on the floor in a shiny blonde heap. 'Hi,' she said.

'That's Star,' Leo said.

'Hi, Star,' Archie said.

There was music in here, too. Archie didn't know what it was. Something electronic and moody.

Archie took a seat next to Leo on the sofa. It was a relief to sit down.

'We haven't done this in a while,' Leo said.

Leo had been twenty-one when Archie had met him after his sister's murder, already older than his years, and already his father's son. He had all of Jack's best attributes: his looks, his physical confidence, his brains. He was being groomed to take over the family business, but he wanted out.

So Archie had introduced him to Raul Sanchez, his contact at the FBI. Archie hadn't anticipated that the Feds would convince him to do exactly what his father wanted him to. In the end, it had worked out better for Jack than it had for Leo. Unbeknownst to him, it was the reason he was allowed to continue doing business. Leo had access to drug operations all over the world. And as long as the FBI and the Drug Enforcement Administration knew the ins and outs of Jack Reynolds's operation, they were fine with it.

People were going to get their heroin somewhere.

It was one of the reasons that Archie had kept in such close touch with the Reynolds family. Leo had access to all sorts of criminal contacts that Archie had accessed more than once during his tenure as leader of the Beauty Killer Task Force.

Star hooked a knee around the pole and spun. It was a small room and Archie could smell her, the sweat on her body, the gel in her hair.

Leo lifted his drink to his lips and took a sip. 'Sorry about my brother,' he said. His eyes were bloodshot, the pupils large.

'How long have you been here?' Archie asked.

'A few hours,' he said.

More like all afternoon. 'You're wasted,' Archie said.

'Yes.'

The stripper sashayed back and forth in front of them, fluttering her fingers over the tops of her breasts.

'She's beautiful, isn't she?' Leo said.

'She's very fit,' Archie said.

Leo laughed. 'You don't like her?'

'She looks like Gretchen,' Archie said.

Leo clapped his hand on Archie's knee. 'Sometimes a blonde is just a blonde.'

Archie tried to get a read on Leo. 'Did you know?' he said.

'Give us a minute, Star,' Leo said. The stripper stopped sashaying, picked up a silk robe that lay in a puddle on the floor, put it on, and left without a word.

Leo frowned. 'The triangles bothered me,' he said. He took another swallow of his drink, holding it in his mouth for a moment. 'Jeremy was always jealous of Isabel. He thought Jack loved her more. When Jack named the *Isabel* after her, Jeremy lost it – tried to wreck the boat, tore the sail, cut the lines.' Leo warmed his drink in his hands. 'I always wondered if that's what the triangles carved into Isabel were – boats.'

Maybe Jeremy had convinced himself that Gretchen had actually killed his sister. Or maybe he had just been lying all along.

'When did you know for sure?' Archie asked.

'He had this fascination with eyes as a kid. Used to pop them out of Isabel's dolls and carry them around in his pocket.' Leo looked in his glass. 'The eyes. That's when I knew for sure.'

'Gretchen came to see me tonight,' Archie said.

Leo looked up from his glass.

'Jeremy's dead. She killed him. She brought me his eyes.'

Leo was quiet for a long time. Then he drained his glass in one swallow and set it on the sofa. 'Just the eyes?' he asked.

'Jesus Christ,' said Archie. 'He's still alive.'

61

Susan's mother was teaching a yoga class at the Arlington Club, and Susan was trying to figure out how to get *Project Runway* to stream on her laptop, when she looked up to see Archie Sheridan standing at the front door. She was wearing black sweatpants and a threadbare University of Oregon T-shirt that she slept in, and Uggs. It was not the outfit she imagined wearing when she pictured Archie Sheridan showing up at her front door at night.

She closed her laptop and padded to the door.

Her bandage was off, but the two puncture wounds on her face had bruised and swollen, and a black eye was coming in. As she opened the door, she caught sight of her reflection in the glass and winced.

The porch light was on, and gnats batted against the fixture. August was the only month of the year in Portland that Susan felt comfortable outside at night without a jacket.

'What's going on?' Susan asked. She'd been burning incense. Patchouli. And a cloud of it drifted out around her on the porch. She hoped Archie wouldn't notice it.

'I need the phone,' Archie said.

She knew which phone he meant. But she was surprised by his confidence in the fact that she had it, that it wasn't still sitting in her glovebox unnoticed.

The only way he'd know that she'd found it was if he knew that she'd used it to try to contact Gretchen. And the only way he'd know she'd tried to contact Gretchen was if he'd been in touch with Gretchen since.

'Sure,' she said.

She left him on the porch, went into the dining room, retrieved the red purse she'd hung on the back of a chair, and returned to the front door. Then she dug out the phone and held it out to him.

He took it, and for a moment their fingers touched. Archie scrolled through the messages. He blinked in disbelief. 'You texted her?' he said.

Susan shrugged and looked away. 'You were in trouble.' She tried to make up for it. 'I plugged it in,' she said. 'I have the same charger.'

Archie finished going through the messages. 'There's nothing here,' he said. He dialled a number and walked away a few steps on the porch, the phone to his ear. Then his shoulders fell and he turned back around to face her. 'The number she was calling from is disconnected. There's no way to find her.'

'What's happened?' she asked.

Archie steadied himself on the door jamb. 'Gretchen has Jeremy.'

Susan had seen his injuries – he had to be in pain. He

was probably delirious. 'Do you want to come in and sit down?' she asked.

'No time,' Archie said, shaking his head. 'Gretchen didn't kill Isabel Reynolds,' he added. 'Jeremy did.'

Susan's hand rose reflexively to her cheek. She flashed on Isabel – tortured for two days before she died. It couldn't be true. What kind of thirteen-year-old kid was capable of that?

'How do you know?' she asked.

Archie pressed his forehead against the door jamb. 'She's going to kill him, if he's not dead already,' he said. He lifted his head and banged it against the wood. 'He played me. He told me that he remembered everything, that Gretchen killed Isabel in the woods. But Isabel was gagged. Wherever Jeremy took her, it wasn't the woods.' He knocked his forehead against the wood again, as if trying to jog a thought loose. 'If they were in the woods, he wouldn't have had to gag her. But he would have had to take her somewhere private, somewhere he could hide the car. Somewhere people might hear if she wasn't gagged.'

And suddenly Susan knew.

'Derek said that house on Fargo's been empty for fifteen years,' she said. 'The Rose Garden. Pittock Mansion. The old produce warehouse. They were all Beauty Killer crime scenes.'

Archie lifted his head off the door jamb and looked at her.

Susan continued. 'There's a foundation for a garage. Maybe twelve years ago the garage was still there.'

'He parked the car in the old garage and tortured his

sister to death over two days,' Archie said slowly. 'Three-nine-seven.' He closed his eyes. 'March 1997. He practically spelled it out for us.'

'You think Gretchen is there, right now?' Susan asked. 'With Jeremy?' She waved a hand. 'So call the SWAT team. Call everyone. Drop a bomb on the whole fucking block.'

Archie just looked at her.

'Oh, God,' she said. 'You're going by yourself, aren't you?'

He turned and started down the steps, one hand held to his side, one hand on the railing.

Susan was filled with terror – terror of Gretchen, terror that she would never see Archie again.

She grabbed her purse from inside the door and sprinted after him. 'I'm going with you,' she said. 'I've been inside. I know the house.' She took him by the elbow, letting him lean on her. 'I'm not going to let you face her alone.'

62

Gretchen is already there, clad in blue inmate denim and manacled at the table, when Archie walks into the concrete-block interrogation room at the Oregon State Penitentiary.

A month in a medically induced coma, a month of physical therapy, and he still can't walk across a room upright.

Gretchen smiles when she sees him and the oxygen rushes out of the room as if she'd swallowed it.

Archie can't look at her. He glances away – at the one-way glass Henry waits behind – but sees only the two of them reflected back at him.

The thick metal door closes behind Archie and locks. It's an electronic lock, controlled by a set of buzzers near the door and a master board in the adjacent observation room. Two guards stand armed in the hallway outside. But inside, in that room, it's just the two of them. Those were her terms.

'I've missed you, darling,' she says.

The smell of the room reminds Archie of the basement she kept him in, concrete and cleaning solvents. 'What do you miss exactly?' he asks, his voice still hoarse from the poison she'd fed him. 'The smell of my blood?'

She folds her hands on the table. 'I've hurt your feelings,' she says.

Archie looks at her, flustered. He has no idea how to respond. 'You fed me drain cleaner and cut out my spleen,' he says.

Her look of concern seems unsettlingly genuine. 'How are the scars healing?' she asks.

She was still beautiful. Even in these surroundings, in the shapeless prison garb, no make-up, his body still responds to her. He hates himself for it.

'You're high,' she says.

'I'm on painkillers,' he says. She had fed him pills in the basement, rewarding him with them when he'd choke down the drain cleaner, dropping them down his throat when he could no longer sit up to swallow them.

He doesn't take them for the pain any more.

She lifts her cuffed hands and gestures to the chair across the table from her. 'Do you want to sit down?'

His broken ribs are still healing, making sitting difficult. The cotton of his shirt chafes his raw scars. The heart-shaped scar on his chest still bleeds sometimes. 'I think I'll stand,' he says.

She nods in understanding. 'Of course,' she says.

It's warm in there, and Archie pulls at the collar of his shirt. He is there for the victims. This is what he's told himself, what he's told Henry, Debbie. No one expected him to give in to her crazy demands to meet with him. She'd nearly killed him. But he's dragged himself there to help with the identification project, for the victims.

The victims.

It wasn't the whole truth.

It has been two months since her arrest, and he's got tired of waiting for the other shoe to drop. She hasn't told anyone about their relationship. He is prepared to deny it. He can explain the time they had spent together in the context of the case. But wondering why she has remained quiet is killing him.

'What do you want from me?' he asks Gretchen.

'You've read the plea agreement,' she says. 'I'm going to confess. I'm going to tell you everything, every person I murdered. You can close all the cases.'

'Just like that.'

'You'll earn it,' she says, and Archie feels the promise of that statement heavy in the room.

'Why did you do it?' he asks her. He doesn't mean the murders. He means the affair.

'For fun,' she says. But he's not sure which question she's answering.

He leans back against the door, feeling weak.

'Sit down,' she says again. 'Please.'

He does this time, making his way to the table and lowering himself painfully onto the chair.

'Don't be sad,' she says. 'You caught me. You're a hero. You got exactly what you wanted.'

A hero. He's been manipulated from the start. Amativeness. He wonders if it is even a real thing.

'Name a case you want to close, a case that's important to you.'

Archie rolls his head back and looks at the ceiling. His scalp tingles from the Vicodin. He just wants to go home. To beg for forgiveness. *It's all right*, she had said when he was dying in her arms. And he'd believed her. He lifts his head and glances over at the one-way glass. Something good might as well come out of all this.

'Isabel Reynolds,' he says.

Something changes in Gretchen's face – a tiny lift of her eyebrows, a minuscule furrow between them. Her mouth tightens almost imperceptibly.

'She's special,' Gretchen says. 'She will be a prize. I'll tell you about her, darling. When you're ready.'

Archie sits up a little. Gretchen's face has reverted to a convivial mask. But for a second, he's seen through her.

She had manipulated him, toyed with him, tortured him, but in the process she'd let him see her. He knows her – at least some small part of her. And it might be enough to work to his advantage.

'Matthew Fowler,' Archie says.

Gretchen smiles. 'You called it a glass rod,' she says. 'It was a swizzle stick.' She lifts a hand and rotates a finger in the air. 'I worked a swizzle stick up Matthew Fowler's urethra.' She looks off in the middle distance, a slight smile on her face, as if she is reliving a fond memory. 'It took almost half an hour. I had to be very delicate, very precise. Once it was completely inserted I wrapped my hand around the bottom of the shaft and I broke it.' Her hand tightens into a fist. 'I just kept squeezing. I could feel the snap inside him under my hand.' She relaxes her hand and her smile widens. 'All at once, this blood full of tiny pieces of glass came pouring out of the tip of his cock.'

Archie reaches into his pocket, gets his new pillbox out, dumps some Vicodin in his hand and swallows them.

She looks up. 'Should I continue?' she asks.

'I'm here,' he says.

63

The house on North Fargo was dark. There were two streetlights on the block, one at each corner. The abandoned house sat in the middle of the block, with two empty lots on each side and a new FOR SALE sign in the yard. An enterprising billboard company had erected a standing billboard on the left-most lot, nearest the freeway exit. Plastered on it was a huge photograph of a woman jogging. EXERCISE CAN SAVE YOUR LIFE, read the slogan along the bottom.

'Twelve hundred people die every month jogging,' Susan said.

Archie held Henry's gun on his lap. The perimeter of the house was taped off with crime tape tied to wooden stakes. The front door would be sealed with more crime tape. But Archie couldn't see it. It was too dark.

'How did you get in before?' he asked.

'Through a broken basement window,' Susan said.

Archie raised an eyebrow at her.

'I didn't do it,' she said.

'Show me.'

They got out of the car. Susan's Saab was the only car parked on that block. He held the gun at his side, but he disengaged the safety. She was in there. He could feel her.

Susan directed him up the mossy concrete steps, through the overgrown yard, around the side of the house. As he followed her lead, he managed to keep a step ahead, one arm out in front of her, as if that small attempt at protection would make a difference.

They got to the window. It had been covered with new plywood. Archie sank to his knees in the soft dirt in front of it.

The plywood was screwed on tight, no way to pry it off. All the windows had probably been reinforced. The front door was certainly padlocked.

'Here,' Susan said. She knelt beside him, rummaged through her bag, and came up with a pocket tool. She opened it with a flick of her wrist, folded out the screwdriver, and set about unscrewing the screws that held the plywood in place.

He watched her in amazement as she quickly twisted out the screws and then lifted the plywood aside.

Susan's face was suddenly flooded with colour, her hair a blaze of purple. There was a light on in the basement. Archie pushed Susan to the left of the window, out of view of anyone watching, and held the plywood back in place.

'She's here,' Susan whispered in the darkness.

Archie reached out and sealed her lips with his finger.

He waited a moment, letting his heartbeat slow. Then he moved the plywood back aside, and peered in the window. He could see broken glass below on the basement floor. The light wasn't coming from the main room. There was another room. Off the basement stairs. A boiler room.

Archie tucked the gun in his pants, placed his hands on either side of the window, and lowered himself through.

The glass crunched under his feet. He looked back at Susan, concerned face framed in the window, and motioned for her to stay there. He drew the gun and moved towards the light.

The door to the old boiler room was open, and light from it spilled in a warped rectangle on the concrete floor. The room was large, maybe a quarter of the basement's square footage. The boiler was long gone, replaced by a dust-covered furnace. There were fixtures for a washer and dryer and a hot-water heater. A laundry line stretched across one corner, wooden clothes pegs clipped along it in a neat row.

Naked, suspended from his own hooks, in the middle of the room, was Jeremy. The hooks pierced his chest, torso, and legs, so that he was lying flat, face-up, table-height from the floor, like a specimen about to be dissected. His wrists were duct-taped behind his back.

'Coma position', Jeremy had called it.

The flesh tented at each hook site, strange triangles of strained skin that looked as if they might give in to gravity at any moment. Jeremy's head lolled back, his pale neck arched, Adam's apple protruded. The one eye socket Archie could see was a bloody hole. A black rubber-ball gag sealed Jeremy's mouth, but in the silence of the basement, Archie could now hear Jeremy's pitiful moan.

Gretchen stood on the other side of Jeremy, facing

Archie, elbows out, brows knitted, a scalpel in her hand. Freckles of blood splattered her bare arms. She'd been busy. Jeremy's chest was raw with wounds. His torso was striped with blood trailing down his ribcage and dripping onto the concrete floor.

Archie tucked his gun behind him and took a step to stand in the doorway.

She lowered the scalpel into Jeremy's chest and drew it towards her, as Jeremy choked against the gag. The Palmar grip. All those years, Archie and his task force had hunted her, always five steps behind. He had stood at so many crime scenes, seen so many bodies, reviewed so many autopsies, trying to put himself in the moment of the victim's terror. Then he had experienced it first-hand.

'Hello, darling,' she said to Archie. She didn't look up. She just knew he was there. 'Have you come to watch me work?'

'I've seen you at work,' Archie said. 'Remember?' He heard the faint sound of crunching glass, as Susan's feet hit the basement floor.

'This is different,' she said. She smiled up at him. 'Come on. Come take a closer look.'

Archie wanted to keep Gretchen's attention on him, so she wouldn't notice Susan, so he walked towards her. Jeremy, hearing Archie, lifted his head and struggled, causing his body to swing, but Gretchen put a hand out and steadied the rigging. Blood ran from Jeremy's eye sockets like tears.

Archie stood across from Gretchen, Jeremy suspended between them. The room reeked of urine. A dark puddle stained the concrete below Jeremy. He'd wet himself. Gretchen bent over again, getting back to work, pressing the scalpel into Jeremy's flesh. His torso was shredded. The wounds varied in depth. Some were mere slivers of red; some gaped open exposing fat; some gurgled blood.

'You were special,' Gretchen said to Archie. 'You got special treatment.' She frowned at Jeremy's brutalized skin. 'This is hardly any pleasure at all.' She moved a stray piece of red hair off her forehead with the back of her wrist. 'But work can't always be fun, can it? That's what makes it work.'

He realized then what she was doing. She was excising the scar tissue of the wounds that Jeremy had self-inflicted, the badges he had not earned.

'You think Jack Reynolds was going to let this go to trial?' she said, still focused on the scalpel. 'He would have had Jeremy killed. On the street. In jail. He would have found a way. Because Jeremy going on trial for multiple murders, that would lead to some discussion of Jack Reynolds's business interests.' She lifted the scalpel and dragged it along the heart Jeremy had carved on himself. 'Jeremy is dead one way or another. You know that.'

'Go ahead,' Archie said. 'Kill him. I didn't come here to save him. I came here for you.'

Jeremy started to sob, the ball gag bobbing, slippery with saliva.

Gretchen sized up Archie's groin. 'Are you going to try to strangle me again?'

He could shoot her. But she had a scalpel in her hand and she would finish Jeremy off if she could. And Susan was behind him, somewhere. He didn't want to risk the bullet ricocheting off one of the concrete walls. Not yet.

Archie smoothed a hand over Jeremy's sweat- and blood-matted hair. 'He told me that he fantasizes that we're lovers,' Archie said to Gretchen. 'He likes to think about me hurting you.'

'Well, he *is* a psychopath,' Gretchen said. She nicked at the heart-shaped scar, peeled a piece of the tissue off with her fingers, and flung it to the floor at her feet.

Archie squatted down, so that his face was level with Jeremy's. It felt good to sit. 'Actually, you're very intuitive, Jeremy,' Archie said. Jeremy twisted his head to face Archie, a black ball for a mouth, bloody craters for eyes. 'We had an affair,' Archie told him. 'Before I knew who she was.' It was a relief to tell someone, to actually say it. 'Two weeks. That's how long it took. She appeared, with her fake psychiatric degree, and offered to help us with the case.' Archie slowly shook his head, his lips curled in a dark smile. 'Fifteen years of faithful marriage and I lasted two weeks before I fell panting into Gretchen Lowell's arms.'

'I'm the best fuck you've ever had, darling,' Gretchen said sweetly.

'Indisputably,' said Archie. He wondered where Susan was, and if she could hear him.

Jeremy gnawed at the gag and pushed at Archie with his head, pleading for help. Had Isabel pleaded for help like that? Had she begged her brother for mercy?

'Anyway,' Archie continued, 'a month into our affair, she poisons me, takes me into a basement like this one and tortures me.' He pictured Susan, behind him, in the shadows, listening. 'I deserved it. I'd betrayed my family. And even after I was out of the hospital and she was in jail, she was all I could think about.' Archie leaned forward, his mouth inches from Jeremy's ear. 'It was just me, in bed, thinking about how much I wanted to fuck Gretchen again.' He glanced up at Gretchen. 'I kept asking myself why she'd done it. Why *then*? What was her plan for me?'

Gretchen stood motionless, the scalpel still in her hand.

He laughed. He sounded crazy. Maybe he was crazy.

Archie put his mouth back to Jeremy's ear. 'Here's the thing,' Archie said in a stage whisper. 'I don't think she had one.' He looked up at Gretchen. 'I think she infiltrated the investigation for her own amusement. I think the affair just happened. For a long time I thought she tortured me because I was the head of her task force, to show the world that she was all-powerful. But I don't think that's it. I think she tortured me because we were having an affair and she thought that I was going to break it off.'

Gretchen's mouth changed. It was something no one else in the world would notice. But that was his gift. No one knew her like he did.

Archie stood. 'Am I right, sweetheart?'

Gretchen sank the scalpel into Jeremy's chest, sliced, and peeled up the rest of his heart scar. 'I don't do anything without a plan,' she said, and she dropped the bloody yarn of flesh on the floor.

'You want to know what's funny?' Archie said. There was no amusement in his tone. 'I wasn't going to leave you.' He paused and looked at her, really looked at her, trying to see her as he'd seen her before he knew what she was. 'I was going to leave Debbie.'

Jeremy emitted another low moan. The gun in Archie's waistband pressed against his back. He couldn't hear Susan. He hoped that she'd climbed back out of the basement.

'Why did you come here?' Gretchen asked.

'To kill you,' Archie said.

'How badly do you want it?'

'Pretty badly,' Archie said.

Gretchen sank the scalpel into the fold of Jeremy's groin. Jeremy howled against the gag, and Gretchen seized Archie's right hand and pushed his fingers inside the warm wound, positioning Archie's thumb and forefinger together around Jeremy's throbbing femoral artery.

'The femoral artery is the second biggest artery in the body,' she said. 'You take your finger out of the dike and he'll bleed out in about a minute.'

Bright red blood spurted between Archie's fingers with each one of Jeremy's heartbeats. All cops were required to take some emergency medicine. Heimlich. CPR. How to treat someone in shock. But the one you paid special attention to was how to treat a wound in the field, because if you were ever shot, it could save your life. Archie couldn't leave him. If he pulled his hand away, Jeremy would die. Archie pressed his left hand on top of his right to get enough pressure to slow the blood flow.

Gretchen backed away.

'You can save him,' she said. 'He'll live. You can put him

on trial.' She came around Jeremy's body to Archie's side and set the scalpel down on the floor at Archie's feet.

'Or you can come for me.'

The pulse of blood against Archie's fingers increased as Jeremy's heart rate quickened. Archie's hand was halfway inside Jeremy's body. He could feel the heat and life of him.

He thought of Isabel Reynolds, of three homeless people Jeremy had killed, of Fintan English who'd died in this very house. He looked up at Gretchen. At the scalpel on the floor between them. And he released Jeremy's artery and lifted his hands.

Jeremy made a noise. 'No.'

Archie took two steps towards Gretchen and scooped up the scalpel in his bloody hand. Gretchen stiffened and took a step back, against the wall. He was on top of her in a moment, their bodies a few inches apart, his palm flat on the wall next to her head.

He could hear Jeremy struggling against the nylon ropes, making strangled cries.

The scalpel was light in his hand, pretty, the same model she had used to carve him up.

'Whatever made you think that I don't support the death penalty?' Archie said.

He stabbed her below the left ribcage.

The scalpel went in all the way to the handle, and Archie held it there, his fist against her heaving abdomen. He looked down between them and saw blood. He tried to ignore Jeremy's whimpers.

'Look at me,' he told her.

She looked up at him with her perfect blue eyes. He had wanted to see surprise. He had wanted to do one thing, take one action, that she had not predicted and orchestrated.

Her lips parted. She tried to speak.

Jeremy made one last strangled sound and then was silent.

'Twist it,' she said.

Archie turned the scalpel and she opened her mouth and cried out, her cheeks flushing. Then she cupped his face with her hands. They were wet with Jeremy's blood. Archie could smell it.

'Men are so simple,' Gretchen said. Her hands were warm and her touch soft. 'With Jeremy, I just went a little younger. I wanted to see if I could take a child and turn him into a monster. So I took him and his sister to this house and I murdered her in front of him.' She beamed.

Archie couldn't think straight. She was lying again. Jeremy was a psychopath. He'd been born that way. He'd killed his sister. He would keep killing. He tightened his grip on the scalpel. 'No,' he said.

Her hands trembled against his cheeks as he pushed the blade in deeper, and he could feel the heat of her blood spreading between them.

'It was an experiment,' she said, slowly sliding her hands down his neck to his chest. 'I wanted to see if I could create something evil. Anyone can be a murderer, given the right set of circumstances.'

She glanced at Jeremy. 'I guess I was right.'

Oh, God, Archie thought. *No. Please.*

She gave Archie's chest a gentle push, and he stepped

back, and the scalpel, his hand still clenched around the handle, slid from her body. 'Jeremy didn't kill his sister,' she said. 'He didn't kill any of them. He was just a poor little boy I manipulated. I talked him into getting his little club to perform the splenectomy. I suspended you from the hooks. I was there the whole time. Jeremy was innocent.' Her smile widened as she revelled in her victory. 'And you just let him die.'

Archie opened his hand and let the scalpel drop. It bounced noisily on the concrete, and as Gretchen glanced down at the sound Archie reached behind his back and drew his gun. By the time she glanced up, the muzzle was pressed into her forehead. Archie's hand was shaking and he had to press the gun to her head hard to steady the thing. He had never wanted anything as badly as he wanted to blow a hole in Gretchen Lowell's head.

'You were right,' he said. 'I was leaving you. That night I came to your house. I was going to end it and tell Debbie everything.'

He moved the muzzle down her face, between her eyes, along the bridge of her nose, and pressed it against her closed lips. 'Take it,' he said. 'Take it.'

He could see the pulse in her throat flutter as she opened her lips and let him slide the barrel of the gun into her mouth.

Pull the trigger and he'd rip open the back of her head.

Who would blame him?

And then he would be a killer. Just like her.

He wasn't going to let her win.

He pulled out of her mouth slowly and lifted the gun back to her forehead. And in that heartbeat, he felt something unfamiliar. He felt like his old self.

'You're under arrest,' he said.

Archie glimpsed the barest hint of movement to his left before he felt the gun barrel on his ear.

'I didn't come alone,' Gretchen said.

And then Archie caught it. A wave of musk. Patchouli.

'Neither did I,' he said.

'If you move,' Archie heard Susan say, 'I will stab you in the neck.' She stepped forward into his peripheral vision. She had the knife out of her pocket tool and was holding it to Frank's neck.

'Hello, Frank,' Archie said. Frank's chin was down, his eyes unblinking, and his doughy face was flushed and sweaty. Archie had seen him like this before. It usually ended with Frank throwing a chair.

'Hello, Archie,' Frank said.

'She's not your sister,' Archie said. 'You know that, right?'

'Shoot him,' Gretchen said flatly.

Susan adjusted her stance, angling the knife higher against Frank's neck. 'Don't even think about it,' she said.

'Are you still mad at me?' Frank asked Archie.

'No,' Archie said. 'I'm not mad.'

'Shoot him in the head,' Gretchen said again.

'Yeah,' Frank said. 'Okay.'

Archie tensed, waiting for the shot, and then he heard it.

He'd never been shot before. He'd had nails driven into his ribs with a hammer. He'd been forced to drink drain cleaner. He'd been cut up and sliced and stabbed. But shot? No.

It didn't hurt. That's what they said. People had been shot and gone several minutes before even noticing. Some people described it as a sensation of heat. Other people said the pain was excruciating.

Being shot in the head, you probably couldn't feel that. You probably just died.

And he wasn't dead.

Frank was.

SWAT snipers came through the boiler-room doorway in pairs, all in black, headlamps shining. They had probably come in through a basement window. The gunshot Archie had heard was not meant for him – it was a sniper bullet meant for Frank. Archie heard the heavy, running footsteps of reinforcements entering upstairs.

It was all a fog.

Archie didn't move, didn't let up the pressure of the gun to Gretchen's head, until there were five other weapons trained on her.

'Sir?' one of the SWAT officers said.

Archie leaned close to Gretchen. 'I'm breaking up with you,' he whispered in her ear. And he lowered his gun.

64

Archie could see Venus from the porch of the house on Fargo. It was the brightest light in the night sky. Venus, the Roman goddess of love and beauty. The fly trap. So often depicted in paintings with red hair.

'We may never know what really happened to Isabel,' Henry said. 'Or the others.'

Jeremy was dead. Shark Boy was dead. Pearl was on her way back to her parents. The two other goons from the boiler room might never be found.

'I know,' Archie said.

Henry had arrived behind the SWAT team, unarmed, as he was officially on desk duty. That left Claire in charge, and she had banished them both to the porch, where Henry had taken Archie's statement.

News vans crowded the street, their satellite dishes battling for the best signal. The empty lots on either side of the house were filled with TV correspondents reporting live. The lights from their cameras looked like stars.

Gretchen was gone, bound on a stretcher, and carried off

by four anxious-looking EMTs and six cops. The cops had had to fight their way through the media horde that had set upon Gretchen like paparazzi on a movie star.

'Gretchen could have proof,' Archie mused. 'One way or another.'

'No,' Henry said, shaking his head. 'You're not reinstituting the victim-identification project. It's not worth it. There is no information she can give us that is worth you having to see her ever again.'

Archie reached into his pocket for the flash drive Gretchen had given him back at Henry's house, and held it up. 'She gave me this,' Archie said, examining the small device. 'Information on a guy named Ryan Motley.' He didn't know whether to believe her, if this guy even existed, or if it was just another game. 'She said she trained him, that he's a child killer.'

Archie held the flash drive out to Henry.

'Goddamn it,' Henry said, taking the drive.

Archie patted him on the shoulder and stood up. They both knew that Gretchen Lowell was not done with them, but for the moment at least, Archie was done with her.

There was really only one person he wanted to see right now.

He found Susan leaning against the side of the house, smoking a cigarette. The light coming from the old living-room window illuminated the side of her face.

The SWAT team had shown up just in time. And there was only one way they could have got there that soon. 'You called Henry,' he said.

'You were in trouble,' she said.

Archie leaned up against the house next to her. Gretchen was in custody. They were safe. He was alive.

'Thank you,' he said.

Susan took a drag off her cigarette. 'Four hundred and forty thousand,' she said.

'What?' he said.

'That's how many people die of tobacco-related deaths in the US each year.' She looked at the cigarette. 'I'm going to quit.'

She didn't move to extinguish the cigarette.

A news helicopter hovered in for an overhead shot of the house and they were quiet until it lifted and went off east.

'You were going to leave your wife for her, weren't you?' Susan said.

'Absolutely,' Archie said.

He still didn't know what she'd heard down there in the basement. What she knew about what he'd done. 'The taser was named after a Tom Swift book,' Archie said. '*Tom Swift and His Electric Rifle*. They added the *A*.'

Susan brushed a stray purple lock behind her ear. 'And you're telling me that because?'

'Because I want to tell you things,' Archie said.

She nodded and seemed to consider that. 'Do you know what the most popular line in movies is?' she asked. '"Let's get out of here."' She smiled in the dark. 'Seriously,' she said. 'Listen for it. It's in every movie. It doesn't matter what kind of movie it is. You'll be amazed.'

The puncture wounds in her face had bruised and her eyelid was a shiny purple. 'You have a black eye,' Archie said.

Susan took a drag of her cigarette and blew the smoke in his face. 'You have hook holes in your back,' she said.

There was a loud sustained car honk and Archie turned to see a shuttle bus trying to force its way past several emergency vehicles in order to get closer to the house. A bus wrap graphic covered the entire shuttle. Archie couldn't make all of it out, but in the headlights and flashing emergency lights he could see Gretchen's face on the side of the bus, and on the hood below the windshield, a scalpel.

'What the hell is that?' Archie said.

'That,' Susan said, 'is the midnight Beauty Killer Body Tour. Thirty-five bucks. Twenty crime-scene stops. No-host bar.' Her mouth turned up wryly. 'They got their money's worth tonight.'

The bus hopped the kerb across the street and people started to file out and spill into the street. Regular people, people who'd read *The Last Victim* and saw an article in *Vanity Fair*, and wanted a piece of the fun. They hollered and pumped their fists in the air.

'Free Gretchen!' they yelled.

Archie stepped back into the shadows.

'Are you hungry?' Susan asked. 'I have some potato chips in my car.'

Archie suddenly couldn't remember the last time he had eaten. He extended his arm and Susan took it.

'Let's get out of here,' he said.